THE TROUBLE GIRLS

E.R. FALLON
KJ FALLON

www.bloodhoundbooks.com

Print ISBN 978-1-914614-18-7

ALSO BY E.R. FALLON

1

W hen Camille O'Brien was a girl her mother liked to tell her that her father, if he had lived, could have been the king of New York City. Camille never knew her father. Colin O'Brien had been murdered when she was just a baby, in the early 1960s. It was the 80s now and Camille was in her twenties. Her mother Sheila had raised her alone after Colin's death, until she remarried when Camille was in high school. Camille's stepfather was a high up Italian mob guy named Vito Russo, and she and she had hated him ever since he had attacked her when she was at her when she was a teenager, something she never told her mother.

Still, her mother talked about Camille's father all the time and Camille knew that he had been a gangster, but he was still her father, and every day she had a desire to avenge him, because she was, after all, her father's daughter. Her father's absence in her life had affected her profusely and she'd started taking an antidepressant medication a few years ago to help her cope.

Camille and her mother had coffee in the diner around the

corner from the church, as they did every Sunday after attending morning mass together. Camille had always known her mother to be a devoted churchgoer, but her mother had told her that Colin's death had brought her closer to the church.

Camille made a joke and Sheila laughed then put her cup to her lips. Then they were silent for a moment and Camille waited for her mother to ask how she was and if she was dating anyone, which her mother always asked. So Camille spoke before she could ask.

"I'm doing good. Work is good. No, I haven't seen anyone since Billy."

Billy was the guy she'd almost married. Now it was just her and her cat.

"Have you seen Billy since you ended things?" Sheila asked.

"No."

"You and Billy were together for a long time." Her mother shook her head as though the breakup had been shameful.

"Yeah, we were together since high school," Camille said. "Can we please talk about something else?"

"How's your job search going?" Sheila asked her after a while.

Camille's mother had encouraged her to find better work than being a bartender, a job which she happened to enjoy. No one in Camille's family had gone to university, and neither had Camille. But in high school she'd been considered smart.

"Yeah, I'm going to be becoming a banker any day now, Ma."

But she'd always been good with numbers and had taken business and accounting courses at night school.

"You have your father's sarcasm," Sheila replied. Then she seemed to be thinking of something pleasant and smiled to herself. "You remind me so much of him."

"How?" Camille asked because she liked hearing why, even though her mother had told her how countless times before.

"You know how. You look just like him, for one thing. You have his dark hair and light eyes. He was a very handsome man, but you can already tell that from the photos you've seen." She continued when she saw that Camille wasn't going to drop the subject. "You're tall like he was, and charming. Oh, he was a charmer. He had a certain way about him that made people like him even though he was an intimidating size." Her mother blushed and Camille smiled to herself as she thought about how much her mother still loved her father.

Camille set down her coffee cup and looked across at her mother. "And how am I *not* like him?" she asked her mother quietly, because she had never asked it before, and it was something she'd always wondered.

"You're not a gangster," Sheila answered honestly. "He'd been to prison and had a darker side that you don't have."

Camille's mother had always been very open about her late father's profession.

"But I'm strong," Camille said.

"You are, yeah, and he was too," Sheila said. "But you don't have that dark side like he did. It's different than strength."

But Camille had always felt that she had some of her father's darkness in her.

"He did things you wouldn't want to know—you or any woman shouldn't know about," Sheila said. "Unless she chooses that lifestyle."

"How come you know about them, then?" Camille asked.

"He told me things, late at night."

Camille figured her mother meant in bed. "What was his childhood like?" she asked her mother, because she felt that there had to be a reason for the way her father had been.

"It was very sad," Sheila replied. "You know all this already," she chided her, then she went on. "He and his family came to this country as poor Irish immigrants—his mother was half

3

Welsh—and his father got involved with some bad characters and it resulted in his death. After that, his mother, who had a mental illness, became involved with someone who wasn't a good guy and your father ended up killing him for hurting his sister. Your father was still a teenager when he got sent to jail. He drank too much when he was young but stopped when he got older. The jacket you're wearing, that was his favorite."

Camille touched the leather jacket she had on; she always wore it outside no matter what the weather. She had heard the story of her father's short and tragic life many times over the years, and his story was reason she hardly ever drank, but every time her mother told the story to her it was like she was hearing it for the first time. She had never met her father's family, who didn't live in the US. It had just been her and her mother while she was growing up.

"Is that why he became a gangster and did those bad things?" Camille asked. "Because he went through all that stuff as a kid?"

"I'm not sure. He was a gangster, and that's what he had to do to succeed. He was smart, like you, but not traditionally educated."

"But didn't he have a choice? Couldn't he have chosen to do something else?" Camille asked. She would often think of what she would do if she had been in her father's shoes.

"A lot of guys became gangsters in the neighborhood he lived in when he came to New York. It was a way of life there."

Camille had heard her mother tell stories about her father's neighborhood, the Bowery, and although Camille worked right near where she lived, a few streets away from her mother, she had considered finding a job at a pub in the Bowery to feel closer to her father, but her mother had discouraged it because she considered the neighborhood dangerous.

4

"Of course, his neighborhood was better when he and his family lived there than it is now," her mother continued.

Camille looked around the small, crowded diner where she sat with her mother, which was near the neighborhood where she and her mother and stepfather both lived—Camille lived in the same apartment her father had lived in when he was single —and the glare of the bright sunlight pouring in through the bare windows hurt her eyes. Her mother knew that Camille didn't like Vito, but not why, so they had coffee at the diner instead of her mother's and Vito's apartment. Camille hadn't taken Vito's surname when her mother married him.

The whole place smelled of coffee and fried food, and the people in the diner were mostly young professionals with the day off or policemen taking a break. The neighborhood had changed a lot over the years Camille had lived there and had shifted from being a more working-class area to being wealthier, although there were still many holdouts from the old neighborhood, people like Camille and her mother.

Camille checked the time on the clock above the diner counter. "I better leave. My shift starts soon."

"Do people drink more on Sundays after church?" her mother suddenly asked.

Camille nodded. "I think they drink more than ever," she said with a smile, and her mother laughed.

"Do you like working there? Are they good bosses?"

"I like the owners. The tips are good, better than at the other place I worked. But there's this guy named Max who works there, and he doesn't seem to like me very much."

"Oh?" Sheila said. "That's his loss." She patted Camille's hand.

Their server came to their table with the check and she grabbed it before her mother could.

"I got it this time, Ma," she said.

"You got it the last time," Sheila replied.

"I know but let me pay. Okay?" Camille smiled. She wanted to do something nice for her mother.

"Okay, but I know that bartending must not pay much." Sheila patted Camille's hand.

Camille took some money out of her pocket and paid the check. Then Sheila rose, and she hugged Camille goodbye.

Camille left the diner after her mother had and the heat of the New York summer hit her as soon as she stepped outside and the sounds of traffic, car horns and emergency sirens. She breathed in the heavy smell of the warm city as she stood on the sidewalk and waited for the traffic to clear so she could cross the street. A truck beeped at her and a man inside whistled from his open window and Camille scolded him. She had her father's spirit, after all.

Once the traffic had paused, she made her way across the street and headed for *McBurney's* pub, where she had an afternoon shift that day. She had worked there for Violet McCarthy, a woman a few years older than her, for the last few years. Before that, she had tended the bar at another place nearby that had closed.

Violet owned the place with her mother, Catherine, who was one quarter French, and they both ran the operation with a guy named Max, who everyone referred to as "No-Last-Name" Max, and who she didn't know very well because he had seemed to avoid her. He talked to everyone else, and for reasons unknown to her, he didn't seem to like her. Violet had inherited the pub from her grandfather, whom Camille knew very little about.

Camille got on well with Violet, and they had sort of become friends over the years, and although she didn't know Catherine that well, Violet's mother had always treated her with respect, and Camille considered both women to be decent bosses. She didn't know much about Violet's background but she knew that Violet had lost her father, a politician from Boston, when she was young, just like Camille. Violet had a twelve-year-old son she had when she was in her late teens but wasn't married to the child's father, who was involved with the Italian mob. One thing Camille had heard whispered throughout the neighborhood was that her own father had a connection to the McCarthy family, but she didn't know what it was.

A gust of hot city air pushed down on Camille as she opened the door to the pub and stepped inside. The place wasn't air-conditioned and given the warm time of the year, the windows were all opened in front and the door was left ajar by a brick placed at the bottom.

The pub opened in the late morning and a few patrons were already there. It would begin to fill up about an hour after her shift started. Violet, with her long, ginger hair in a ponytail, was tending the bar until Camille's arrival.

Camille greeted her.

"How was mass this morning?" Violet asked her.

The McCarthys were Catholic like Camille and lived in her neighborhood but she'd never seen them at the local church, and neither Violet nor Catherine had brought up the subject, so Camille didn't ask them.

"It was nice," Camille said. "I had coffee with my mother after."

"Oh, and, how is she?"

Violet didn't really know Camille's mother and Camille reasoned she was just being polite.

"She's doing well," Camille said, because she didn't want to get into how her mother had suffered ever since her father had died. Violet didn't know much about Camille's background either except that both had lost their fathers when they were very young.

Violet's mother Catherine came downstairs and said hello to Camille.

"How is your mother?" she asked Camille. "Is she well?"

Catherine McCarthy always spoke of Sheila as though she knew her.

"She is. We went to mass together this morning and then had coffee," Camille said.

"Did you hear that, Violet?" Catherine said to her daughter with a smile in Camille's direction. "*She* attends mass with her mother."

"She's always trying to get me to go with her so she'll go," Violet explained to Camille. "But I'm always telling her if she wanted to go so badly then why doesn't she just go on her own?"

"I'd be more likely to go if I went with somebody," Catherine replied to her daughter.

"Maybe you can go with Camille and her mother," Violet suggested, not sarcastically.

Catherine went pale, and Camille wondered why. What was she so afraid of?

"It'd be fine if you wanted to join us," Camille said.

"No, I wouldn't want to intrude," Catherine mumbled, increasing Camille's curiosity.

"You wouldn't be. Honestly," Camille said.

Catherine didn't reply, and Camille didn't bring it up again. What was going on, exactly?

Max, an older, heavyset man with whitish hair, entered the pub from outside.

"Good afternoon," he said to Violet and her mother, ignoring Camille.

Camille didn't know just what Max did at the pub. He worked out of the upstairs and a parade of desperate-looking men would come in and out of the pub and go up to visit him then leave after a little while. Camille figured he must have been something like a bookie and Catherine and Violet probably got a cut of his profits. That was just the way things were in the neighborhood, and it hadn't changed much despite the influx of rich, young professionals to the area.

As usual, he walked behind the bar and helped himself to a cup of coffee then went upstairs, without so much as acknowledging Camille's presence.

"What's his problem?" Camille asked Catherine, who seemed to have a soft spot for her, as Violet lugged in the two cases of whiskey that had been delivered to the front by mistake.

"Who? Max?" Catherine asked.

"Yeah, he doesn't seem to like me, and I don't know why. I used to try to be friendly to him, but it didn't work so now I just don't bother."

"Max's an old grouch," Catherine said.

But Camille felt it was more than that. "Sure, but it feels personal."

Catherine shrugged. She usually wasn't this evasive, so it piqued Camille's curiosity and she pushed further for information. "Do you have any idea why he doesn't like me?"

"Maybe it's because—" Catherine started to say when Violet came back inside.

"Mom, weren't they supposed to deliver a case of vodka?" Violet asked, distracting her mother.

"It might be around back," Catherine said.

"I already went back there and checked while I was outside and there was nothing there. I think the distributor forgot the vodka."

Catherine sighed. "I'll have to call them." She stepped away from Camille and went to use the phone near the kitchen.

Camille hung up her jacket in the employee break room and then helped Violet unpack the crates of liquor.

"I asked your mother why Max doesn't like me, and she started to answer me but never finished. Do you know why he avoids me?" she asked her.

"I'm not sure," Violet said. "He's nice enough to my mother and me, but he knows us well. Maybe it's just that he doesn't know you very well."

"I've been working here for years," Camille replied. "He's never given me the chance to get to know him, he just seems to avoid me."

"Max is a peculiar guy," Violet said. "I wouldn't let it worry you." She smiled.

Camille nodded. She went behind the bar counter to put some of the whiskey bottles on the shelf and prepare for the afternoon influx of drinkers. Camille checked the money jar, which they kept filled to bribe away any of the more youthful police they knew who responded to noise complaints when the packed bar roared with music and laughter and conversation well into the night. It looked a little low and she pointed this out to Violet.

"I'll ask my mother to refill it when she's done with her call."

Camille could hear Catherine scolding the distributor on the phone.

A group of men in construction worker garb entered the pub and sat down at the bar. All three ordered beers and Camille served them.

"Is Max around?" one of them, the thinnest of the group, asked her.

"Yeah, he's upstairs," Camille replied. "Why, you want to place a bet?"

"Yeah, how did you know?" he replied quietly, confirming she'd been right about Max.

"I took a good guess."

"I look that desperate, huh?" the guy asked with a smile and Camille saw he was flirting with her, which she experienced often in her line of work.

A man, tall, handsome and youngish looking, burst into the bar and approached the group of men.

2

"When are you gonna pay me what you owe?" the young man demanded from the thinner guy at the bar.

"I'll get it to you soon, I'm gonna place a bet today and then I should have it," the guy answered.

"And if you lose?"

"I won't. I feel lucky today."

"You better hope you're lucky," the young guy said, and for a moment it seemed like he might strike the other man.

Camille stepped out from behind the bar. "Hey, take it easy," she told the young guy. "Or else I'll have to get the big guy to throw you out."

There was no 'big guy', it was just a phrase Camille had learned to use over the years when patrons got out of line. And in this kind of neighborhood situations like that—guys barging in and demanding money from other guys—happened quite a lot.

"Relax, miss, I'm not gonna do anything to him. At least not inside this place," the young guy responded with a spark of mischief in his nice brown eyes. His short, wavy dark hair was styled elegantly. "What's your name?" he asked Camille with a grin, revealing good teeth, just then seeming to comprehend that she was young and good looking. But she didn't easily fall for that kind of charm.

"Wouldn't you like to know," Camille replied.

"Come on, tell me."

"Maybe I will."

"Maybe?"

"Yeah, it depends."

"On what?"

"Are you going to buy a drink? Otherwise, you're distracting me from the customers."

"I don't really drink," the guy replied.

"What's your name?" she asked him.

He held out her hand for her to shake. "Johnny Garcia Jr."

Camille swallowed and was still for a moment. Johnny Garcia had been the name of her father's best friend, and he had died long ago, before Camille's father had, according to her mother. But Camille didn't know the circumstances.

How common was the name? Possibly, they were related, and this guy could have been his son. But Camille didn't mention it. She shook his hand and his skin felt smooth and cool. "Camille O'Brien," she said, but the surname, a common one, didn't seem to register on his face.

He held her hand for longer than he needed to. "Thanks for telling me. I'll buy a soda or something."

"We only have cola," Camille replied and went behind the bar again.

"That happens to be my favorite."

She couldn't tell whether he was serious or was just saying it to amuse her. She dispensed seltzer water in a glass from the sprayer and got out the syrup and squirted some in a glass to make the drink. Johnny watched her stir it with a knife.

"You live in this neighborhood?" he asked her.

Camille nodded. "I've never seen you around."

Johnny shrugged. "I've been around."

Just when she thought he'd forgotten about the guy who owed him money, Johnny slammed his fist down on the bar in front of the guy as the guy and his friends got up to walk away.

"Where do you think you're going?" Johnny asked them.

The man's friends started to intervene, and Johnny indicated to a gun tucked into his waistband that Camille hadn't noticed before.

"Take it easy," she told him, although the sight of guns in her neighborhood wasn't uncommon.

"I never use it unless I have to," Johnny said with a wink while eyeing the men.

One of them grunted in anger and then they all sat down again. Camille figured that maybe that had something like a knife on them but that wasn't any match for a gun.

"You'll need to pay for your beer before you try to leave again," Camille told them.

"Yeah, you need to pay the lady," Johnny said to them.

"I got to go upstairs to place my bet," the guy who owed Johnny told him. "That way, I can win enough money to pay you."

"You think I'm so stupid that I'm gonna let you out of my sight?" Johnny asked the man.

"You're gonna come with me?" the guy said.

"You can go upstairs when *I* say you can."

"You gonna come with me?" the guy asked him again.

Johnny contemplated something then said, "I'm not gonna come with you, but I do expect you to pay me in twenty-four hours, by tomorrow afternoon. Understand?"

"Or else what happens to him?" one of the man's friends asked.

"You know what'll happen to him," Johnny said, and his voice filled with dark undertones.

"We're gonna go with him upstairs. Okay?" the other friend said to Johnny.

"Are you asking me or are you telling me?" Johnny said, eyeing the man, and the room felt smaller with tension.

"Asking," the guy finally said, in a whisper, and Johnny backed down.

He nodded at them to go.

"Look at them," Johnny said to Camille as the group of men got up from the bar and went upstairs. "The guy already owes me money and he's gonna place a bet with someone else to try to pay me back and then he's gonna owe them money."

"It's a vicious cycle," Camille observed.

"What was that?" Johnny asked, having not heard her.

"Nothing. You sure know how to make an entrance," Camille said to Johnny when the three men had disappeared upstairs.

"The guy owes me a lot of money. What else was I supposed to do? Otherwise, he'll never pay me back," Johnny said with a smile.

Camille thought that Johnny's way might have been like her father's, if she had known him. But she kept that to herself.

Catherine came out of the kitchen and glared at Johnny from across the room. Violet joined her and both women stared at Camille talking with Johnny.

Johnny seemed to feel the women's wrath towards him. "I should go," he told Camille. "I'll see you again soon."

"I wouldn't count on it," Camille replied with a grin, and Johnny laughed.

She watched his tall, well-built frame leaving the pub and as soon as he'd left, Violet and Catherine pounced on her.

"What was he doing in here?" Catherine demanded. "Do you know him?" she asked Camille.

"I only just met him now," Camille responded.

"Honey, I care about you," Catherine continued speaking, and Violet's face flushed with jealousy, "and I'm going to warn you to stay away from him."

"Yeah, I don't know his name, but I know his face—he's the leader of the Cuban gang that moved up here over the years. He's bad news," Violet chimed in.

"His name's Johnny Garcia. And thanks, ladies," Camille replied. "I appreciate your concern. But I don't need anyone telling me who I can or can't talk to. I have my mother for that."

Gang guys didn't scare her. Billy, the guy she'd almost married, and whom she met through her stepfather, worked for the Italian mob but wasn't a made member because he wasn't fully Italian. Besides, Camille didn't know the full extent of Violet and her mother's involvement with Max's bookie operation upstairs, but they knew enough to let him operate it and probably took a percentage. She stopped short of telling them they were hypocrites.

"How do you know him anyway?" she asked Violet and her mother.

"We've seen them in the neighborhood, causing trouble. Lots of them moved here from the East Side over the years," Violet said.

"So, you don't really know him, you're just making an assumption about him," Camille countered, her voice becoming emotional because she was convinced of Johnny's connection to her father.

"Honey, we know enough to tell you he's bad news," Catherine said.

A customer came in and sat down and Camille breathed a sigh of relief.

"What can I get you?" she asked the woman and didn't pay

any mind to Violet and her mother, who were still standing nearby. As far as Camille was concerned, that conversation was finished. She would decide for herself what kind of person Johnny Garcia was.

3

Violet McCarthy's grandfather, Sean, had doted on her when she was a little girl. In the streets Sean McCarthy was considered a brutal leader of the Irish mob, but to Violet, he was her kind grandfather. His death a few years ago from a stroke had devastated Violet, but she and her mother had stepped up to take his place and lead the gang. Women gang leaders weren't common at the time, but once word got around that the brutality of Violet and her mother matched Sean's, most men didn't have a problem doing business with them, not even the more traditional Italians.

In the wee hours of the morning, Violet closed the pub for the night and cleaned up the place. *McBurney's* was named after her Scottish great-grandmother.

Her mother sat at the bar, drinking, as she sometimes did after closing. Over the years, Violet had come to realize that her mother could be considered an alcoholic, though her mother didn't like to think of herself in that way.

Max paused as he put on his hat and headed out the door.

"Vi," he called to her. "Do you need my help tonight?"

Sometimes Max assisted her in bringing her intoxicated mother to her mother's apartment over the pub.

"I think I'll be okay tonight, Max, but thanks," Violet replied. Her mother's behavior embarrassed her, as it had embarrassed her grandfather, and she didn't like anyone witnessing it, not even Max, whom she'd known since forever.

Max looked at Catherine, who was pouring her fifth or sixth drink of straight vodka into a shot glass. "You're sure?" he asked Violet.

She nodded. "Yeah, we'll be fine. Thanks."

He waved goodbye and opened the front door to leave and a trickle of cool evening air blew inside and carried with it the smell of food from the restaurants outside.

Once he'd left, Violet approached her mother at the bar.

"Mom," she said quietly, to not startle her.

Sometimes when people got drunk, they became tougher, but Violet's mother was the opposite, the more she drank, the frailer she became. Violet wondered why her mother drank. Her family didn't have a history of alcoholism, and her grandfather hardly touched a drop, so did Catherine drink because of some deep sadness that was unknown to Violet? Violet's father had died when she was very young, so maybe that was the cause. She felt that if she asked her mother, she might cause further sadness, so she didn't ask.

Catherine looked up at her from the bar. Her mother was a very attractive woman and had a lot of charm, but she had never remarried and barely dated over the years after Violet's father's death. Violet figured her mother must have missed her father a lot.

"Mom," Violet said again, touching the vodka bottle in her mother's hand. "I've finished closing. It's time to go home."

"Just one more drink, sweetheart," her mother replied, her voice shaking.

"Come on, you've had enough." Violet pried the bottle out of her mother's hand and held it out of her reach.

Catherine grabbed at the bottle and tried to get it back from her. She started to fall off the bar stool and Violet steadied her.

"You've had enough," Violet repeated.

"Don't scold me," Catherine said from the bar seat, wagging her finger at her daughter. "I'm your mother, not the other way around."

"Please don't make this any more difficult than it has to be," Violet said. "Just let me take you home."

"Where's Max?" Catherine asked, looking around the room for him.

Violet realized her mother hadn't noticed him leaving. "He already left. You didn't see him leaving?"

"He didn't say goodbye."

"He said goodbye," Violet said. "You were too busy to notice."

"You're accusing me of being rude to Max?" Catherine said, becoming oddly emotional with the drink.

"No, you were drinking and weren't paying attention."

Violet couldn't quite figure out her mother's relationship with Max. It wasn't romantic, and he treated her mother more like an uncle or father would, and she treated him like a niece or daughter would. She didn't know Max as well as her mother did, for he was a difficult man to become close to. One thing Violet was certain of was Max's loyalty to her and her mother, which he had proven to them many times over the years. Earlier on, he had even killed for them.

"When did you get to be so bossy?" Catherine smiled, and Violet saw that all was well between them, the previous tension having faded away.

"I inherited it from you," Violet smiled. "Come on, now," she said after a moment. "Let's get you home." She leaned over the bar and put the vodka bottle behind it so her mother couldn't sneak another drink.

Catherine started to stand up from the bar and Violet caught her before she fell to the floor.

"Aren't I a sight?" Catherine laughed, but Violet didn't find it funny because it happened quite often.

"Did you want to ask Max something?" Violet asked her mother.

Catherine nodded. "Earlier today, he was telling me that there's this guy who owes us a ton of money through the bookie operation. Max allowed the guy's tab to get too big, which I wasn't happy about, and now the guy's not paying up."

"You're thinking we might need some of the guys to take care of him?" Violet asked.

"Yeah. If we don't make an example of him then others in the neighborhood will think they can do the same."

Violet had never enjoyed the messy side of the business, as her grandfather had seemed to, but sometimes bad things needed to be done, and that was the way it had always been. They had guys who took care of that sort of thing these days, although in the past it hadn't been that way and they had to carry out the unpleasant tasks themselves.

"Call me when you're sober enough to make a decision," Violet said.

She and her mother ran the gang together, but the opinion of her elder mother weighed more in their decisions. Though, sometimes, on nights like tonight, Violet felt she was the true leader, during those times when her mother could barely function.

Catherine nodded. "I will, but as of now, I'm thinking we should cut him out."

"Grandpa once told me not to make any big decisions when drunk," Violet said.

"My father was a wise man," Catherine chuckled.

"What do you think of Camille chatting with that Garcia character?" Violet asked after a while. Camille had left the pub hours ago.

"I don't think it's good. I try to do my best to look out for her, like I think her own mother would want me to, but she doesn't listen. She's so stubborn."

She'd asked the question in part because her mother seemed to have a soft spot for Camille—like how Camille had suggested they feature live music acts in the pub once in a while and her mother thought it was such a great idea. This had always annoyed Violet, and she didn't understand it, and she'd wanted to test her mother. In fact, she didn't care what Camille did, and that included talking with Johnny Garcia.

"Why do you care so much what happens to her?" Violet asked her mother.

"You seemed to care too."

"I acted like I did because you did."

"You don't like Camille?" her mother asked.

Violet shrugged. "I don't dislike her. I don't know her that well."

"I thought you two were friends."

"I'm nice to her because you like her. But I don't hate her. Why do you like her so much, anyway?"

"It's complicated," her mother stated, and after a minute, Violet comprehend she wouldn't elaborate why.

She considered pushing her mother for an answer then thought better of it because the answer might make her more jealous.

"Let's go," she said, and put her arm around her mother's waist. She assisted her mother with standing up from the bar stool. "Max offered to help me walk you home."

"I take it you declined. Why?"

22

"I did. I don't like him seeing you throw up."

"I don't throw up."

Violet looked at her mother. "You've done it plenty of times. Most of the time you're just not conscious enough to remember."

Catherine's face reddened in embarrassment. "I'm sorry, sweetheart. You know I've tried programs to help me get sober, but they never work."

"That's because you never stay at them long enough to work."

"They're expensive," her mother insisted.

"Grandpa left you some money when he died."

"I don't want to spend it. That money is supposed to be for you and Tommy."

Tommy was her twelve-year-old son, who she had with a guy in the Italian mob named Kevin Carmine but who she'd never married.

"Yeah, but you're always saying how soon we'll be making enough to retire comfortably. I think you just don't want to stay sober."

"It's my business," her mother snapped.

"What you do affects me also. What about going to a support group?"

"You know how I don't like those. Let's just drop this. Okay?"

Violet reluctantly agreed as she often did when the topic came up.

Violet escorted her mother out of the pub, and with Catherine leaning against her and swaying with drunkenness, she locked up the pub and then walked her mother up the side stairwell outside the building and up to the apartment her mother had lived in ever since Violet's grandfather's death. Violet herself lived nearby.

Outside the apartment door, Catherine handed her the key

and Violet opened the door. She felt for the light switch and brought her mother inside the apartment. The couch was close to the door and Violet set her mother down there.

When Violet first started bringing her drunk mother upstairs to bed, when Violet was in her teens, her mother had thanked her for the help. But as the years went by it became a sort of routine and the 'thank yous' had stopped.

After Violet had locked and bolted the front door—it was New York and the neighborhood wasn't exactly safe—she got her mother up from the couch and led her into the bedroom and turned on the lamp.

Violet and her mother owned all the apartments above the pub and, since they were fair landlords, many of their tenants had rented from them for years. Most of the other landlords in the neighborhood had kicked out their years-long tenants in favor of the new professionals who had moved into the neighborhood in the last few years and who could pay more rent, but Violet and her mother had remained loyal to their own kind.

Violet helped her mother into bed and undressed her. She got her nightgown out of the drawer.

"Raise your hands up," she told her mother, and when she did Violet slipped the gown over her mother's head.

Her mother looked up at her with tears in her eyes; she often become emotional when drunk. "Thank you," she said to Violet.

"You're welcome," Violet said. "Why are you sad?"

"I have my reasons," Catherine said faintly.

"Do you want to tell me them?" Violet asked gently.

"Not tonight. Maybe someday I will."

Violet nodded. "All right." She went into the bathroom to get her mother a glass of water and handed it to her. She set down a bottle of headache relief medicine on her mother's nightstand.

"I figured you could use that later." She indicated to the bottle.

"Smart girl," her mother said. "Thanks for looking out for me."

Violet handed the water glass to Catherine and she got under the covers and Violet turned off the lamp.

"Don't forget to take a pill when you wake up," she told her mother as she left the room.

"I won't."

Violet left her mother's apartment building and walked to her own apartment. She and her mother both owned unregistered guns and Violet carried hers, a small piece, in her purse for when she walked home alone at night in the dangerous city, which was often. She had frightened away a knife-carrying, would-be robber more than once. And if they'd had a gun themselves, what would she have done? She'd learned long ago that most didn't have enough strength to pull that trigger, but that she did.

A homeless woman asked her for money, and she gave her a few dollars. The woman grinned from ear to ear. She enjoyed doing random kind things like that sometimes, because she figured that in the eyes of God, it might make up for all the bad things she'd done and would do.

She made it home safely that night and entered her apartment building, smiling to herself when she thought of how immaculate her building looked compared to Camille O'Brien's place. Her mother might have had a soft spot for Camille but at least Violet lived in a better building. If things kept going the way they were, she would have enough money to move to the suburbs. She wanted Tommy to finish growing up with fresh air and green grass, under clear, blue skies.

Her live-in boyfriend Anton was home with Tommy, but both would be asleep at that hour. Anton, American born and half Irish and half Russian, used to work for a rival Russian gang, but after meeting Violet, he now worked for her and her mother.

The apartment building was quiet, as it often was during the late nights she returned home. On her floor she got her keys out of her purse and unlocked the door. The light inside was on, but at first it looked like the living room was empty and she figured that Anton and Tommy were probably asleep. Well, Tommy better be. She set her keys on the table by the front door and shut and locked the door. Then she entered the living room and saw a shirtless Anton seated on the couch in front of the low coffee table, injecting what looked like heroin into his rubber-banded arm. He was using again, when he'd promised her over the last few months that he was clean. She should have known better than to trust him.

"V," he said quietly. "This isn't what it looks like."

"Like hell it isn't," Violet exclaimed. "You're using again."

4

Anton set the needle down on the table and sat back into the couch. "I really tried not to, but I couldn't stop."

Violet shook her head in anger.

Her first concern was Tommy—had he seen Anton shooting up? She went to check on him and breathed out in relief when she found him asleep in his bedroom. She didn't want him seeing things like that; she didn't want to ruin his innocence too soon, like her own had been. She made it a point to keep him away from the darker aspects of her life and her business, and Anton had brought that reality straight into her home, where Tommy could have seen.

Violet shut the door to keep Anton out and knelt on the floor of Tommy's room. She stroked his hair and watched him sleeping peacefully.

Tommy heard her in his room and stirred. "Mom?" he asked sleepily. "What's going on?"

"It's all right, sweetheart, go back to sleep." She kissed his forehead.

She would have to deal with Anton. Violet rose. She'd taken her purse with her into Tommy's bedroom and she removed her silver gun. Anton had a gun himself, and it wouldn't be easy to get him to leave, but she would make him. She left Tommy's room and closed the door behind her. Violet marched into the living room and pointed the gun at Anton, who had fallen asleep in a drug-induced stupor on the couch.

"Get out of my apartment," she ordered. "This is the last time you'll expose my child to this. I don't ever want to see you again."

But Anton hadn't been sleeping like she'd thought; he was awake with his eyes shut. He chuckled and opened his eyes.

"That's pretty ironic coming from you, who used to be a junkie yourself," he said smugly.

Violet shook with rage and wanted to pull the trigger. Anton often brought up her own past during their arguments about his using drugs because he knew it bothered her.

"I won't let you expose Tommy to this," she said calmly. "Leave now."

"They took Tommy away from you," he replied. "Because you were such a big junkie."

"That was years ago," Violet said, trying not to let her voice crack. "I was just a kid."

A social worker had temporarily removed Tommy from her care a year after his birth because she had been arrested for heroin possession. The charges were later downgraded to a misdemeanor and she'd been granted probation instead of jail time. Anton knew how to get her where it hurt the most, through Tommy.

"Once a junkie, always a junkie. You're a junkie, too, V, and don't you forget it."

Violet wanted to scream at the top of her lungs, but she had Tommy to think about in the other room. She didn't want to wake him, and she didn't want him to see her pointing a gun at someone.

"Anton, I'm warning you, I won't hesitate to use this on you," she said.

"Yeah, and then you and your mother will have some of the guys dispose of my body. I got people, family, who'll miss me, so you might want to think twice about that."

But Violet knew that in this neighborhood when it came to the matters of her and her mother, people didn't dare ring the police. Still, Tommy would hear if she shot him and he'd come out to look and see everything, and she didn't want him to have such an unpleasant memory.

"Get up and go," she said. "I'm not going to ask you again."

Anton looked at her and seemed to be deciding what to do then he started to rise, unsteadily.

"I guess this means I'm no longer working for you and your mother," he mumbled.

"You've guessed right," she replied, figuring the Russians would just cajole him back into joining them. Anton was the kind of guy that was useful for a gang to have around because he would do almost any task asked of him, no matter how gruesome.

"Good," Anton said tersely. "I don't like taking orders from my woman anyway."

"I never was your 'woman'," Violet snapped.

Anton looked at her and smirked. "On most nights you were. I didn't hear you complaining then."

Violet cringed at the innuendo. "Get out, and I never want to see you again."

"I'm sure you will. You'll come crawling back because you miss me so much." He blew her a kiss.

"I wouldn't count on it." Violet still had the gun pointed at him just in case he tried something, and she kept her eyes on his hands instead of his face.

Anton put on his shirt and seemed to be taking forever and

she wanted to yell at him to hurry up, but she didn't want Tommy coming out of his room. Tommy had never seen her gun or her mother's, or Anton's. He didn't know about the violence in their lives. The irony was that Anton had always treated Tommy well. That was a big rule she'd had over the years of dating: the guys had to like her son.

"Can I get my things?" Anton asked.

"I'll come with you," Violet said and trailed him into their bedroom.

Anton had moved in recently, after convincing her of his sobriety, so he didn't have much to pack. He got his clothes out of the drawers and tossed his gun on top then he zippered the bag and grabbed it from the bed.

"Go," Violet gave a quiet order; Tommy's bedroom was adjacent to theirs.

Pointing the gun at his back, Violet followed Anton into the living room. She gestured at the implements on the coffee table.

"Take those with you," she said. "I don't want them in my home."

"Why, afraid you'll be tempted to use it?" Anton remarked with a cruel smile.

Violet didn't answer him. Anton grabbed the materials, opened his bag and shoved them inside under her watch. She followed him to the front door.

"One more thing," she said. "I need the key I gave you." With her free hand, she opened her palm in front of him.

Anton grunted. "You're really serious about me not coming back, aren't you? I thought you'd cool off after a couple of days."

"I want you gone for good," Violet replied. "And you no longer work for me and my mother. You know we don't tolerate junkies. We already gave you a second chance because Tommy likes you."

Anton took the spare apartment key out of his pocket and

gave it to her with a sigh. "You know, it's too bad we had to end it like this, with you pointing a fucking gun at me, when the beginning was so nice."

Violet shrugged, although she knew Tommy would be disappointed to see him go. Anton left and Violet shut and bolted the door behind him. As she started to go check on Tommy, the phone rang in the kitchen.

Violet ran in and answered.

"Hello?"

"It's me," her mother said.

"How are you feeling?"

"Better," she said. "I went and got some fresh air when I woke up."

"You didn't sleep for very long," Violet said.

"You know me, I don't need much sleep."

"Why are you calling at this hour? You wanted to talk? I threw Anton out."

"What happened?"

"He's using again."

"That's too bad. I liked Anton."

"He's gone, this time for good. I can't have that in the house with Tommy."

"I know. I'm sure you did the right thing. How's Tommy going to take it? I know he liked Anton."

"I'll worry about that when he gets up," Violet replied.

"About why I'm calling," Catherine said, "you know the guy who's been giving Max the runaround?"

"Yeah, what about it?"

"I've been thinking about it—that's what I've been doing since getting some fresh air—and I think it's time to say goodbye."

Violet knew her mother meant the man who owed them thousands through Max and wasn't paying up. Her mother wanted him whacked. They would discuss those matters in a roundabout way just in case they were being wiretapped.

"Should I meet you at the pub?" Violet asked her mother.

"Yeah, in a half hour. I'll call the guys and tell them to meet us there."

A middle of the night or very early morning in person 'meeting' at the pub to discuss a problem wasn't uncommon in their business, and often occurred when they needed to deal with something and her mother didn't want to discuss it on the phone.

Violet didn't like leaving Tommy alone when he was sleeping, especially at that odd hour, but with Anton gone, it wasn't like she'd be able to easily find a babysitter in the middle of the night.

She went into the bathroom and saw she didn't look well so she washed her face and put on some fresh makeup. She fixed her hair and then went to check on Tommy in his room. She saw him breathing softly under the covers and smiled to herself. If the rest of her life was a mess, Tommy was the one thing she had gotten right.

"I'll be back in a while to walk you to school," she whispered to Tommy, but he couldn't hear her.

She closed the door to Tommy's bedroom and put her gun in her purse and walked out the door, locking it behind her.

Out on the dark street, the hot city air dampened her bare arms. She passed by a group of prostitutes who were on the lookout for clients.

"Hello, ladies," she said, because she knew them from the neighborhood, and knew they wouldn't ask her questions about where she was headed at that late hour. They knew she owned the pub down the street and that sometimes she gave them a hot meal when they were in need, but that was all.

"Hi, sugar," one of them replied.

Violet continued walking to the pub, keeping her purse with her gun inside tucked under her arm just in case she needed it. Sometimes, she carried her gun in her waistband, but it was more noticeable when she did so, and she had to be careful. She made it to the pub even before her mother who lived upstairs, so she unlocked the door but kept the lights off so they wouldn't draw suspicion given the hour and couldn't as easily be photographed inside. The meeting would take place in the locked backroom behind the kitchen, which everyone thought was an unused supply closet, and was a place only Violet, her mother, and Max and their men knew the truth about. Not even Camille had been allowed inside it.

With her purse on the bar, Violet sat and waited for her mother and their men to arrive. Max wouldn't be coming because they mostly respected his wish to not be bothered in the wee hours at his age but would be kept informed of what unfolded. She could make out the clock in the dark room, and seeing that her mother and men would be late, she reached over the bar and helped herself to the bottle of fine whiskey she kept there. Like heroin had once been, drinking was another one of Violet's weaknesses, and so it was something she didn't indulge in often. But after throwing out Anton, she figured she deserved a drink.

"Just one," she whispered to herself. "Just one."

Not bothering to use a glass, she opened the bottle and put it to her lips. It had been a while since she last drank, and she enjoyed the strong, refined taste in her mouth. She set down the bottle on the bar then reached for it again, held it in her hand for a moment and considered taking another drink. It would be easy to become like her mother and drown her sorrows in the bottle. And just what was her mother so sorrowful about? Violet supposed she had her reasons, like everyone did. Then Tommy's smiling face appeared in her mind, like a reminder not to indulge. Violet pushed the bottle off to the side of the bar.

She watched the clock. Where were they? Then something unpleasant crossed her mind. Had something happened to delay them, such as an arrest? Her mother was directly upstairs and probably just running late, but the men were out of her sight and she didn't know what was going on with them.

There was a knock on the door, and then Derrick, Violet and her mother's top man, besides Max, walked inside the pub.

"Derrick," she said.

He recognized her voice in the dark. "No lights?" he remarked. "Are you all right, Violet?" he asked as though she was being unnecessarily paranoid.

"You know better than anyone that we have to be careful," she replied.

"Yeah, but I might trip and crack my head in the dark," he joked.

"Have a seat at the bar." She smacked the bar stool next to hers. "We'll be going into the back once the others arrive."

"All right. Got anything to drink?" he asked as he sat down.

Violet moved the whiskey over to his side.

"Got a glass?" he asked next.

Violet reached behind the bar for one.

"Thanks," Derrick said as she handed it to him.

Derrick opened the bottle and poured his drink. Back when Violet's grandfather ran the gang, he had a strict rule about no heavy drinking or drugs, and Violet and her mother had continued the rule despite her mother constantly breaking it. They wouldn't even sell drugs, that's what separated them from the other gangs.

Derrick had a drink and then went to pour himself another.

"Careful," Violet said, and she didn't like having to remind him.

34

Aware of the rules, Derrick closed the bottle and moved it back to her side.

Violet looked at the clock. "I'm going to check to see what's taking my mother so long," she said to Derrick.

She got up and as she made her way to the front door, it opened with Catherine and the remaining two men, Jake and Patrick, who everyone called Pat, appearing.

"I can't see anything," Catherine said then turned on the light.

"Mom," Violet said. "You know why it isn't on. Someone could see us." She got up and switched it off.

"Who? The police?" Catherine said. "They've barely noticed us before. No one's out there, sweetheart."

Violet sighed because she knew about her mother's stubbornness.

"Yeah, Violet, I'm sure we have nothing to worry about," Pat said.

"Yeah, Cathy's right," Jake said.

The circumstances weren't unusual because the men, even Max, frequently took her mother's side, which wasn't too surprising to Violet since some of them had worked for her family going back to her grandfather and had known her mother longer than they'd known her.

"I'm leaving it off. Let's just go into the back, all right?" Violet told them. "Then we can stop debating about this. I'm getting a headache over this nonsense."

"Do you want us to kill someone, is that why you called us here at this God-awful hour?" Pat, the blunt one of the group, asked.

Catherine shushed him. "We don't talk about that outside the backroom."

Pat shrugged. "Sorry, Cathy."

Jake leaned over the bar.

"What are you looking for?" Derrick asked him.

"A drink," he replied.

"Violet's got a bottle of whiskey on the bar."

"Oh, I didn't see it." Jake felt for the bottle and grabbed it. He held it up in the moonlight trickling into the pub. "I'll bring it in the back with us in case one of us gets thirsty."

"You know the rules," Catherine said.

Violet saw the irony in her mother's retort. It wasn't like Catherine's drinking problem was kept secret, but no one talked about it.

"We'll just have one each," Jake said.

"Derrick's already had one," Violet said. "And to be fair, so have I."

They made their way into the kitchen and Violet turned on the light there since it wasn't visible to the outside. Catherine took out the key to the secret room and Violet and the men waited for her to open it. Jake took a swig from the bottle and Violet grabbed it from him.

"You aren't even gonna use a glass?" she said.

"I'm sure you didn't," Jake replied.

"Yeah, but it's my bottle."

Violet handed it to Pat. "You want one?" she asked him.

He declined.

Catherine took the bottle from Violet and left it outside when they stepped into the windowless room.

Violet pulled the string attached to the ceiling bulb to turn on the light then she shut the door. There was a table and a few folding chairs in the small room and she and her mother and Derrick sat, while Jake and Pat, who were lower down in the organization, leaned against the wall.

"You were right, Pat," Catherine said, looking at him.

"Who's the lucky bastard?" Pat asked.

"Name's Joseph O'Connor. He owes us thousands through

Max and keeps brushing off Max every time he confronts him about it. He doesn't take us seriously, so we'll have to show him just how serious we are."

"Want us to give him a beating?" Pat said.

"I think we're already past that," Catherine replied. "Max sent Anton over to the guy's house to give him a beating and even that didn't work. He's still not taking us seriously. He thinks he doesn't have to pay up. We need to send a message to those in the neighborhood who are considering doing the same thing."

"Maybe Max shouldn't have let him place all those bets," Jake remarked.

"Max ain't his minder," Pat countered. "You know how this business works, and these people know what they're getting into when they get involved with us. We're not saints, and they know it."

"It isn't just the bets that are the problem," Catherine said. "He borrowed money from us to place those bets."

"Where's Anton anyway?" Derrick asked.

"Anton's not going to be joining us tonight—or ever again," Catherine said.

"He's dead?" Jake asked, and his face whitened. From his tone, Violet wondered if he thought that Catherine had killed Anton.

"No," Violet said. "I caught him using again."

The men nodded and didn't ask questions; once Catherine made a decision, it was final.

"About this O'Connor," Violet said. "Keep it quick and get rid of it clean. We don't want a mess like that last time."

The last time the guys had eliminated someone, they used the warehouse Violet and her mother owned on the waterfront to butcher his remains then put them in oil barrels to drop into the Hudson River at night. They'd never cleaned up after themselves after, so Violet and Max had to deal with the disgusting mess, and Max had complained he'd ruined his favorite shoes.

"What do you mean?" Jake asked.

"Put a bullet in his head then break his bones and shove him into a barrel in one piece, is what I mean," Catherine said bluntly. "Don't chop him up like the last time. When it's done, call the pub and one of us will answer the phone. I'll need confirmation it's done."

While some gangs hired contract killers for the type of deed Catherine was asking, Violet and her mother's crew had continued Violet's grandfather's reign of brutality and chose to carry such grim tasks out themselves, which was why even the Italian mob respected them.

"You'll get a bonus, of course," Violet told the men. "For your trouble."

The men grunted in approval, but it wasn't as though they had much choice; if they denied Catherine what she wanted, then they might find themselves on the other end of her wrath.

Catherine handed Derrick the man's address. "But don't do it near his home."

"He's got a wife and kids?" Derrick asked.

"A wife. No kids," Catherine replied. "Follow him, get him into the van. And then do it somewhere far away. We aren't monsters."

They kept the van in the warehouse and used it to transport those that they needed to deal with, and when they weren't using it for that, they were using it to pick up supplies for the pub.

"Any special requests?" Pat asked. "I know you had said you wanted to send a message."

Catherine shook her head. "His death will be clear enough."

Back in the day when Violet's grandfather ran the mob, he'd

sometimes leave a severed finger or two where someone could find them.

Violet swallowed at the thought and was thankful her mother lacked his morbid humor.

Violet checked the time. "I should be going. I don't want Tommy to wake up and I'm not there," she told her mother.

"How is the big guy?" Jake asked her with a smile. Her mother had thought Jake had a crush on her, but Violet felt he was just the most outgoing member of their crew.

"He's well," she said. "But he won't be happy about Anton leaving."

"Yeah, I remember you said he really liked Anton," Jake replied. "That's too bad."

"Go," her mother gestured for her to leave.

Violet got up and said goodbye to the men. She knew her mother wouldn't give them their bonus until the act had been completed.

She exited the dark pub for the city streets. Daylight was fast approaching and Violet hurried home to get Tommy ready for school before he woke up and saw she wasn't home. She crossed the street quickly and avoided getting hit by a taxicab. The women she'd said hello to earlier were leaving for the day and one of them yelled at her to be careful.

"You're gonna get killed someday if you keep doing that," the woman said.

Violet nodded and smiled at her, but the truth was that there was so much danger in her life that risks like that didn't seem like much.

Violet entered her apartment building and ran up the stairs. She quietly put the key in the lock and entered.

"Mom?" Tommy said in front of her. "Where did you go?"

"Hi, big guy," she replied, ruffling his hair, but he was already almost as tall as she was. She thought about what to say, not the truth. "I needed to go for a walk to clear my head."

"You do that a lot," he said.

Violet smiled at her son but was saddened by his words. Tommy was right; there were a lot of middle-of-the-night meetings at the pub, and sometimes people were killed afterwards and Violet knew about it, and although she had helped clean up after the killings, she had never participated in them directly.

"Come on," she said. "You need to get ready for school."

Tommy looked around the living room. "Where's Anton?"

"He had to . . ." Violet paused. "He's gone, Tommy. I had to throw him out because he wasn't being honest with me." There wasn't any other way to put it.

"He lied to you?" Tommy asked.

Violet nodded.

"What did he tell you?" he asked.

"Anton had a problem," she said delicately, to preserve her son's innocence. "It wasn't good. He couldn't live with us anymore."

"Will he still work for grandma?" Tommy asked. Her son knew that Anton had worked for his grandmother but not the true nature of their business. Tommy thought that Anton worked at the pub, which had been easy to pretend since Anton had hung around there a lot. But that would stop.

"I'm afraid he can't anymore," Violet replied.

"Why not? Does it have to do with his problem?"

Violet nodded. Tears pooled in her eyes at her son's virtue, and she wiped them away.

"It's okay, Mom, you don't have to tell me more." It was in Tommy's nature to not want to see people upset, especially his mother.

Tommy went to his bedroom to prepare for school and

Violet made them some breakfast. After they had eaten, Tommy put his backpack on his shoulders, and they left the apartment to walk to the local Catholic school he attended.

Her son looked dashing in his school uniform and Violet patted his shoulder tenderly as they walked. Tommy looked over at her and smiled.

"You know, I'm old enough to walk to school," he said.

"I know, but we live in New York City. It's dangerous," she replied. "Let's wait until you're at least a teenager, okay?"

Tommy nodded.

Once they arrived, she said goodbye. He was at that age when he didn't want a hug, or, God forbid, a kiss, from his mother in front of his schoolmates. His school wasn't far from the pub so she went to the shop at the corner for a cup of coffee and then headed there. Halfway on her way there, her hands shook as she thought about what her men could be doing at that very moment and she dropped the cup on the ground. Was she getting soft, or was it because each time they did something like that it meant they were one stop closer to getting caught?

She sighed and picked it up and threw it away in a trash can.

She made it to the pub and found her mother already there, perhaps she had been there since Violet left her—Catherine never seemed to need much rest despite her drinking. Camille hadn't arrived yet but was due to come at any moment.

Catherine poured a cup of coffee for each of them and gestured for Violet to join her at the bar before they opened for the day.

"Hear any news from the guys yet?" she asked her mother.

Catherine shook her head.

Violet put the coffee cup to her lips but was suddenly too anxious to drink any. She put the cup back down and watched her mother drinking her coffee.

"How can you drink when I'm too nervous to?" she asked.

Catherine shrugged. "I've gotten used to it over the years, and you will soon."

"I know, but some things you just don't get used to. These kinds of things, especially, could attract the police. I worry."

"Don't, sweetheart." Catherine touched Violet's hand on the bar. "It's never been a problem before."

Violet nodded but her mother's words wouldn't quell her worries.

After a few minutes, they got up to prepare to open for the early drinking crowd, and in this neighborhood, there were many. Max came in a few minutes later, followed by Camille.

Hours later evening arrived, and the pub began to get crowded for the night. The phone rang in the kitchen above the noise and Violet looked at her mother and then ran to answer.

"Hello?" she said, putting her hand to her other ear to block out the sounds of the pub.

"Job's done," Derrick said on the other end of the phone.

Violet hung up and walked out to the barroom and approached her mother, who was chatting with a few customers. She motioned for Catherine to come with her. They checked to make sure no one was in the ladies' room and then stepped inside.

"Derrick called. It's done," Violet told her mother by the sink.

"That's good to hear. I'll make sure the fellas get their money."

"I'll let Max know," Catherine said. "I'm sure he'll be pleased."

5

Camille sweated as she worked behind the bar and tried to keep up with the orders of the big crowd in the pub. Out of the corner of her eye, she watched Violet leaving the ladies room with her mother and wondered what they were up to. Catherine walked upstairs, presumably to talk with Max. What about? Camille could only guess.

The pub door opened, and Johnny Garcia strode in. Camille was surprised to see him, but maybe she shouldn't have been, since he'd said he'd return to see her. One thing was for sure, he wasn't going to give up easily.

He grinned at her from across the room and approached the bar. He found room at the end of the bar and waved to get her attention, but she'd already seen him and was ignoring him. When he started calling her name, she had to look at him.

She threw her bar towel over her shoulder and went over to face him.

"What are you doing here?" she asked.

"I'm here to see you. I said I'd see you soon, remember?" Johnny smiled. "Where did you learn bartending?"

"From working at various places," she said, then stopped

when she realized he was trying to have a conversation with her. "I'm busy, as you can see."

"I realize that," he said.

Violet eyed them from across the room.

"My bosses don't know why you're in here," Camille told him.

Johnny glanced at Violet. "I can see that."

"Why don't they like you?" she asked, but she thought that she already might have known why. "I know you're a gangster."

"Who told you that?"

"They did."

"They're trying to get you to stay away from me," Johnny replied. "Are you going to listen to them?"

"I haven't decided yet," Camille said with a smile. "Did that guy you were hassling in here the other day ever pay you?"

"No, but I'll make him."

"And if you can't?" But Camille thought she already knew the answer, yet she wanted him to tell her, to confirm what Violet and Catherine had said he was.

"Me and my guys will have to hurt him."

"So, it's true, then, you are a gangster. Is that why they don't like you?"

"They probably don't like me because I'm Cuban."

"That's terrible," Camille said. "But I don't think that's why."

"Me and the Irish don't exactly get along," Johnny said.

"I'm Irish," Camille replied.

"I know."

"Why don't you like us?" she asked.

"It's personal."

"Tell me."

"Okay, I will. They killed my father and his gang leader, a guy named Tito Bernal, Irish gangsters did."

"I'm sorry, I didn't know that."

"Thanks. But why would you have known that?" Johnny asked.

Camille realized she'd slipped up. "No reason," she quickly said.

"It was a long time ago," Johnny said after a while. "I took over recently. I used to have a real job before that, but this is more lucrative. I'm taking a risk by even setting foot in this place, but I knew the guy frequented here and I want my money, and then I just had to see you again."

"I hope I'm worth it," Camille cracked a joke.

"I'm betting you are," he flirted.

"What are your plans for the gang?" she asked him.

"I got lots of them, one of them is to avenge my father."

"Why are you telling me that?" she asked, thinking how they had something in common.

"Because while I don't know you well, I have a feeling I can trust you."

"You're taking a big risk."

"Then it's one I'll just have to take." Johnny smiled. "Go on a date with me."

"Maybe. When?"

"When does your shift end?"

"In an hour."

"How about then? There's a late-night movie playing at the cinema."

"I'm not sure," she replied.

"Why, what's there not to like?"

"You're pretty confident," she said.

"In my line of work, I ought to be."

"All right, I'll go with you. But if I have a bad time I'm leaving. I'm not staying out of politeness."

"It's a deal. I like a blunt woman." Johnny smiled. "I'll be waiting outside in an hour."

"All right, I'll see you then. Meet me in the back."

After Johnny left, Violet approached the bar.

"What was he doing in here again?" she asked Camille.

It really wasn't any of Violet's business, but it was her pub so Camille replied, "He was just saying hello."

"I should have thrown him out," Violet remarked. "Next time, maybe I will."

Camille didn't dare tell her about her date with Johnny. "Why? To protect me? Why do you care so much anyway, Violet? I get why your mother does, but why do you?" Camille felt that Violet might just be trying to cause trouble for her.

"Because you work here, and I thought we were friends." Violet sounded hurt.

Camille looked at her. "I'm sorry."

Violet nodded but didn't say anything. Perhaps Camille had been too harsh. A customer ordered another drink and Camille had to step away. She watched Violet walk away to speak with her mother, who had returned from upstairs. Violet pointed at Camille and Catherine shook her head. Violet had probably told her mother about Johnny's visit. Oh, well, Johnny seemed like an all right guy, and she didn't care what they thought, but at the same time she knew they could make things hard for her.

Max came down from upstairs and joined Violet and her mother in staring at Camille. Why were they talking to Max about it? To hell with all of them. If she wanted to spend time with Johnny that was her choice.

The hour seemed to take forever to pass, and by the time Camille had finished her shift she felt so tired that she somewhat regretted agreeing to the date, when all she really wanted to do was go home and sleep.

Camille didn't have time to go home and change for her date. She sneaked out of the back and Johnny wasn't there. She looked around for him, but no luck. *Just great. I've been stood up.*

She started to walk home.

"Camille," Johnny called out from down the street. "Wait!"

She glanced at him over her shoulder. Then she stopped. After all, she had left the pub a little early so technically he wasn't late.

"Hi," she said.

"Were you leaving?" He smiled.

"Yeah, I thought you were late." Camille laughed, and so did Johnny. "I thought you stood me up."

"I wouldn't do that. I thought that maybe *you* were ditching me," he said.

"I'm sorry I doubted you," she said. "I'm not great at trusting people."

"It's okay, I'm not either."

They began to walk to the cinema a few blocks away.

"Do you know what's playing?" she asked him.

"I heard that *Back to the Future* is playing. Have you ever seen it?" Johnny asked.

Camille shook her head. "But I heard it supposed to be good."

They passed a couple of restaurants that were closed for the night, but the air still smelled of the food prepared there earlier. The heat made it difficult for Camille to talk and walk at the same time, but she tried anyway.

"Did you grow up in this neighborhood?" Johnny asked her.

"Yeah. What about you?"

"I grew up in Brooklyn. Do you have any brothers or sisters?" he asked.

"No, I'm an only child. You?"

"I have a sister, but we're not very close. She still lives in Brooklyn."

The traffic had thinned out given the late hour but there were still cars driving past them as they walked.

"My father died when I was a baby," Camille told him, perhaps unconsciously she hoped he would realize his father's possible connection to hers.

Johnny stopped walking. "I'm sorry to hear that."

"Yeah, I didn't know him at all, just from what my mother tells me."

They continued walking.

"What about your parents?" she asked him, but she already knew.

"My father died when I was a kid, but older than a baby," he replied. "My mother is still alive, but we aren't that close. Are you close with yours?"

Camille nodded.

He had to have been the son of her father's friend. She didn't know why she kept the revelation a secret from him, the right time to tell him just never seemed to come.

"In the pub, you said you wanted to avenge your father, what did you mean by that?" she asked him.

"Just what I said, Irish gangsters killed my father."

Camille paused. "So you plan to kill them?"

"If I can."

His blunt answer should have shocked her, but it didn't. They walked in silence for a while, and soon they made it to the cinema and bought tickets for the midnight showing from the box. Johnny insisted on paying for hers despite Camille's protest. He also bought popcorn and sodas.

"I enjoy treating you," he said.

Camille was sort of relieved at seeing a movie for their date because that meant that they didn't have to talk for a while, because she didn't know how long she'd be able to keep the secret from Johnny, or when would be the right time to tell him. She didn't want him to be reminded of his father, because that seemed to bring out a sadness in him.

Halfway through the movie, the popcorn bag was empty, and Johnny looked over at her in the crowded theatre and smiled then took her buttery hand and held it in his. Camille sipped her soda and kept her hand there until the ending credits rolled. He waited until everyone else left the room to kiss her, which was the first kiss she'd had since Billy.

"When can I see you again?" he asked after the usher had asked them to leave the theatre.

"Soon," Camille said, and gave him her phone number.

Neither of them had a paper or pen.

"I'll remember it," Johnny said, but Camille didn't know if he would. Perhaps she'd never see him again. It wasn't like he was welcome at the pub.

He smiled. "Let me walk you home."

"Thanks, but I'll be fine." She didn't trust herself enough to resist him once he was at her door.

"Please," he said. "It's late, and this is New York."

"All right."

They were some of the last ones to exit the theatre building and a crowd had gathered outside on the street to watch a young guy in a baseball cap, a bright top, and jeans break-dancing on the sidewalk. Loud music played from a radio on the sidewalk near him. The kid was very talented, and people cheered and whistled to encourage him to keep going. A few people left dollar bills in his hat on the sidewalk. Johnny and Camille stopped to watch for a few moments.

"Hey, this guy is pretty good," Johnny said to her with a smile and she nodded in agreement, mesmerized.

After a few minutes the kid stopped, and a couple asked him when his next show would be. He shrugged and replied he wasn't sure. When the sidewalk cleared, the kid walked up to Johnny and Camille, the only ones remaining.

"Hey, man, this your girl?" he asked Johnny as he looked at Camille.

"I hope she will be," Johnny replied with a grin.

"You should hope so man, she's fine." The kid grinned. "Rafael sent me to come get you. Some of our guys got into a fight."

"With each other?" Johnny scowled.

"*Si.* Rafael had to fire his gun to break it up."

"What was it about?" Johnny asked.

The kid shrugged. "They were squabbling over something stupid."

Johnny shook his head. "They're acting like a bunch of cowboys."

"Anyway, Rafael called a meeting and he sent me to come get you," he said, again.

Johnny looked at Camille and apologized. "I have to go deal with this." He looked at the kid. "Walk her home, will you?"

He nodded, and Johnny hugged Camille goodbye, his arms felt strong around her and he smelled faintly of cologne, then he took off down the street.

"Where do you live?" the kid asked as she watched Johnny leaving.

"Not far," she replied. "What's your name?" she asked him.

"Pedro," he said. "Yours?"

"Camille."

They shook hands.

"Do you work for Johnny?" she asked him.

"Yeah, something like that."

They'd started to walk toward her apartment building, with him carrying the radio.

"How do you know him?" Pedro asked. "If you don't mind saying. Johnny wouldn't like me bugging you."

"It's okay," Camille said. "I haven't known him very long. We only met the other day. He came into the pub where I work."

"Are you a waitress?"

"No, a bartender."

"Johnny's a good guy," Pedro said. "I like him a whole lot better than Rafael, but don't tell anyone that." He smiled.

"Don't worry, I won't. Who's Rafael?" she asked.

"Johnny's number one guy, but I think he'd like nothing more than to be Johnny. Don't tell anyone I told you that."

"I won't. How long have you known Johnny?" she asked him.

"Since I was in diapers," he said with a laugh.

"Really?"

"Yeah, our mothers were friends when they were girls. Johnny sort of looked out for me over the years. He's like a big brother to me."

"So, you think he's a good guy?" Camille asked him.

"Johnny? Yeah. He's the greatest. He'd be embarrassed if he knew I told you that 'cause he's kinda shy when it comes to stuff like that, but he's the man."

"Okay, I'll take your word for it." Then she asked him something just in case, because she didn't like surprises. "He doesn't already have a girlfriend, does he?"

Pedro seemed to hesitate and for a moment Camille thought he'd answer yes. Then he shook his head. Still, it seemed like he wanted to tell her something.

"What is it, Pedro?" she asked.

"Nothing. He hasn't got one. I have a girlfriend."

"What's she like?"

"Her name's Fiona. What, you thought her name was gonna be Maria or something?" Pedro grinned when he saw the look on her face. "She's Irish. Her father would probably kill me if he knew we were dating."

"Do you live in this neighborhood?" she asked him.

"Yeah, but no matter where I was, he'd still find me. He isn't a wise guy or anything like that, he's an electrician. But he doesn't like Cubans."

"That's awful," Camille said. "I hope it works out for you two."

"Thanks. I want to marry her someday."

"You already know that at your age? What are you, fifteen?"

"Sixteen," he said.

"You should be thinking about school."

"I might leave school to marry her. She's a year older than me and wants to finish."

"Pedro, you shouldn't leave school." Camille stopped in her tracks and looked at him. "You can still be with her and finish school."

"How do you know? You don't even know me, no offense."

"Because I saw your dancing, and with your talent, if you finished school, you could go places."

"I already work with Johnny and Rafael."

"Places beyond that," Camille said.

"No one ever told me that before, so thanks. But I like where I already am."

"Do your parents know you aren't planning to finish school?"

"My dad died when I was little."

"I'm sorry to hear that. I lost my father when I was really young also. What about your mother, what does she think?"

"She doesn't know. I have brothers and sisters who are younger than me so she's busy with them all the time."

"All the more reason to set a good example for them," Camille said.

"My mother would like you," Pedro said with a smile. "I think I'll tell Johnny that I approve of you."

"Thanks," Camille replied with a smile. They passed by a group of teenagers running around in the street, laughing, as they neared her apartment building. "My place is just down the street. I can walk the rest of the way if you want to go. You really should be at home this time of the night. Your mother will probably worry."

"She won't notice," Pedro said. "I promised Johnny I'd walk you home, so I better come with you the rest of the way."

"I'll be fine," she insisted.

"Johnny will be angry with me if I don't, so I have to. Okay?"

Camille nodded.

They reached her building and said goodnight. The street was very quiet that time of the night, and the streetlamps cast an ethereal glow on the sidewalk. Pedro stood there waiting as she walked up the steps. Camille turned around.

"You can leave, you know," she said.

"Johnny would want me to make sure you got inside okay."

Camille smiled to herself at the importance he gave the matter. She walked inside all the way and then through the small, narrow window at the side of the door, watched him leaving holding the radio.

6

Early the next morning, Camille's phone rang while she was still sleeping. She rolled over in bed and reached to answer it. She checked her clock and saw that she had another hour of sleep left before she had to rise to run some errands before going to work. There was only one person who could be ringing her at this hour.

"Sweetheart, how are you?" her mother asked on the other end.

"I was still asleep," Camille replied.

"You should get up earlier. Getting too much sleep is just as bad as not getting enough," Sheila said, and Camille had to smile at her mother's advice.

"I went to bed late last night."

"You were working late?"

"Not exactly."

"What's that mean?"

"I went out with someone after work."

"A friend?"

"No, a date."

Her mother paused. "With Billy?" Hope lifted her voice.

"No, Ma. Billy and I are done, you know that."

"Then who did you go out with?"

"His name's John, Johnny."

"Last name?"

"Johnny Garcia." Then she said, "I think he's the son of Dad's friend." Sheila was so quiet on the other end that Camille said, "Hello?"

"His son? What are you talking about?" Sheila finally spoke.

"I'm pretty sure that Johnny Jr., is the son of Dad's friend Johnny Garcia, you know, the one you told me about?"

"You really think he is?"

"Yeah, he has to be."

"Camille, you shouldn't get involved with him."

"What are you talking about?" Camille couldn't hide the hurt in her voice. First the McCarthys had given her trouble about Johnny, and now her mother. "Why would you say that when you don't even know him?"

"Trust me, it's for the best."

"What do you mean?"

"It's for the best."

"Tell me what you mean. You don't know him, or do you?"

"I don't."

"But you knew his father?"

"Not really. If he's even his son."

"I think he is."

"What's he do for a living anyway? His father was in a gang."

"Like my own father," Camille retorted. "It's no wonder I'm attracted to him," she snapped back. But she didn't answer her mother's question because she didn't want her to judge Johnny. "I had a nice time, in case you're wondering."

"I'm not saying he isn't a fun guy."

"He's a good guy, he isn't just 'fun'."

"Honey, see it from my point of view for a second—is he a gangster like his father?"

"Dad was one and you married him."

"So, the answer is yes. But before you accuse me again of being a hypocrite, the reason I think you should stay away from him isn't that. You need to trust me about this, Camille. There's a history there that you don't know about, there are things I've never told you."

"Did something happen between Dad and his father?"

"I don't have anything to say," Sheila replied.

"There is something, but you're not going to tell me?" Camille asked in exasperation.

"Sweetheart, there are some things about your father that are best you don't know. You don't need to know everything about him."

Camille took her mother's words to mean that the secret would be devastating to her.

"Trust me on this one," Sheila said. "Leave Johnny alone. It's better if you two don't carry on. There are lots of other guys out there."

"Yeah, but none of them are like him."

"You don't know that. Maybe you can call Billy and see how he's doing?"

"I know you liked him but please don't keep bringing him up, we're through."

"What you had with Billy will never be over," her mother insisted. "There's always a second chance."

Camille checked the time. "I have to take care of some things before work."

"Okay," Sheila said. "I didn't mean to spoil your day. You were excited about your date and I understand why. But there's a history, and it's more complicated than you know."

"He and Dad were friends, what more is there to know? How I am supposed to understand when you won't tell me anything?"

"There are some things you don't need or want to know. Trust me."

Whatever it was, it was momentous. A lump formed in Camille's throat and she couldn't speak. Her mother said goodbye and Camille hung up the phone. Just what was the secret between her father and Johnny's?

She sat up in bed and the phone rang again. It could be Johnny. Camille considered whether to answer it after what her mother had told her.

She lifted the receiver and put it to her ear. "Hello?" she said and braced herself to hear his voice.

"Morning, beautiful," Johnny said. "I can't stop thinking about you. Sorry I had to leave you last night. I hope Pedro walked you home all the way."

"Pedro was an absolute gentleman," Camille said. "If a little young to be working for you."

"I know, I tried to tell him that, but he won't stop hanging around us. If I kick him out, I figure he'll just get into trouble elsewhere, but if I keep him close by then at least I can keep an eye on him."

She smiled at his reasoning. "Make sure he finishes school," she said.

"For you, I will."

Camille could almost feel Johnny's warmth. "How are you?" she asked. "Did everything work out with your guys last night?"

"Yeah, I put them in line."

"Did you ever get that guy you hassled in the pub to pay you?"

"It was taken care of."

"Does that mean you beat him?"

"You ask a lot of questions."

"You should know up front that I won't be one of those women who you can keep in the dark."

"That's all right, I like that. I got the guy to pay me, minimal beating required. I won't lend to him ever again, that's a rule I have. If someone won't pay up, then I don't work with them a second time. It minimizes unneeded violence."

"That's a good rule," Camille said.

"Are you working today?"

"Yeah, later. I have a couple of errands to run beforehand."

"You have time for breakfast?" he asked, shyly.

Camille checked the time. "Sure." She paused. "My mother told me to stay away from you. Give me a reason not to."

"Why doesn't she like me, because I'm Cuban?"

"I'm not sure why," Camille replied, not wanting to give away her secret about her father and his. Then again, maybe Johnny already knew, and if so, why wasn't *he* saying anything about it?

"Let me take you to breakfast and I'll prove to you I'm worth it."

"All right," she said. "I'm not an easy woman to be with," she said, thinking of the difficulty Billy had with understanding her depression and her family's history of it. If she would defy her mother, she needed to be sure Johnny was worth it.

"Give me an example and I'll give you an answer, then you can decide if I can deal with it."

"I take medication for depression. My grandmother had depression as well."

Johnny didn't hesitate. "That's okay, I understand. My sister takes medication for something similar."

"Really, or are you just saying that?" she asked.

"No, she really takes pills. What she has, it's one of the reasons I'm not as close to her as I would like, because she has a hard time letting people get close to her because of what she has going on. She isn't close to my mother either."

Camille found herself wondering what his sister might be like.

"That's too bad," Camille said, and then she thought that his sister sounded a little like her.

"When do you have time to get breakfast—now?" Johnny asked.

"Sure, I can meet you in a half an hour."

"Great, what's your address?"

Camille gave it to him.

"I'll wait outside for you," Johnny said.

Camille liked that he was gentlemanly enough to avoid stepping into her apartment until he knew her better. "How about I treat you since you paid for the movies last night?" she asked.

"You don't have to do that," Johnny said. "I enjoy treating you."

"I insist," she replied sweetly.

"Okay, then. Thanks."

They said goodbye and Camille rose to take a shower and get dressed. She would run her errands after meeting Johnny.

She left her building and found Johnny already waiting for her outside.

He smiled. "I got here early so we wouldn't have a repeat of the last time. I actually live not far from here."

"Interesting. We have an excuse to see one another often, then," she replied with a smile.

"I heard there's a good diner not far from here," Johnny said.

"Yeah, I've eaten there many times."

"So, you must like it then. I assume it's a good place. I've never been there myself."

"Yeah, it's pretty good," she said, as they began to walk there.

Johnny's warm hand reached for hers, and thinking about her mother's warning—how bad could the secret have been?—

she hesitated for a second before holding his. In silence she considered asking Johnny if he knew what the secret was, but that could be risky.

"Pedro said you look out for him," she said instead.

"Yeah, I make sure the little man stays out of trouble. Pedro's a good kid, if a little lost at the moment."

"That's why he wants to be a gangster?" Camille asked honestly.

"Yeah, I guess so."

"I think I can understand why he feels that way," she said, thinking of her father.

"You sound like you know from experience," Johnny said, and then paused as though waiting for her to elaborate.

How could Johnny not have known who she was? But he didn't seem to. Unless he did, and like her, was pretending not to, but she didn't want to think that way.

"Not really," she lied. "But I could see what that would feel like. You should make sure Pedro stays out of trouble. He's a good kid."

"You're really worried about him, aren't you?" Johnny said with a smile. "You have a soft spot, Camille, and I like that. It's not often you find that in this neighborhood."

"I certainly don't get it from my mother," she said, thinking of Sheila's toughness.

"Maybe from your father, then?" Johnny suggested.

"Maybe. I never knew him," she said quietly.

"I'm sorry. What happened, if you don't mind my asking?"

"I don't want to talk about it, if that's okay."

Johnny became quiet and she didn't know if she'd offended him. "Sure, that's okay, I didn't mean to intrude," he said in an easy-going way.

"Maybe later, at some point," she said, for she knew that if they were to continue seeing one another into the future then she couldn't keep secrets from him. Sooner or later, the truth would have to come out, but she planned to keep it until later.

They reached the diner and he held the door open for her. Camille walked in ahead of him.

She turned around and smiled at him over his shoulder. "Remember, I'm treating you this time."

The woman at the front of the diner seating people eyed Johnny warily and Camille wanted to shake her. How dare she judge Johnny. Camille glared at the woman and took Johnny's hand in hers, making it clear they were together.

"Table for two," she said to the woman.

The woman stared at them with an unfriendly expression and then nodded. She picked up two menus and led them to a table far in the back when there were several empty tables closer.

"We want to sit in one of those," Camille said, pointing to one of the free tables. She wasn't going to let anyone try to hide her and Johnny.

The woman set the menus down on the table and pointed. "You can sit here."

"Why, when those tables are free?" Camille asked.

"What's going on?" Johnny whispered to her.

Camille gestured that she would take care of it.

"Those are reserved," the woman stated.

"For who?" Camille was very familiar with the diner, and it didn't look like the tables were being set aside for anyone.

"I know why you want to sit us in the back," Johnny said to the woman, realizing what was going on.

"Please calm down or else I'm going to have to ask you to leave," the woman responded and gestured to a large man in a chef's hat behind the counter.

"I'm just trying to have a nice meal with my girl," Johnny replied.

"Maybe it's better you two ate elsewhere."

"What is that supposed to mean?" Camille snapped at the woman. "I've eaten here plenty of times before with no trouble."

"You can't force us out, we've done nothing wrong," Johnny said.

"Me and my husband own the place, so I can do whatever I want," the woman replied.

Camille had lost her appetite but didn't want anyone to get away with treating Johnny and her that way. She looked at Johnny and he seemed to feel the same way.

"You're a terrible person," Camille said to the woman.

"And I'm sure your food is terrible also," Johnny added.

The woman gasped and scowled at them. "Get out of my diner!"

With few other options, Johnny grabbed Camille's hand and they walked away. Outside, Camille felt like she might cry, something she didn't do often, but the experience had rattled her—and angered her.

"What a horrible person," she said.

Johnny shrugged. "I'm used to it."

"What do you mean?"

"Some people in this neighborhood aren't exactly welcoming of guys like me."

"Because of where your family's from?"

"Yeah, and they also might know who I run with. I'm sorry about this whole thing."

"It isn't your fault," Camille said.

"Let's go somewhere else to eat," Johnny suggested. "If you have time."

"There's a fast-food restaurant a few blocks down, we could go there."

"Sounds good," Johnny said. "I know where it is."

They walked to the restaurant without a lot of conversation, there was a quiet sadness between them because of what had happened at the diner.

Then Johnny suddenly said, "It'd be a shame to let that lady ruin our morning. Unfortunately, I'm used to it, but you seem really upset."

"I've heard of people being that way, but I've never experienced it until now."

"I have," Johnny said, "And you never get used to it."

"I'm sorry, Johnny," she said. "I've lived in this neighborhood my whole life and I'm ashamed at how that woman acted."

"You aren't like them, I can tell. You're different. There's something about you that's special."

"I'm not sure how special I am," Camille said, and felt her face becoming warm.

"I think you are," Johnny said with a smile.

At the fast-food place there were few free tables left by the breakfast crowd, but they eventually found a vacant one and sat down with their food.

"I still can't believe that happened," Camille said with a sigh. "I've gone in there countless times."

"Yeah, but that was when you were alone or with someone who didn't look like me, right?"

"I'll never set foot in that place again," she declared.

"I like you," Johnny suddenly said as they began to eat. "A lot. Go out with me again, even if your mother doesn't like it."

Camille smiled to herself. "All right," she agreed.

7

Violet wasn't having a good day. She'd woke Tommy up late and then decided to take the public bus with him to his school because she thought it'd be faster, but they had encountered traffic and so he ended up being late for school anyway. And last night she'd found Catherine had had too much to drink, again, after the pub had closed, and Violet had to tend to her and help get her into bed.

Violet poured her and her mother a second cup of coffee so they could enjoy it before the pub opened for the day. They were alone in the pub, as Max and Camille hadn't arrived yet.

Her mother held her forehead as she drank her coffee.

"I guess it's not true that you never get a hangover," Violet observed.

Catherine smiled grimly. "Did Camille go somewhere with that Garcia character last night?" she asked after a moment.

Violet shrugged and rolled her eyes out of view of her mother. "I don't know. Why?"

"I'm just looking out for her, the same as I would for you."

"Yeah, but she's not your daughter," Violet replied carefully, for she knew her mother had a temper and didn't like anyone talking back to her.

"It's complicated."

"What's that supposed to mean?"

"I knew her father a long time ago."

Violet wondered what her mother meant by 'knew'. Catherine, a beautiful woman still, had been quite a beauty in her day, or so Violet had heard, and she wondered about her mother's relationship with Camille's father.

"Her father, the one who died?" Violet asked.

Catherine nodded.

"How did he pass anyway? No one seems to want to talk about it."

Her mother shrugged. "There's not much to say really."

"Well, how did it—"

"Violet," her mother cut her off. "I don't want to talk about this right now. Okay?"

"I don't understand, why is it such a big secret?"

There was a knock on the door that kept her mother from answering her.

"We aren't open yet," Violet called out.

The person kept knocking.

Violet sighed and trudged over to the door. She looked outside and saw a man in a suit. When he kept knocking, she opened the door. "Listen, I said we aren't open. You're gonna have to wait..." She stopped when she saw that the person standing in front of her, a tall man in his forties with a black mustache, was clearly a cop. He just had that look of authority about him.

"Detective Seale," he said, holding up his badge. "Violet McCarthy?"

He must have looked up her driver's license because he recognized her. "Yeah. What's this about?" Given her and her mother's line of work, she was used to dealing with the police, who were mostly friendly because a lot of them lived in the neighborhood themselves, but something about Detective Seale seemed different. For one thing, Violet didn't recognize him from around the neighborhood.

"Is your mother around also?" he asked.

Violet gestured behind her. "Yeah, she's right over there. What's this about?"

"I need to speak with you both," he replied. "I'd like to come in."

Violet could say no but that would make them look suspicious, so she nodded and stepped aside for him to enter. She tried to think of which crime he might be talking about.

"What kind of detective are you?" her mother turned in her bar stool and asked the guy before he even opened his mouth. She, too, knew right away that he was law enforcement.

"I'm a homicide detective," he answered.

Violet tried to think of which homicide he could have meant, and she knew right then that he wouldn't be going anywhere and would be a force in their lives from then on.

"What's this about?" Catherine asked, not offering to shake his hand like she did with the other cops they knew and liked, and Violet saw that her mother would take the lead on this one.

"The death of Robert Shane," he answered.

Robert Shane. Violet remembered him. He was a union leader of the dockworkers who was resisting paying them off like his predecessor had. Dating back to Violet's grandfather, the McCarthys controlled the waterfront. Catherine had ordered their men to kill Shane over a year ago, and when nothing had come of it afterwards, Violet and her mother had figured they were in the clear.

"I don't know anything," Catherine replied.

Detective Seale looked at Violet.

66

"I don't know anything either," she said.

"It happened around a year ago. He was shot in front of his home. Whoever did it sped away."

"I'm sure you have the license plate, then, so I don't know why you're bothering us," Catherine said.

"Actually, we do. The car was registered to a man named Frank O'Rourke."

Violet's body tensed. Frank O'Rourke was a guy with bad teeth who had worked for them on and off for years until a few months ago when he disappeared, and no one knew what happened. He was an alcoholic and Violet and her mother had assumed he'd died.

"Does that name sound familiar to you? Mr. O'Rourke said he used to work for you two."

"So, maybe he did. So what?" Catherine replied.

"At the pub?" Detective Seale asked.

"Yeah, here," Catherine said, and Violet knew it was a lie. "I don't see what this has to do with us."

"Frank O'Rourke is claiming you asked and paid him to shoot Robert Shane," Detective Seale said to Catherine. "He only mentioned your name, but I'd like to hear what your daughter has to say." He looked at Violet.

So, they had a confession. Violet tensed further.

"She knows nothing," Catherine told the detective. "We know nothing. O'Rourke is a liar. Can't you see he's trying to blame us for a crime he committed? Imagine the nerve of that guy, blaming two women!"

Detective Seale ignored her and kept his gaze on Violet.

"Did this victim have a family?" she asked, when she already knew the answer, but she wanted to play innocent.

"He was single, but he has elderly parents, and a lot of friends, me among them."

That explained Seale's determination. He'd been friends

with Shane. Violet knew that she and her mother wouldn't get out of this easily. Her mother appeared calm as she often did in these situations, when Violet imagined she herself looked stressed. She tried to control her emotions so as not to look guilty in the detective's eyes but struggled.

"You can't threaten us," Catherine said. "How dare you come in here and—"

"I'm very sorry to hear about what happened to Mr. Shane," Violet said to the detective, interrupting her mother. "But I have to echo my mother's words. Mr. O'Rourke isn't being honest with you. He must've had an issue with Mr. Shane himself and killed him. We have nothing to do with it."

"That might be true, Miss McCarthy. But I think it goes without saying that your family has quite a reputation in this city," he told Violet and her mother. "It's well known around here how the McCarthys own the waterfront."

"I can't help who my father was," Catherine said. "But I'm not like him, and neither is my daughter. O'Rourke is just dragging us into this because of my father."

Violet thought about how good of a liar her mother was.

"O'Rourke used to work for my father," her mother added.

"Ms. McCarthy," the detective said to her mother. "Your father died before this murder was committed."

"So, because we're related to him, we must be like him?" Catherine nearly knocked over her cup of coffee as she stood up from the bar to face him.

"I never said your daughter was," Detective Seale replied, as though her mother had put the idea in his head. "Are you denying that Frank O'Rourke worked for you after your father's death?"

"No, he worked at this pub, like I said."

"And what did he do here? Why did you let him go?"

"He helped behind the bar sometimes. Look, I did him a

favor because my father knew him. But he turned out to be lazy, so I got rid of him. That's the extent of our contact with him. Did he commit a crime or something and is now lying to you and giving you false information in the hope that he'll be let go?"

Detective Seale looked at Catherine and seemed to be deciding what to say.

"We arrested Frank O'Rourke for a robbery, yes, but I believe he's telling us the truth about Robert Shane."

"He's obviously lying and hoping you'll release him."

The detective ignored her mother's conjecturing.

"What is this O'Rourke guy saying exactly?" Catherine asked the detective when he remained silent.

"That you ordered him to kill Robert Shane and then gave him money afterwards as an incentive to keep quiet."

"What would I have against this man that I'd want to kill him?" Catherine asked.

"Shane headed the dockworker's union, and from what he told me back then, you had been squeezing him for money ever since he was elected. But he refused to pay you. So, you had motive. The man who replaced him, I assume he's paying you."

"I don't like your accusation," Catherine said. "We're decent, family-oriented people, not murderers. We've lived in this community forever. Do you have a warrant?"

Seale shook his head. "Not at this time."

"Then I think you should leave now," Violet suddenly spoke up. Just his presence made her uncomfortable.

"I think you ordered the killing of Robert Shane and your daughter knew about it," Detective Seale said to her mother. "I'll be keeping an eye on both of you," he said to them, as though he couldn't resist getting in the last word. "Good day." He nodded at them then left.

Violet made sure the door was closed after he left.

"We're screwed," she said to her mother as she watched the detective walk down the street to his car from the pub window.

"Don't say that," Catherine replied. "Frank O'Rourke is a moron who'll tell anybody anything. Soon this detective will come to see that."

"Yeah, but it's the truth, and you know it. O'Rourke's not lying. You asked him to eliminate that guy and I knew about it. I don't like this detective sniffing around us. It means we're being watched and have to be very careful."

"We're good people," her mother insisted, and Violet thought it was perhaps to make herself feel better. "We don't sell drugs or do any of that. We care about the neighborhood. Robert Shane knew that we've always overseen the waterfront, and that we do it so nobody else can move in and take advantage of the people who work there. We've always treated them fairly and saw that nobody bothered them. Then he had to go and act like he was a tough guy."

"I told you that you shouldn't have had O'Rourke kill him. I knew he was unreliable. We should've had a professional do it, or Max."

"Max doesn't do that anymore."

"Then Derrick then."

"O'Rourke was cheaper," Catherine reasoned.

"Cheaper isn't always better."

"What's done is done. We can't change that."

"This is going to put a lot of pressure on us," Violet thought out loud.

"No charges ever stuck to your grandfather or us before, so why should this be any different? And believe me they tried really hard with your grandfather."

"That was a different era," Violet said. "They had a different relationship with law enforcement back then. I've been reading about in the newspapers lately how the district attorney is cracking down on organized crime."

"Yeah, but they're talking about drug dealing. We don't dabble in any of that, we stay clear of it."

"I think you ought to be a little more concerned."

"I'm not relaxed about it, all right? I'm just not as panicked as you are. I've got years of experience on me, honey, and I know from seeing your grandpa experience what he did, that these things usually pan out. The DA will probably not bother to press charges because they'll know how bad this O'Rourke, a career criminal, will look testifying in court. It'll never go to trial, trust me, sweetie."

"I'm not sure about that. Can we somehow talk to O'Rourke and coax him back to our side? Maybe we can offer him something in exchange—money."

"Maybe, but once a rat, always a rat," Catherine said. "We couldn't trust him not to decline the offer and tell the police we tried to bribe him. It could backfire badly."

"So, you think that, what, the best thing to do is to wait it out and see what happens?"

"Yes, I think that's best."

"I disagree. I don't think this detective is going anywhere. I think he's going to be watching us around the clock. This guy was his friend, he's not going to take what we did lightly."

"What would you have us do, then? I already told you that trying to bribe O'Rourke isn't a good idea."

"I don't know. Maybe we should take care of O'Rourke."

"We could," Catherine said, sitting down at the bar again and finishing her coffee. "But that detective would suspect us immediately, and it could make things worse. Better to wait it out and I'm sure nothing will happen."

Violet walked behind the bar and touched her coffee cup

and it felt cold, so she didn't drink it. She was so quiet that her mother asked her, "Don't you agree?"

"I'm not sure," she replied. "I don't know what to do so I guess we shouldn't do anything."

"You don't sound happy," Catherine remarked as she set her coffee aside.

"You know that I told you we shouldn't get rid of Shane, that we should find a way to try to work with him. Grandpa always said don't kill anyone unless it's really needed."

"It was needed," her mother interjected. "Sometimes that's how we have to deal with someone. Your grandfather knew that very well. Shane would never have backed down and worked with us. He was a very stubborn man, and you know that."

Her mother had a point, after all, the guy who had replaced Robert Shane as the union representative was being much more cooperative with them.

"I hope you're right," Violet said as she watched Max approach the entrance door outside.

He opened the door and greeted them. Then he said, "What's wrong? Both of you look like death warmed over."

"Thanks, Max. That's just what every woman wants to hear," Catherine joked.

Max removed his hat and held it in his hand. "What's going on, ladies?" he asked.

"A detective was in here before, asking about Robert Shane."

"Shane—isn't that the guy we bumped off last year?"

Catherine nodded. "Violet thinks this detective fellow is going to cause us trouble."

"He was close friends with Shane," Violet explained.

"Then he has no business investigating it," Max replied.

"That won't stop him. You know how these cops are, they think they're gods," Catherine said.

"Still, any jury would see that he had no business," Max said. "What have they got on you?"

"Frank O'Rourke—remember him?"

"Yeah, he's not a very reliable fellow, are you sure the cops aren't just messing around with you hoping you'll confess?" Max asked.

"I think he's serious," Violet said.

"What's this O'Rourke saying?" Max asked her mother.

"That we asked him to eliminate Shane and then paid him as an incentive to keep quiet."

"He's trying to get out of a charge?"

"Yeah, robbery."

"What a no-good rat," Max grumbled. "But he's an unreliable witness. My take is that the police are using him to make you sweat. His words give them an excuse to keep an eye on you. They're hoping to catch you somehow."

"You don't think we should be worried either?" Violet said to him, exasperated.

"I think that anytime something like this happens it's cause for concern, but I wouldn't worry too much," he replied. "The thing is, Violet—"

The door began to open, and Catherine shushed him. Camille walked inside.

"Good morning," she said, cheerfully.

What did she have to be so happy about?

Max eyed Camille in a guarded way. Violet didn't know why he didn't like her, but she was beginning to like Camille less and less herself. Catherine and Violet greeted Camille but Max retreated upstairs without so much as a glance at the girl.

"What did that Garcia fellow say to you when he was in here?" Catherine asked Camille. "What did he come back here for anyway?"

"Don't worry, he knows he's not welcome," Camille replied, rather sarcastically, thought Violet.

"He certainly seems to have no problem coming in here," Catherine retorted.

"Oh, who cares?" Violet said angrily. "No offense," she said to Camille. "But why do you care who she sees?" she asked her mother. "She isn't your daughter."

Catherine ignored Violet. "Does your mother know he's been bothering you?" she asked Camille.

"He isn't bothering me," Camille replied.

"You welcome his attention?" Catherine said.

"I like him, and, yeah, my mother knows," Camille said.

"And what does *she* think about it?" Catherine asked her.

"She doesn't like it."

"Exactly," Catherine said. "Yet you'll ignore her and continue seeing him, am I right?"

"I'm a grown woman."

"You girls," Catherine remarked, "have no idea what you're in for with a man like that. He'll get you into trouble. Your mother is right, Camille, listen to her."

Violet disliked how her mother included her in the statement about 'you girls' since she had nothing to do with this Garcia person.

"Thanks for the advice," Camille said as she stepped behind the bar and tied her smock around her waist. "But I know what I'm doing." Camille frowned.

Violet looked at her mother and thought that it was time for her to realize that Camille wasn't perfect.

8

McBurney's filled with customers as the night began. Camille had trouble keeping up with the drink orders, something that rarely happened to her, there were so many people in the place. Violet and her mother helped her with the orders and even Max came downstairs to assist on the floor while ignoring Camille. Just before midnight a guy at the end of the bar spilled his drink on the man seated next to him and they started arguing.

"Did you do that on purpose?"

"I didn't."

"I think you did. You've ruined my jacket."

"It's nothing your old lady can't wash out with soap and water."

"I don't have an old lady, so I'll have to do it myself."

"It was an accident."

"Like hell it was."

The drink spiller threw a punch at the other man, who ducked out of his way. Then both men stood up and faced each other.

"Fight! Fight!" a few of the rowdier patrons started chanting, but most of the customers retreated away from the pair and looked around for the owners to intervene. The drink spiller threw another punch at the guy and hit him in the face.

The man held his bloodied chin and said, "You cut me!"

McBurney's didn't need a bouncer because most people knew better than to fight in Catherine McCarthy's establishment, but the big Max, who sometimes acted as one when needed, ran over to the two men and intervened. He grabbed the fighter by the sleeve of his jacket.

"You. Out," he said.

"He started it," the man pointed at the other. "He spilled a drink on me."

"Yeah, well, you shouldn't have hit the guy," Camille overheard Max replying as she watched the scene play out.

Suddenly, the taller drink spiller swung at the other guy and punched him in the forehead, and blood trickled out.

"Hey!" Camille shouted. "Stop it!"

To her surprise, Max, who was taller than either of the men, yelled at the man who'd just been punched and ordered him again to leave. He seemed to know the drink spiller.

"Are you okay, Jim?" he asked the man and patted his shoulder.

The other guy shook his head and mumbled to himself and then stumbled out of the bar. Camille signaled to Catherine to take over the bar and then followed the man outside to make sure he was all right. He had been hit hard and seemed unsteady on his feet and Camille didn't want him to fall into traffic and get hurt.

The guy sat on the sidewalk outside the bar and leaned against the building's façade. The neon sign flashed above him, creating an ethereal glow across his pale face. He sighed and held his head in his hands.

"Are you all right?" she asked the man.

He took his hands away from his face and looked up at her. "Are you an angel?" he asked with a grin.

Camille shook her head and couldn't help laughing. "I think you're fine," she told the man.

"What's with the big guy in there?" the guy asked her.

"Who, Max?"

"Yeah."

"Do you know him?"

"Sort of, but not that well."

"I think he's friends with the guy who hit you, but you did hit him first."

The guy shrugged. "He spilled beer on me, what else was I supposed to do?"

"You could've just forgotten about it," Camille suggested.

"True, but he should've apologized. What's your name, anyway, sweetheart?" He smiled up at her. He was a heavy, older man, and he had a friendly face.

"Camille."

"That's a lovely name. What's your last name?"

"O'Brien," she said.

"Are you Colin's daughter?" he asked her.

Camille took a step back because he'd surprised her. She didn't know how he knew her father and if she should be concerned about his intentions. "Yeah, I am. Why?"

"I knew your father, young lady. He and I were sort of friends. I knew him when he lived around here."

Camille thought about how the guy had said he 'sort of' knew Max and thought that the guy probably 'sort of' knew a lot of people, so she didn't know how well he really knew her father.

"What's your name?" she asked the man.

"Albert Peters," he replied, reaching up to shake her hand.

She held her hand limply in his, then shook his, still unsure of what he wanted from her.

"I'm surprised you work here," he said.

"What do you mean by that?" she asked, letting go of his hand.

"Don't you know your father's history with this place and these people? I don't come here that often and this is the first I've seen you, or else I would've told you already. But . . ."

Camille retreated farther away from him. "I don't know what you want."

"I don't want anything. I was friends with your father, I'm telling you as a favor to him." Albert stood up from the sidewalk and dusted off his pants. Standing, he towered over her and Camille felt unsure around him. He didn't seem threatening, but she didn't quite trust him.

"What are you saying?" she asked at a distance.

"The McCarthys killed your father," he said.

"No," Camille said, stepping farther back. "You're lying."

"I'm not," Albert said. "I'm afraid I'm telling you the truth. I'm sure it comes as quite a shock to you."

"No. Why are you saying this?"

"Because it's the truth. Your father—he'd want you to know about it. He wouldn't like you working here, for the people who betrayed him."

Her mother had never given her the precise details of her father's death, just that he'd been shot. But had she known the truth all along and kept it from her? And if so, how come she'd allowed her to continue working at *McBurney's*?

"How well did you know my father?" Camille asked, suddenly believing Albert.

"Fairly well. He and I used to play cards with some other guys every week. I couldn't believe it when I'd heard he'd been shot in Los Angeles. That's where the McCarthys killed him, you see. They waited until they got him out there, so it was far away from the friends he had here, friends like me."

"Did you know my mother?"

"Sheila? Yeah, I knew her back then."

"Did she know what really happened to my father?"

"Yeah, I think so. She must. Why? She doesn't seem to have told you, otherwise I'd doubt you'd be working here."

Camille didn't know this man, yet she felt he wasn't lying, and if he wasn't, that meant her mother had lied to her and allowed her to continue working at *McBurney's*.

"What's the name of the person who killed my father?"

"Sean McCarthy, who ran the Irish mob back in those days, ordered him to be killed, he didn't actually do it himself. They used Catherine McCarthy—she was a quite beauty back then— to lure him out there, and Max..."

Camille couldn't believe what she was hearing and had trouble standing.

"Max was the one who shot him," Albert finished speaking.

"How do you know all this?"

"I've heard things over the years, and I knew a couple of Sean's, that's Catherine's father, Violet's grandfather, men."

Camille put her hands on her knees and leaned over to prevent herself from collapsing in the street. Albert approached her.

"Are you all right?" he asked.

"Not really. My mother might have lied to me." She didn't know Albert, but she felt comfortable talking with him because there was an air of calm about him.

"I'm sure she had a good reason to," he said. "Maybe she was trying to protect you."

"From the McCarthys? Then why did she let me work in this place? I've worked here for a few years."

"I'm sure she had her reasons," Albert offered.

Camille reasoned that Violet and Catherine headed the Irish mob ever since Sean McCarthy died. Max didn't just work out of the pub, he worked for the women, and the truth was probably why he was uncomfortable around her. And what had gone on between her father and Catherine?

Camille started to stumble away from Albert down the street.

"Where you going?" he called out to her.

"I'm not going back in there," Camille answered over her shoulder. How could she have faced Violet and her mother given what Albert had just told her? They'd wonder where she went but Camille didn't care what they thought. She had everything on her that she needed, and she had to just get away from them for now.

She walked down the street and a woman ran past her and bumped into her.

"Watch where you're going!" Camille shouted at the woman, still angry over what Albert had revealed.

The woman looked back at her and scowled. Camille was in a mood for a fight, but the woman kept walking away from her, and Camille didn't pursue her. She had someone else she needed to see.

Camille walked quickly to her mother's apartment. She wondered about Albert. Could she trust him? Yet she felt he was being honest with her. The streets were crowded despite the late hour and Camille brushed past a group of musicians playing for money on the sidewalk. It made her think of Pedro's dancing and that made her think of Johnny. Could she count on him to be there for her? She considered seeking out a payphone to give him a call but telling him what had happened would reveal to him who she really was. And she wasn't prepared for that just yet.

She continued to her mother's place and bypassed a

homeless man sleeping on the front steps to enter. The man tossed and stirred as she walked past him. The front entrance wasn't locked despite the hour, as it never was, so Camille entered directly into the corridor. She walked toward her mother and stepfather's apartment in the back of the building. She knew her mother would be upset that Camille was disturbing her at a late hour, but Camille didn't care. If her mother had been untruthful with her then she had to know why.

Camille knocked quietly on the door so as not to disturb the other residents lest someone call the police on her. She knocked again when no one answered.

The door opened and her stepfather Vito opened the door with a gun in his hand.

"Camille, I didn't know it was you," he said. "It's very late."

Camille pushed past his bulky frame. "I need to speak to my mother."

"She's sleeping," Vito replied. "What's this about? You really should come back another time."

Vito sounded worried. Camille faced him and smirked. "Don't worry, I'm not going to tell her what you did to me."

His face paled. "You little bitch," he murmured.

"Yeah, I'm a bitch all right," Camille whispered heatedly. "A bitch with a big secret for when I want to use it." She smiled at him.

Sheila exited the bedroom in her dressing gown. "What's going on out here?" she asked, rubbing her eyes. "Camille, what are you doing here?"

"I need to talk with you," Camille stated to her mother. "It's very important."

"All right, but can't it wait until the morning?"

"No, it can't."

Sheila sighed and Vito closed the front door. Sheila gestured to the couch and Camille sat. She eyed Vito, who hadn't left the room.

"I need to speak to you alone," Camille said to her mother.

Sheila motioned to Vito and he left the room. Camille could hear him fidgeting around in the kitchen and assumed he would be listening in. Sheila sat down next to her.

She took Camille's hand in hers. "What's going on? You have me frightened."

"I know what the McCarthys did to my father," Camille blurted out, pulling her hand away from her mother.

"What they did?" Sheila acted like she didn't know what Camille meant.

"You know what I mean, Mom. They killed him, Catherine and her father, and that Max guy. How could you let me work in that place with them almost every day?"

Sheila sighed and looked away from Camille for a moment. "I knew this day would come."

9

"How could you have lied to me?" Camille asked her mother.

"I didn't lie to you," Sheila said. "I just never told you the whole story even when you asked. You knew your father died, that he'd been shot, but you didn't know by whom, and when you asked, I'd change the subject. The truth is I was protecting you, to keep you out of it. I didn't want them harming you because you knew. I also knew that once you knew you'd want revenge, because you are your father's daughter, and I feared that once you wanted revenge, you'd stop at nothing to get it."

"I wasn't sure if you knew—but clearly you did. You let me work with these people," Camille said in distress. "How could you do that?"

"I assumed you heard whispers over the years and that someday you'd find out yourself, gradually."

"I heard things about the McCarthys, but nothing like this."

"Who told you?" her mother asked.

"This guy named Albert something," Camille said, not recalling the man's last name. "He knew Dad."

"I can't believe he just told you. What was his motive?"

"I don't think he had one, he was friends with Dad and couldn't believe I'd be working in the pub, so I asked him why and he told me."

"It wasn't his place to," Sheila said.

"Who would have told me if he hadn't? You weren't going to."

"Still, he had no right."

"It doesn't matter now. Why didn't you say anything when I started working for them?"

"You seemed to like it there. By the time I found out where you were working, it was too late for me to intervene. You were already settled. I told myself that someday I'd tell you, but I never got around to it."

"Was that why you were always encouraging me to find a better job?"

"That was part of the reason, yes, the other reason was I thought that you could do better for yourself. I didn't know the entire truth about what happened to your father. The word on the street, according to Vito, is that Catherine betrayed him, and Max shot him."

"How come you never went to the police to have them arrested?" Tears filled Camille's eyes when she thought of what probably and been her father's last moments. Betrayed then murdered. Then Camille's blood boiled, and she shook with rage at the mistreatment her father had endured.

"We aren't the kind of people who go to the police, Camille. They wouldn't have taken your father's death seriously because of who he was. To them it would have just been another gangland murder."

"Even today?"

"Even today. It was a long time ago. No one's going to pay any mind to it. It also happened in another state, one where Sean McCarthy wasn't known to the police."

"But why did they do it?"

"Your father worked for McCarthy, and when he longer had use for him, he killed him. Your father had worked for another gang before meeting Sean McCarthy."

Camille took her mother's words to mean that her father had betrayed his former gang to work for McCarthy and she didn't like to think of her father as a traitor, so she chose not to think about it.

"Why did Catherine betray Dad?"

"That I'm not sure about. Probably because her father told her to. Like you, she was her father's daughter. Still is, I've heard. I think she might have been sweet on your father, but I was never sure. I had my suspicions, though."

"And she still betrayed him?"

"As I said, she's her father's daughter."

Camille and her mother sat in silence for a moment.

"Do you forgive me?" her mother asked after a while.

"I'm going back to sleep if anyone cares," Vito said from the kitchen.

Camille heard him going into the bedroom and closing the door.

"I'm not sure," Camille told her mother. "I want to. But I don't like that you kept it a secret from me for all these years, although I understand why."

"What are you going to do about it now that you know?"

"What do you mean?" Camille turned to face her mother on the couch.

"Their gang would have been your father's if he had lived, I'm sure about that. It would've been yours also."

"I don't know anything about being a gangster," Camille said.

"It's in your blood. Your father taught me, and I can teach you. Wait here." Her mother rose from the couch and walked over to a chest of drawers by the fireplace. She opened one of the drawers and took out what looked like a key. Then she went to a cabinet at Camille's right and opened the door. She removed a faded wooden box and brought it over to the couch. She sat down with it and set it in her lap. She opened it carefully and Camille saw that it contained a gun.

"This belonged to your father. He had two, the other one the police confiscated after he was killed. But this one I've saved all these years."

What did her mother expect for her to do with the gun?

"I'm not going to hurt anyone," Camille said, turning away from her mother, as though she couldn't believe what she was seeing and hearing.

"Not yet. But we all will eventually, before they hurt you," Sheila replied. She closed the box and handed it to Camille, who held it in her hands as if it were harmful. Growing up in her neighborhood, she had seen guns, but she had never held one.

"I don't know how to use it," Camille said, and started to give the box back to her mother.

"Your great grandmother taught your father to shoot back in the old country when he was a boy," Sheila said. "He might have taught you if he had lived. There's a box of bullets in there as well."

"I'm not going to use it," she said, but her mother wouldn't accept the box back.

"You probably won't have to. But it's time for you to take what's yours, and the McCarthys don't play around, so if it comes to that, you're going to need to protect yourself."

Camille reluctantly accepted the case. "How will I learn how to use it?" she asked her mother.

"You'll figure it out." Sheila patted Camille's hand.

Johnny owned a gun, she had seen it on him at the pub, and she thought about going to him for instruction.

"Penny for your thoughts," her mother said to her with a smile.

"I was just thinking that I know someone who could teach me to shoot," Camille said.

"Who?"

"Johnny."

"You're still seeing him?"

Camille nodded. She wanted to make it clear to her mother that she had no plans to stop.

"Even after what I told you?" her mother asked.

"You wouldn't tell me why so unless you tell me and it's something relevant then I don't see why I shouldn't."

Sheila sighed. "He knows how to shoot?"

"I assume so."

"Why, you saw a gun on him?"

Camille hesitated then nodded.

"Why can't you find a nice guy, like Billy?"

"Billy works for the Italian mob," Camille replied. She stood up. "I have to go," she said, because she didn't want to discuss it further.

"Where are you off to?" Sheila asked.

"To see Violet and her mother."

Sheila smiled. "That's my girl. But don't do anything that could get you into trouble, unless you can get out of it."

Sometimes Camille doubted she was her father's daughter, but she never doubted that her mother might have been as tough as her father. She took the gun out of the case and tucked it into the small of her back, like gangsters did in the movies, and gripped the box of bullets in her hand.

"Don't worry, I'll be fine," Camille replied over her shoulder as she left, because she imagined that was what her father had told her mother countless times.

She had an urge to call Johnny and tell him about everything she'd learned over the past few hours. But that would reveal who she was, his father and her father's complicated and painful histories intertwined. She walked to *McBurney's* with a newfound sense of where she belonged and who she was. She had enjoyed being a bartender, but it had never felt like it was her destiny. Perhaps continuing her father's legacy was.

She sweated in her leather jacket in the night's warmth and removed it as she walked and put it around her shoulders. She put the bullets in her pockets and threw away the box. From the window outside the pub she saw that the lights inside were dimmed, and Violet and her mother had closed the pub and were cleaning up for the night. Knowing that the door would be locked, she knocked to be let inside.

Violet looked at her through the glass then opened the door. She seemed surprised to see her.

"Where did you disappear off to earlier?" Violet asked her as she entered.

"I had some business to take care of," Camille answered bluntly.

"Killing Moon" by Echo and the Bunnymen played on the jukebox in the background, the music faint.

Violet continued looking at her as though she wanted Camille to explain and when she didn't, she said, "Come in," and shut the door behind Camille.

Catherine watched them from the back of the room and Max wasn't there; he sometimes left before closing.

Camille stood near the door, unsure, and kept her hand close to her side to reach for her gun if needed, although it wasn't loaded and she could only use it to scare them.

"Camille?" Violet said.

"I have to talk to you," she finally said to Violet.

"Okay. What about?" Violet didn't sound worried, and Camille wondered if she already knew what her mother and Max had done to Camille's father or if it would come as a shock to her.

"It's about my father." Camille kept watching Violet's hands as she spoke and she also kept an eye on Catherine, who remained standing, watching them as she cleaned the tables with a white rag.

"Camille, what are you talking about?" Violet looked at her like Camille wasn't making sense.

"My father was murdered, he was shot," Camille replied. "I don't know if I ever told you that."

"I'd heard that," Violet said softly. "Are you all right, Camille?"

"Max shot him, and your mother helped," Camille said quickly before she could lose her courage.

Violet stared at her in silence and her face blanched. She burned a hole in Camille with her gaze. "No, you're lying."

So, she hadn't known, it had been kept a secret from them both, which had allowed a friendship of sorts to form between them.

"I'm not, multiple people have confirmed it, including my mother," Camille said.

Violet made a quiet sound, not quite a word. Then she repeated, "No," firmly. "That isn't true. It can't be." She looked back at her mother, who seemed too cautious to approach Camille, as though her mother wasn't sure whether Camille would harm her but continued watching them from a distance.

"Your grandfather ordered his killing," Camille continued.

"If it's true then why have you come here?" Violet seemed defiant but also a little afraid and uncertain.

Catherine moved closer to them but remained far from Camille.

"Why are you here?" she asked Camille.

Camille looked from one woman to the other. "I quit."

"Fine. You can leave now," Catherine said.

"No," Camille said, looking at Violet. "My father would have

89

been the rightful leader of your organization had he lived."

"You don't know that," Violet replied.

"It's a real possibility," Camille said.

"You should go now," Catherine told Camille.

"I'll leave when I'm ready," Camille said with determination. "What you have should have been my father's, and now it should be mine. I'm going to make sure that I get my fair share," she told Violet and her mother.

"Camille, sweetheart, I don't know what your mother told you," Catherine said to her as though she was trying to reason with her.

"It wasn't just my mother."

"Who told you, then?"

Camille wouldn't say.

"We've known you for years, you're almost like a daughter to me," Catherine pleaded with her.

Violet's face seemed to redden from aggravation.

"I'm not your daughter," Camille replied to Catherine. "You owe me," she told them both as she filled with courage. "And if you don't give me what I deserve then I'm going to take it."

Catherine's expression darkened. "We don't owe you anything," Catherine said to her, the woman who'd been kind to her for so many years suddenly turning on her. "Get out of my pub."

Camille didn't know why she had even considered that they might give in to what she wanted, but she had to try.

Camille stared at both women and then walked out into the warm evening, feeling their gazes on her as she departed. She would get control of the Irish mob from them even if it took everything she had. In the meantime, she had some money saved up to live on until she started making a real income. Violet and her mother wouldn't make it easy for her, but she had one thing they didn't: her father's tough genes.

10

The music stopped just after Camille left. Violet kicked a chair across the room.

"Who does she think she is!" she screamed.

"Calm down," Catherine touched her daughter's arm. Violet had her grandfather's temper. "She won't be able to do anything, she won't succeed, it's just her against us. Who's going to help her? We have a whole army behind us," she assured Violet.

But there had been something in Camille's eyes, a look of such determination that Violet was forced to take her words seriously. She had something Violet and her mother didn't, a reason to fight for what she wanted.

"I'm not as convinced," Violet said to her mother as she sat down at one of the tables. She fiddled with the rag her mother had been cleaning with. "Is what she said true?" she asked her mother, looking at her closely.

"Your grandfather was a complicated man," Catherine replied, which was her way of saying yes.

Violet shook her head in anger at having been kept in the dark for so long. "Camille's father—did you know him well?"

"Why are you asking me this?"

Violet realized she would be evasive. "I think I deserve to know. She was working in our pub. I never knew you helped kill her father."

"I didn't help kill him," Catherine said. "I didn't actually hurt him. I just...helped set it up so that it happened."

"But you knew about it?"

Catherine nodded and looked down at the ground. "It's why I drink," her mother said, looking at her and sitting down in the seat next to her. "I have guilt over what happened in Los Angeles."

"I remember being in Los Angeles and I remember him a little, but I didn't know who he was. I remember we went there with him and Max. He was a tall, handsome guy, right?"

"Yes, he was," Catherine said faintly.

"When I asked you what happened to him, why he was no longer on the trip with us, you told me he'd 'gone away'."

"Did I say that? I don't remember."

"You did," Violet replied.

"I loved him but chose my father in the end."

Violet touched her mother's hand, her anger dissipating. Was that why her mother had never remarried or dated much, despite her good looks and charm, and why she had a soft spot for Camille? Knowing the reason about the latter made Violet lose some of the jealousy she'd had toward Camille over the years. "That must have been hard for you," she said to Catherine.

"I didn't have much of a choice. Your grandfather would have killed me if I'd defied him, even if I was his daughter. Loyalty meant everything to him, and he did away with those who weren't loyal to him, no matter who they were."

"I didn't know that about him."

"Of course not, to you he'll always be your loving grandfather, and it's better that you remember him that way."

"We could have a real problem on our hands with Camille," Violet told her mother after a while.

"She's all talk, I wouldn't worry so much. It's getting late." Catherine started to get up.

Violet gestured for her mother to remain sitting. "I'm being serious, mother. There's a darkness in her, and I've always felt that. She's different than us. She might be capable of anything. What was her father like?"

"He was a very tough man."

"There you go," Violet said. "She's like him, then."

"She certainly looks a lot like him, but she's her own person."

"No," Violet insisted. "It's in her blood, she's like him, just like we're like grandpa in some ways. I think she could harm someone herself and not hand it off to somebody else like we always seem to do these days."

"We don't have the stomach for it, and that's okay, it's probably better in some ways. In that way, we aren't like your grandfather. You think Camille has the stomach for it?"

"It's possible, yeah."

"We won't let her win," Catherine spoke with determination. "I don't think she's as strong as us. What's she going to do for money now that she's quit? She isn't thinking."

But Violet wasn't as confident as her mother.

"Do you know who her stepfather is?" she asked her mother.

"Of course. He works for the Italians we work with." The Alfonsi crime family. "Just what are you saying?"

"A connection like that could help her, it could draw them away from us toward her."

"The boss is loyal to us because Kevin works for him," Catherine replied. "Anyway, I heard that she and her stepfather don't get along."

"Yeah, but Camille's ex also works for the boss."

"She's no longer with him," countered Catherine.

"Kevin and I aren't together anymore either."

"He's the father of your child."

Violet had a revelation. Was she being overconcerned or was her mother not concerned enough? "You're really not worried, are you?" she said.

"I'm not happy about it, but my opinion is that we should see how things go before we get all worked up about them. I don't think you should worry because if Camille O'Brien has a problem with anyone it would be me because I was directly involved with her father's death."

"I think she has a problem with anyone who's related to grandpa, including me."

"Sweetheart, you shouldn't be so worried," Catherine said and touched her arm.

"I have to go home now," Violet said, disagreeing but not wishing to argue with her mother. A babysitter was watching Tommy, but she would want to leave soon. "I'll get in early tomorrow so we can talk about this."

When Violet arrived at the pub the next morning she found that her mother didn't want to discuss the matter further, rather she seemed content to believe that Camille would be all talk and no action, so to speak, and that they had nothing to worry about. She seemed most preoccupied with trying to convince their other bartender over the phone to work extra shifts since Camille was gone. Violet ended up working the bar. The day went by slowly with few customers and only when the afternoon arrived did the pub start to fill up.

A handsome, blond man in a suit and tie, carrying a briefcase, entered the pub and sat at the bar. He ordered a beer and Violet didn't really pay much attention to him until she felt him watching her. Why was he even looking at her? Normally a man in a suit wouldn't give her a second glance. Not because she wasn't attractive, but because businessman-types weren't usually interested in her.

"I recently moved to the neighborhood," he spoke to her. "Have you lived here long?" Her had a slight accent that definitely wasn't a New York accent.

Violet couldn't help but smile. He was much too friendly to have been from New York. People in New York didn't start conversations with strangers.

"I've lived here my whole life," Violet replied. If he'd been someone else, she might have ignored him, but he was quite good-looking, and she was single.

"A lifelong New Yorker? You're the first I've met," he replied.

"There are quite a few of us in this neighborhood," Violet said.

"Most people aren't friendly," the guy said.

"This is New York City. What did you expect?" Violet teased. "Where are you from, anyway?"

"Ohio."

Violet smiled to herself. "Figures," she said.

"What's that mean?" he asked her with a smile.

"It means where you're from is pretty obvious."

He leaned over the bar to shake her hand and introduced himself as, "Sam Paul."

Violet shook his hand, which felt large, smooth, and warm in hers. Most of the men she knew had rough hands. "Violet McCarthy," she said.

"You're Irish?" he asked.

"Part," she said.

"A lot of people in this neighborhood are," Sam said. "Most of the ones I've met don't seem to like us new people who've moved in lately."

Violet assumed he was one of the wealthy younger people buying up apartments in the area, something many of the locals resented, that was, those who weren't getting rich from it.

"That's because when people like you move in here you drive up the rents and force them out," Violet said bluntly. "What do you do for a living anyway?"

"I'm a banker," he said.

"I never would've guessed," she said with a smile. "You might not want to keep your briefcase on the floor."

"Why?"

"Someone might steal it."

"No. Really?"

Violet nodded and he picked it up and set it in his lap.

"What do you do for a living?" he asked.

"I work here," Violet said with a frown.

"I'm sorry, I didn't mean to insult you. I just thought that maybe you went to school or something and worked here on the side."

Just how young did he think she was?

"My family owns this place," she said. Of course, her family did more than own a pub, but she couldn't tell just anyone about that.

Sam seemed more impressed. "Oh? That's great."

"I went to college," she said.

He seemed surprised. "Of course. I'm sorry, I didn't mean to offend you."

"You haven't," she said. "I never finished college."

"Everyone has their own path," Sam said, as though he was trying to clear the air, but Violet realized that they probably had very little in common.

"Have you ever been in here before?" Violet asked, although she didn't recognize him.

Sam shook his head. "No, it's my first time."

"Your beer is on the house, then," Violet said with a smile.

She was flirting with him, yes, but it also didn't hurt to attract new regulars to the pub.

"Thanks," Sam said. "You're a lot nicer than I would have thought, being a New Yorker and all."

"Don't get used to it, Sam, most of us aren't like me."

"How long has your family owned the place?" he asked as she continued to take orders from the customers seated around him.

A small, red-haired woman put money in the jukebox and a pop song started playing.

"Since my grandfather opened the place many years ago. The neighborhood was pretty much all Irish back then."

"It must have been a tight-knit place," Sam said.

"Yeah, there was a genuine sense of community," Violet replied, thinking of her childhood.

"Is your grandfather still around?"

"No, he died a while ago."

"I'm sorry to hear that. So, it's just you and your parents who own the place now?"

"My mother and me," Violet said.

Sam might have been a friendly Midwesterner, but he didn't know her well enough to ask what happened to her father.

"Are you and your mother close?" he asked.

"Yeah, I'd say we are."

"I'll admit that my mother and I aren't," Sam said. "My dad died when I was young."

So, they had something in common, and Violet felt more relaxed around him and started to open up. "I'm sorry to hear that. I lost my father when I was young as well."

"I'm sorry, Violet."

They were silent for a moment as she continued to work then he asked her, "Would you like to go out with me sometime?"

Violet stopped and stared at him. "On a date?" she asked in surprise.

"Yes."

"Why do you want to go out with me?" Then something occurred to her: did he think she would be easy because she was a local girl? Was he looking for a one-night stand?

"Because I've enjoyed talking with you," he replied.

"I don't think that would be a good idea," she said quickly.

Sam looked down at his hands and then at her. "Is there any way I can change your mind?"

"I just don't think it would be a good idea. We come from two different worlds; I'd doubt we'd have much in common."

"I'm from Ohio, not Mars," he said jokingly.

"Same thing," Violet laughed.

"Would you reconsider?"

Violet shook her head. "You seem like a nice guy; I just don't see us being a good fit."

Sam shrugged and smiled. "I had to try."

He left a few minutes later and Violet didn't think any more of it then the next morning the phone rang in the kitchen while she and her mother were setting up for the day. Catherine still seemed content with believing that Camille wouldn't be a problem for them, and they'd been arguing about it as the phone rang.

"Believe me, I've known that girl for years, and people like her are all talk. She isn't going to do anything. She's quit her job and we won't hear from her ever again, I'm sure of it," Catherine said. "She's gone from our lives."

"I'm not as relaxed about the situation as you are," Violet replied. "I think she could spell trouble for us." She ran into the kitchen from the barroom to answer the ringing phone.

"*McBurney's*," she said.

"Can I speak to Violet?" the man asked.

Violet didn't recognize his voice. "This is she," she said. "Who's calling?"

"It's Sam," he said.

"Who?" She pretended to not know who he was.

"Sam Paul, from yesterday. I was at the bar and we talked?"

"Oh, right," she said when she saw he wasn't going to go away. "What can I do for you?"

"I was just calling to see how you are," he said.

"Why? You don't even know me." Violet knew she sounded cold, but the situation with Camille made her stressed and she couldn't take it out on Tommy or her mother, so she took it out on Sam because she could.

"I just thought," he started to say. "I'll be blunt here, I like you. A lot. And I'm not going to go away until you agree to go out on a date with me."

Violet smiled to herself. His candor turned her on. A man hadn't been that direct with her since Tommy's father Kevin.

"All right, I will," Violet said.

There was a pause on the other end of the phone. "Really?"

"Yeah, sure."

"Okay, great. When are you free?"

"How about tonight?" She and her mother had hired someone to replace Camille.

"Tonight? That's perfect. What's your address? I'll pick you up."

She had forgotten to test him about Tommy, something she had to do. So many guys had been scared away by her motherhood before. "I have a son," she told him. "Just so you know."

There was a pause and she waited for him to make an excuse about why he couldn't see her. Then he said, "I love kids. How old is he?"

"Tommy's twelve. His father and I aren't together, of course."

Kevin was in Tommy's life a lot less than she wanted, which was why Tommy had been drawn to Anton, seeking a father figure. "I didn't want you to think I was married."

"Thanks for clarifying. I'm glad to hear you aren't because I really like you."

"It'd be best if we met here, outside the pub. I don't know you well enough to introduce you to my son."

"That sounds good. I'll meet you there. I hope that someday I'll get to meet your son."

Violet didn't want to promise him anything, so she didn't reply. She didn't introduce just anyone to Tommy. She'd only had him meet Anton when Anton was about to move in.

"How does eight o'clock sound?" Sam said.

"That works for me."

"Great, I'll meet you outside the pub at eight."

She started to say goodbye then thought of something to ask him. "Where will we be going? I need to know what I should wear."

"I have a very nice place in mind."

So, she would wear a dress. She hadn't gone to a 'very nice' place since she was with Kevin. Anton had been a bit of a homebody. "All right," she said. "Bye."

"Bye, Violet."

As she was hanging up the phone, her mother came in to see who she was talking with.

"Who was that?" she asked Violet.

"This guy I'm going out with tonight. Can you watch Tommy?"

"Sure. Who's the guy?"

"His name's Sam." She knew her mother would ask more questions about him.

"Where did you meet him? Do I know him?"

"No, I don't think so." Her mother had an unspoken rule

about not dating customers, but Violet also knew that her mother would keep pressing for information until she got what she wanted to hear. "I met him here, actually."

"While you were tending the bar?"

"Yep."

"Oh. It isn't a good idea to flirt with customers because then all of the guys will expect it."

"There weren't 'guys'," Violet replied. "Just the one."

"You really like him," Catherine said.

"I'm not sure yet. I'll find out tonight. I'm just not sure I should leave with everything that's happened with Camille."

"No, you should go. What else are you going to do, sit around and wait to see if she attacks us?" Catherine smiled.

Violet cringed at her mother's grim humor. "She threatened us, and I think we should believe her."

"It's not that I don't believe her, but she's on her own, and we've got plenty of men."

"She has that Garcia guy."

"He hasn't got as much manpower as us," Catherine replied.

"Sam's a banker," Violet said, to draw her mother away from an argument and because she knew it would impress her.

Catherine's eyes brightened. "That's interesting. What was he doing in our pub, then?"

"He lives in the neighborhood."

"He's a newcomer?"

Violet nodded. Although she knew her mother distrusted the wealthy newcomers, she didn't want to lie to her. "But he's different than the others," she quickly said. "He's nice."

Her mother became quiet, then she asked, "What's his full name?"

"Sam Paul."

"That's his last name?"

"Yeah, I think so. It must be."

"I've never heard of him, and I read all the newspapers, even the financial sections."

"I don't think he's famous," Violet said.

"All right, that doesn't matter. I'm not the biggest fan of the newcomers, as you know. But if you like him then I'm sure I'll like him. When will I get to meet him?"

Violet smiled at her mother's words. "I only just met him, and this will be our first date. I know we're a close-knit family, but I don't think he's ready to meet my mother yet."

"Of course," Catherine said. "But let me know when I can."

11

Camille knew that every morning her stepfather Vito had breakfast alone at a café around the corner from where he and her mother lived. Camille hadn't slept much last night; she'd spent much of the time thinking. Which is how she came up with the plan to speak with her stepfather and let him know just how much was at stake if he refused to help her.

She found Vito seated at a sidewalk table outside the café, reading a newspaper. The table's umbrella shielded him from the sun. Camille approached him.

"Camille," he said, looking up from his paper. "What are you doing here?" He seemed uncomfortable being alone with her.

"I need to talk with you," she said, sitting down in the vacant seat across from him.

He put down his newspaper on the table. "Would you like a coffee? Something to eat?"

She could have used a coffee and something to eat, but she didn't want to give him the impression that this was a social call. So, she said, "No."

"Camille, if this is about what happened many years ago, I'm sorry."

"I never told my mother, if that's why you're worried," she said. "And it wasn't 'many years' ago, it was when I was in high school."

Vito's face flushed and he wouldn't look her in the eye. He drank his coffee. "I had a problem back then, which I no longer have."

"I'll believe it when I see it," Camille replied.

"I'm just trying to enjoy my breakfast, until you came here and . . . What do you want?" he asked her.

"I need you to do something for me."

"I'm not telling your mother what happened, I'm a changed man," he quickly said.

"That's not it, but, remember, I can tell her any time I feel like it."

"You haven't yet, and it's been years. I doubt you ever will."

"Oh, believe me, I would if I wanted to. But now I want something from you."

"You want money to keep quiet?"

She expected him to take out his checkbook. "No," she said. "I don't care about money." She knew she was different from her stepfather in that respect.

Vito looked concerned. "Then what do you want?"

"I know you work for the Alfonsi crime family; my mother never hid the truth from me. I need you to set up a meeting for me with them."

"You sound like your father," Vito said.

"You knew my father?" Camille asked in surprise.

"Not well, but he was a good man."

She doubted her father would have associated with the likes of Vito, but to tell him that would be insulting, and she needed him to carry out her favor. "I'm not here to discuss my father."

"Why does a woman like you want to meet the Alfonsis? Are you in trouble? Because I can help you."

"I don't need your money, I'm not in trouble, this would be purely a business meeting."

"Why do you want to do business with the Alfonsis? You're a bartender." He chuckled.

Camille's face burned with anger. How dare he laugh at her. "I quit my job. I can't work for the McCarthys any longer."

"Why not?"

"Because they were involved with my father's death. It seems everyone knew except for me."

"Your mother wanted to protect you. But why do you want to meet my guys?"

"I'm going to take what the McCarthys have."

"You want their pub?"

"No, their crime business."

Vito gave her a condescending look. "You're quite ambitious, but you're only one woman."

"That's why I need a meeting with the Alfonsi family, I want them to work with me instead of them."

"The McCarthys have worked with us for a long time, dating back to the grandfather. We take a cut of their profits so that they can continue to operate in a few neighborhoods in the city, because, of course, we control the whole city. What could you possibly have to offer us?"

She didn't really know where to start but was determined to learn quickly. "A larger percentage once I take control from them. What's the split currently?"

"Fifty-fifty."

"I could give you guys fifty-five, sixty percent." She knew she could always add but couldn't subtract.

Vito didn't react to her offer. "You seem very confident you will be able to take control—why?" he asked.

"I'm ambitious," Camille said. "And I don't give up once I've set my mind on accomplishing something. Also, my mother said she would teach me what my father taught her, and you know my mother."

Vito nodded. "All right," he said, leaning back in his chair. "Let's say you're able to take control—why should I help you?"

"Because I'll tell my mother what you did if you don't."

Vito sat straight and watched her in silence with a worried look on his face. A waiter came over to the table and asked Camille if she wanted anything. She declined and the man left.

"I don't think you'll tell her," Vito said.

Camille crossed her arms and stared at him. "How come you're so confident I won't?"

"Because it's been years and you haven't yet."

"I've been waiting for the right moment, which could be now."

Vito smiled. "You really are something else, Camille. You remind me of your mother when I first met her, and of your father."

"I'm not here to trade memories with you. Will you help me or not?"

"Do I have a choice? No. I'll see what I can do. The Alfonsi family doesn't just meet with anyone, and so if I can't convince them to see you, I hope you won't tell your mother."

"I will, so you better try your best."

"Camille, I can't promise you. These guys don't work that way."

"You better try your best," she repeated.

Vito sighed and rose from his chair.

"Where are you going?" she asked him.

"To the payphone across the street to make a call to see if I can convince them to meet with you and when that might be." He gestured to across the street. Vito was a regular at the café and so no one stopped him from leaving without paying.

"All right," Camille said, not quite trusting him. Would he try to bolt? "But you better come back, or else I'll go straight to my mother's apartment to tell her what happened." Camille figured her mother would be home.

Vito turned to look at her. "You're a tough woman, Camille. I didn't know how tough you could be."

"I'm only getting started," she said with a smile.

She watched him walk across the street to the payphone and kept an eye on him to make sure he wouldn't walk away. After about ten minutes, he walked back and returned to the table. He sat down.

"They've agreed to meet with you, because of me," he said. "But just the associates will be there, not the boss."

"It's too bad the boss won't be there, I wanted to meet him."

Vito frowned. "I can't make him do anything."

"I'm disappointed," she said, toying with him. "But I guess I'll take what I can get. Where and when will this meeting take place?"

"They say they can meet with you at one o'clock today in the backroom of *Anthony's Steakhouse*. They own the place."

"I'm aware of that. All right, but you'll be there with me to help move things along since they don't know me."

"Sure, yeah, I'll be there."

"Good. And Vito?"

"Yeah?"

"You better not mess this up."

"Camille, I've tried my best and I'll try my best while we're there, but I can't promise you anything. I have sway in the organization but I'm not in charge."

"They'll listen to you, they respect you."

"I'll see what I can do."

She didn't like his answer, but she understood his reasoning, so she nodded. "Will Billy be there?" she asked.

"Probably. Is that going to be a problem for you?"

"No," Camille said without thinking. "I don't care."

She parted ways with Vito and rose to leave.

"One more thing," Vito said to her.

She turned to look at him. "Yeah?"

"Don't bring any weapons. I know your mother gave you your father's gun."

She knew that just because she was a woman didn't mean the mob wouldn't harm her. "I won't," she told Vito as she left.

Well before one o'clock Camille headed to *Anthony's*. She'd called Johnny earlier and arranged to go to an old pier by the Hudson River early that evening so that he could give her a shooting lesson. It was a place where he and his gang went often to practice. He'd seemed surprised at first that she wanted him to teach her, but then she explained that she recently inherited her father's gun and wanted to know how to use it properly should she ever need it as a woman alone in the city. That got him to agree to teach her, but now she felt guilty for lying to him. She liked Johnny and trusted him to a certain extent, but she didn't want her plans for Violet and her mother to be public just yet. She wanted an advantage over them.

Camille arrived at the restaurant dressed professionally in a pantsuit and heels. She entered and was immediately greeted by the hostess, a tall attractive woman who seemed to know who she was right away. The place smelled of wine and cooked meat and garlic and was filled with people having lunch. The woman smiled at Camille and escorted her toward the back of the restaurant. They walked down a long, dim hallway then the woman motioned for her to step through a door and left once Camille opened it. Camille nearly stopped in her tracks, for she came face-to-chest with the very tall and handsome Billy.

"Camille," he said, looking down at her. "I couldn't believe it when Vito said you wanted to meet with us. Is everything okay?"

He seemed concerned, and Camille realized he still had feelings for her.

Camille nodded. "Yeah, I just have some things that I need to figure out and I thought that maybe you guys could help me. It's been a long time, Billy."

"Too long," he said. "How's your mother?"

"She's well. She still talks about you; I think she still wishes we were together."

"Sometimes I do too," he said. "Are you seeing anyone?"

"Yes."

Billy frowned. "Who? Do I know him?" he inquired.

She didn't want to reveal Johnny's identity to him because she knew that Billy could be a bit vindictive and she didn't want him to take it out on Johnny.

"No, you don't know him," she lied.

"I might. What's his name?"

"It doesn't matter. You don't know him."

Camille was grateful when Vito appeared in the hallway and walked towards them.

"Camille," he said, and she nodded at him. He walked past Billy and entered the room.

Billy came close to her and whispered in her ear, "It doesn't matter if you won't tell me his name, I'll find out myself."

Was that a threat? She didn't want to make Billy angry because she needed something from his crew, so she didn't react. But she'd wanted to tell him to leave Johnny out of it.

Camille started to go inside the room, but Billy stopped her.

"I have to check you for weapons," he said.

"Is that really needed?" Camille asked. "I didn't bring any. I promise." She didn't want his hands on her because that might draw her to him again.

"I promise I won't bite." He grinned.

Camille nodded at him to go ahead and she tensed as he

knelt and lightly traced over the contours of her legs and waist with his strong fingers. At this proximity he smelled good and masculine, like spicy cologne. She had to tell herself not to be tempted, that they were through.

"Did you want to be here, or did they ask you to come because you know me?" she asked him to keep herself from thinking about his hands on her.

"I haven't seen you in a while and I wanted to come," he said. "To see how you are."

"I'm doing fine," she replied.

"I know, I can see that." He gave her a thoughtful glance and smiled. "All right, you're all set," he said, and took his hands away.

She exhaled and entered the room after Billy and found Kevin Carmine, Violet McCarthy's ex, seated at the table under a bright light, which illuminated his dark good looks. The rest of the room looked rather dark and Camille tensed as Billy shut the door behind her. A coffee pot and cups and a tray of pastries sat in the middle of the table. Would Kevin's presence be an issue because, as the father of Violet's child, he would seemingly be loyal to her? Or perhaps he kept business separate from family. There was only one way to find out.

Billy pulled out her chair for her and Camille sat down and thanked him. Her shoulders relaxed a bit once she was seated.

Kevin greeted her with a smile and a nod. She was familiar with him from the pub when he and Violet were still together. Vito poured himself a cup of coffee and helped himself to the pastries then asked the others if they wanted any. Camille declined.

"I have to say, Camille," Kevin said, "I'm surprised you wanted to meet with us. I didn't know about your troubles with Violet and her mother. But the boss respects Vito and wanted us to come."

"I appreciate your being here," she told him.

"I am grateful you all came here," Vito told the other men.

"The boss knew your father but not well," Kevin told Camille. "So, we were happy to meet with you."

Camille thanked him. The Italians were much more formal than the Irish, so she knew this was all a part of that.

"Now, let's discuss," Vito said, and looked at Camille, and the pleasantries were done.

"The reason I asked to meet with you is I have a business offer of sorts. You say you are aware of my father through your boss so you must know his history with the McCarthys. It's my belief that if he hadn't been killed then the New York Irish mob would have been rightfully his and mine."

"You're making an assumption that he would have obtained control from Violet's grandfather," Kevin said.

"You and I both know that this is a boys' club when it can be," she told him. "I believe my father would have succeeded him. Violet and her mother wouldn't be in the picture."

"All right, let's say you're correct. What makes you think that you, one woman, can take control of that neighborhood from Violet and Catherine?" Kevin asked her, and just as she thought, she realized he would be reluctant given his relationship to Violet. "They've had control going back to the grandfather and they have an army of guys behind them. Who do you have?"

She figured she might be able to convince Johnny and his men to join her but that would be very difficult due to his general dislike of the Irish, except for her, of course.

Unlike Violet, Camille's mother was half Italian, and she decided to use that to her advantage. "There's just me for now, but that will change. I'm determined. My mother is half Italian, and so a partnership with the Alfonsi family would have a special meaning to me."

"I didn't know that about you," Kevin said.

"Yeah, Shelia's mother was one hundred percent Italian," Vito told him.

"Still," Billy said to her. "It's a huge risk for us to even be meeting with you about this. It could spoil our partnership with the McCarthys."

Camille wondered if he would be vindictive and discourage the boss from considering her offer since Camille hadn't reciprocated his feelings.

"I'm not asking you to make a decision today," she replied. "I wanted to use this sit down as an opportunity for me to express how much a partnership with you would mean."

"Assuming you're able to get control from them. We all know they're not going to just hand over their empire to you without a fight," Kevin said. "Violet is the mother of my child, and I have to consider that and her safety. To be honest, given what I've just told you, I'm quite surprised you're even here. But evidently, you take after your father. He was also an ambitious man, from what I've heard."

"I don't plan on harming them," Camille stated, but deep down inside she knew that it might come to that.

"How do you plan on taking control from them, then?" Kevin asked her.

"Take it easy, Kev," Billy told him. "I know Camille very well, as you know, and if she says she won't then she won't."

Kevin looked at Vito for his opinion. Camille eyed Vito and gave him a look that said, "You'd better agree."

"If she gives us her word then I'm sure it's good," Vito told his men.

"All right," Kevin said. "Let's say you get control and we even help you get control, what would you have to offer us that the McCarthys already don't?"

"I'd give you a larger percentage of everything. Vito's told me that right now they give you half."

"That's correct," Billy said.

"I would give you fifty-five percent," she said, starting with the lower number.

Kevin chuckled. "Fifty-five? We're not going to go to the boss with that."

Camille didn't want them to see her face reddening, which she could feel, so she tilted her head, breathed out quietly and sat up. "All right," she said. "Sixty."

"That's better," Kevin said. "How about seventy-five?"

Camille stared at him.

Kevin shrugged. "The boss always wants the highest number."

She looked at Billy.

"What he says is true," Billy told her.

"Sixty-five," Camille said.

"Seventy percent and you're on your own taking control, but if you do get control we don't come in and take it from you," Kevin replied. "We won't resist you operating in the neighborhood. We'll let you operate if you give us our share. That's how we've always done business with you Irish."

Camille wasn't in a position to negotiate and she didn't trust that Kevin would ever help her physically take control from Violet, so she said, "All right."

"It's not set in stone," Billy said. "We'll have to speak to the boss about this, of course, to see what he wants to do."

"Don't make this personal, Billy," she told him carefully.

"No, this is just how we do things," Billy replied.

"Yeah, Camille, we need to see what the boss thinks," Vito said. "If he wants to go ahead then we're good to go. We'll go speak with him and I'll let you know what he says."

A partnership with the Alfonsi family would mean that she would be able to operate her organization once she gained control from Violet and her mother, for if the Italians weren't with her they'd be against her, and without their cooperation they might kill her if she took over the neighborhood and didn't pay them. So, she had no choice but to work with them, and if they wouldn't work with her once she gained control then she wouldn't be able to run the neighborhood. Camille hoped they would want to work with her, and if they wouldn't then she would just have to think of some way to deal with them.

"I think that's all, then," Kevin told her as he stood up. "Vito will let you know what the boss says."

"I hope you know how much I will value a partnership," Camille said as she rose.

Vito said, "Camille, we'll let you know."

She shot him a warning look and he said, "But of course we hope it works out for everyone."

Kevin opened the door for her, and she stepped outside. She felt someone tug her sleeve as she started walking down the hallway and turned around to see Billy standing there.

"You're just going to walk away?" he asked her.

She could see Kevin and Vito speaking outside the doorway behind him. She didn't want Billy to make a scene, something he was prone to doing so she said, "Billy, we shouldn't be having this conversation. This was supposed to be a business meeting, that's all."

"You never told me who you're seeing. Or you won't tell me."

"Because it's none of your business. We have nothing to do with each other anymore."

"I still care about you." He stepped closer and looked down at her with his piercing blue eyes. "I want to make sure he's good enough for you."

Camille didn't trust Billy not to do anything to Johnny if she told him Johnny's name. Johnny was a good guy, but even if Camille told Billy that he might still invent things about Johnny in his head and then snap for no reason.

"He is," Camille said. "And if you trust me, you'll believe me when I tell you that." She could hear the lunch crowd leaving the restaurant in the distance.

"What does he do?" Billy asked. "Does he have a job?"

"Yes," Camille replied.

"What is it?"

"It's like yours," she said.

"He's a gangster?" Billy's gaze darkened.

Camille hesitated then nodded.

"Which one? Do I know him?" Billy asked.

"No, I don't think you know him."

"He's not with Violet and her mother, is he?"

"No, no."

"Then he's, what, with one of the other Italian families?"

"No."

"Then he's, what, Cuban?"

Camille nodded, and Billy crinkled his nose.

"He's a good guy," Camille told him.

"I can't believe you left me for this guy," Billy said, shaking his head.

"I didn't leave you for him. I didn't even know him when we were together. I only recently met him." She almost said, *I left you because I fell out of love with you.*

"Then how can you be so sure about him?" Billy raised his voice and Vito and Kevin stopped talking and watched them.

"Because our fathers were best friends," she replied.

"You knew him when you were kids?"

Camille shook her head. "No, but my mother talked about his father enough that I feel like I knew him."

"Camille, what are you talking about? You don't know this guy. He could be dangerous. What's his name? I'll ask around about him for you."

"I'm not giving you his name. I know better than to do that."

Billy frowned. "Maybe I'll find out on my own. Or maybe if you don't tell me I'll speak with the boss and suggest he declines your offer."

Camille stepped forward and got as close to his face as she could, given their height difference. She pointed her finger at him. "Don't threaten me."

Vito and Kevin stopped as they walked past them to leave.

"Is everything all right?" Kevin asked.

"Yeah," Camille said. "I was just leaving." She glared at Billy, who didn't say anything.

The three men lingered behind while she walked all the way down the hallway and past the hostess who'd greeted her on her arrival. Camille wondered what the three of them were discussing. Her, probably. And would Billy tell the boss not to work with her? She wouldn't put it past him.

The hostess smiled at her and Camille left the restaurant.

12

J ohnny had insisted on picking her up at her apartment in his car rather than her meeting him at the pier because it wasn't safe at night. At dusk she went outside and waited for him on her front steps, wearing her leather jacket with her father's gun tucked inside. She kept a close eye on her surroundings, something she had done ever since confronting Violet and her mother, for she knew what that family was capable of. Her mother had called her earlier and it appeared that Vito had said nothing about the meeting to her, but she didn't think her mother would have minded it if he had. She felt her mother would have been proud of her for thinking so far ahead.

The weather had turned cooler as the night arrived, and there were still plenty of people walking the streets, coming home from work and going out for the night, children playing on the sidewalk and teenagers gathering on the steps of the nearby apartment buildings, smoking and laughing. Sometimes she longed to be that carefree again, to be released from her troubles and the idea of the dangerous fate that might await her, for she knew that being male or female didn't make a difference in the life of crime, you could still find trouble.

Johnny pulled up in a small red car that looked older than she would have imagined him driving and waved to her. She didn't mind the old car. Billy had been a flashy guy and things hadn't turned out well for them. Billy had been too controlling of her, wanting to know what she did and who she saw. How he'd tried to get Johnny's name out of her had been a good example of that. She'd never told him why she felt things hadn't worked out between them, because she knew he wouldn't see what he'd done was wrong. She'd never told her mother about Billy's controlling side, or anyone. But she imagined that she would tell Johnny someday.

There wasn't a parking space for Johnny's car, so he stopped next to two parked cars and Camille hurried to get inside before someone beeped because Johnny blocked the road.

"How are you?" he asked her.

She hesitated then kissed him on the cheek. Soft rock music played on the radio.

He touched his face and smiled. "That was nice."

Johnny drove off and they waited in traffic on the next street.

"I must admit I was pretty surprised when you called me up and asked me to teach you to shoot. It's not exactly what comes to mind when you think of a date."

Camille shrugged. "I don't have a father to ask so I thought I'd ask you."

"And I'm happy to oblige. But I must ask, you aren't planning on doing anything dangerous, are you?"

"I'm going to make a name for myself in the neighborhood," she stated.

"The McCarthys run the Irish side of things in that neighborhood," Johnny said.

"Yeah, and I think they shouldn't."

Johnny looked at her with a puzzled expression. "Why?" Then he looked a little worried.

If she told him the truth then it would mean revealing who her father was, and she didn't know how he'd react, if he'd be bothered that she'd kept it a secret from him.

"I don't know," she replied. "I just don't like them. I think it's time for someone else to take control. I no longer work for them."

"They fired you?"

"Not exactly."

"I don't like them either," Johnny said as the traffic moved again. The wind from Johnny's open window blew her hair in her face and she pushed it out of her eyes. "But the McCarthys have run the neighborhood since forever and that's always how it's been. I wouldn't mess with them if I were you. They're dangerous."

She was tempted to ask him if he would help her, but she didn't know him well enough.

"Why do you dislike them so much?" Johnny asked her. "I don't like them because of the Irish and their history with my father, but why do you hate them?"

If she told him her own history with the McCarthys then he might figure out that she was Colin O'Brien's daughter.

"I have my reasons," she said, and didn't elaborate. Luckily Johnny was polite enough not to press her for more information.

"What did you do today if you weren't working?" he asked her in a friendly way. "Are you going to look for a new job?"

"I'm thinking of becoming an independent contractor of sorts. I have some money saved. How far is this pier we're going to? You said it was on the Hudson River, right?"

"Yeah, there's never anybody there, and there's an old warehouse there where some of my guys and I go to shoot. It's good practice if you want to learn. We should be there soon."

"I met with the Italian mafia earlier," she told him. "That's what I was doing."

His mouth dropped a little and he took his eyes off the traffic to look at her. "Camille, what did you just say?"

"That's the truth. I want to push out Violet and her mother and take over."

"Why? What's your history with them? It must be something big."

"Someday I'll tell you. Okay? Just trust me." She looked him deep in the eyes and he nodded.

"I can help you, you know," Johnny said, with his gaze on the road again. "Is the mafia going to work with you?"

"I'm not sure. And no, I couldn't ask you to do that, not after what you said the Irish did to your father."

"You're not like the rest of them, I can trust you. Let me help you."

"No," Camille said. "I couldn't ask that of you. I also should be able to do this on my own, I don't want a man always having to help me, no offense."

"You're independent, I admire that. We're here."

The car stopped. Camille hadn't been paying attention as he drove, but now she looked at the stark urban landscape around her. They were parked by an old pier that seemed to not be in use any longer. The great river rippled and shone like oil under the steady moonlight. At the other side of the car, the side not facing the river, there was a large, vacant warehouse with its windows broken and trash and rubble piled high around it. She didn't see anybody around, as Johnny had promised.

"You're sure no one comes here?" she asked him just in case.

"Just homeless people sometimes but they never bother us." Johnny gestured at a group of people camped out in the distance. He shut off the engine and the music stopped. He stepped outside, walked around the front of the car, and opened Camille's door.

"So, no cops are going to show up?" she asked him before getting out.

Johnny shook his head. "I promise."

"Okay, I hope so because I don't feel like getting arrested tonight." She smiled at him.

"Only tonight?" Johnny teased her, making her feel like a teenager again.

Outside she walked toward the river and he followed her.

"I haven't seen it this close up in years," she told him. The fresh smell of the water circulated in the wind and it felt like it could rain as a chill touched her skin. "We better hurry, I think it's going to rain."

Johnny held out his hand as if to test the air. "I think you're right. But we have time. Where's your gun?"

Camille took her gun out of her jacket and showed it to Johnny. "It was my father's."

"He gave it to you?"

"No, I was too young when he died. My mother, she gave it to me."

"Your mother must be some kind of woman."

"She is," Camille said with a laugh.

Johnny reached around to the other side of his waistband and removed his gun. "You might want to get a holster," he told her. "It's dangerous keeping it in your pocket like that."

"Where am I supposed to keep it, my purse?" she teased him.

Johnny smiled. "No, but it could go off accidentally if you keep it in your pocket."

"You keep yours close to you."

"Yeah, but I'm experienced."

"I will be someday too," she said in a matter of fact way. "Maybe I'll get one," she said, but didn't promise.

"Have you ever swum in the river?" he asked her, looking at the water.

"No. Have you?"

"Yeah, a couple of times."

"It's too polluted," she insisted.

"Not if you wash off after."

"I'm not going swimming with you," she said. "Not today anyway."

"I'll get you to go with me some time," he said with a smile.

"Are we going to practice out here or inside that old building?" she asked, pointing at the warehouse.

"That's what we're going to shoot at, there are still some windows left to break."

"And the cops really won't come around?" she asked, still unsure.

"They don't come down here, trust me."

"I want to trust you, but I don't know you that well."

To her surprise, he put his arm around her shoulders and pulled her in close to him. "Trust me, I care about you."

She found the gesture sweet and it warmed her on the inside. She slowly rested her head on his shoulder. Now felt like the right time to tell him.

"I'm pretty sure our fathers knew each other," she said.

"What do you mean?"

"My father's name was Colin O'Brien. My mother told me about my dad's friend named Johnny Garcia, and he was in a gang like you said your dad was. I think your dad and mine were best friends when they were kids."

Johnny narrowed his gaze on her.

"You really didn't know, did you?" she said.

Johnny released her from his embrace. "You knew this the whole time and didn't tell me?" He had a wounded look on his face.

"I suspected but wasn't sure," Camille replied.

"Why didn't you tell me?" he asked.

"I'm not sure. I can't put words to it. I like you and I didn't want it to come between us."

"But why would it come between us if they were friends, not enemies?"

"I don't know, I just thought it would somehow change things." Camille disliked conflict so she started to step away toward the road to walk away.

"Where are you going?" Johnny called out.

"You're angry, it's better if I leave," she replied over her shoulder.

"Wait," he said, jogging over to her. "I'm not angry. I just don't understand why you kept it a secret. Please don't leave." He reached for her hand and she let him hold hers.

His moved his finger in circles in her palm and she looked at him. "I don't know why I didn't tell you my suspicions. I thought about it but just never did. I'm sorry," she said.

"That's okay, I'm not angry," he said, touching her hair. "Now that I know, I feel even more of a connection to you."

"The McCarthys, they killed my father," she said, looking up at him.

"Why?" Johnny asked her. "He owed them money?"

"No, my dad was a gangster. He worked for them."

"Your father was an Irish gangster?" Johnny looked hurt that she'd hid this from him also.

"Yes, but he was friends with your father. His death devastated him."

Johnny's eyes showed years of pain. "It's all right, Camille," he said, patting her shoulder, "I believe you."

"You have to believe me," she said. "My dad would never have hurt him. He loved your father."

"I believe you," Johnny said quietly. He brushed her hair away from her forehead and kissed her there.

The air felt heavy and rain seemed imminent.

"We better hurry up," Camille said, pointing at the night sky.

She and Johnny walked closer to the warehouse but were still far enough away that Camille would have to make an effort in order to shoot through the windows. Johnny showed her how to remove and put in the cartridge and turn off the safety feature on his gun. Her father's gun was an older model. She hadn't brought extra bullets with her, but Johnny had.

"You mentioned how old your gun was so I figured you could use them," he said.

"Thanks. Where do you get them from?" she asked.

"This guy I know. But I wouldn't meet him alone if I were a woman. He's a bit strange. I can get you more any time you need me to. Just ask me and I will."

"Thanks, but I'm sure I can handle him," Camille said, not wanting to have a man, any man, control the situation.

"No, really. Just ask me." He paused. "I'm assuming your gun isn't registered?"

"It's not," she said. "Should it be? Is yours?"

Johnny shook his head. "I don't want the police knowing I have it. I'm assuming you feel the same way?"

"Yeah, they don't need to know I have it. It's a hand-me-down, anyway."

"Doesn't matter. The cops will bust you if they find it on you and it isn't registered, so be careful toting it around."

Camille nodded but she'd thought as much. "Thanks for teaching me to shoot," she said. "I imagine it's something my dad would've done if he was still around."

"No problem. I like spending time with you."

Johnny stood close behind her and showed her how to aim at the window on the warehouse and she fired the gun with his hand over hers. Her hand shook with the force of the gunshot and the smell burned her nostrils. She'd missed and the bullet hit an abandoned car nearby.

Camille laughed at herself. "I think I'm going to need a lot of practice."

Johnny smiled down at her. "You'll get better. I'll help you. Let's try again."

He stood behind her and moved her arm so that her aim was more on target. Then he placed his hand on her inner thigh to move her leg and electric shocks were sent through her at the feeling of his touch. She pulled the trigger and hit the area just above the window.

Once again, the smell of the gunshot bothered her. "The smell, and the way it feels—do you ever get used to it?"

"Sure, you will," Johnny said. "Eventually you won't even notice it. Your gun is older than mine, so you'll notice those things more at first."

Johnny moved to stand behind her again, but Camille stopped him. Truthfully, him being so near to her distracted her because it made her think of other things besides firing the gun.

"I want to see if I can do it on my own this time," she told him.

Johnny nodded.

Camille widened her stance like he'd showed her and straightened her shoulders. Once again, she aimed and fired, and the sound of shattering glass filled the night air and the pieces sparkled like jewels as they flew all over the place.

Johnny clapped and whistled, and Camille did a little happy dance and ran into Johnny's arms, and he held onto her and picked her up off the ground.

"You did it," he said. "See, you're better at this than you thought."

"Thanks to your teaching." She smiled at him.

Johnny squeezed her tightly then set her down on the ground. "I like having you in my arms," he said, watching her, "because then I know I'll never lose you."

Camille's face felt very warm, but she didn't know how to respond to him. She aimed again at the building and took another shot at a window, breaking the glass.

"You're amazing," Johnny said, beaming at her.

Camille felt something cool on her face and realized it was raining. Soon the rain began to dampen her hands, her hair. Johnny grabbed her hand from behind and they ran for his car. They made it inside and shut the doors as it started to pour. Johnny took Camille's gun from her and set it on the dashboard next to his.

"How about we come here once a week to practice?" Johnny suggested.

"Sounds good," Camille replied. She rubbed her hands together.

"Are you cold?" Johnny asked.

"A little."

He put his arm around her and started the car. "Head On" by Jesus and Mary Chain played on the radio. Camille leaned her head against his shoulder.

He brushed back her hair and whispered into her ear, "I think I'm falling for you."

Camille liked Johnny but she didn't want to allow herself to become vulnerable after what happened with Billy.

"I like you, Johnny," she said. "I need to tell you that I recently came out of a long relationship—I almost married the guy. I saw him today, actually."

"You ran into him in the street or something?"

"Not exactly. He was at the meeting I went to."

"He's in the mafia?" Johnny seemed taken aback.

"Yeah."

"Did you tell him you were seeing somebody?"

"Yeah, and he asked about you."

"That doesn't worry me," Johnny stated. "I can take care of him."

"No, nobody is going to 'take care' of anybody. I wouldn't give him your name, but he said he'd find out who you are. Please be careful. Billy, that's his name, is quite volatile."

"Billy? He doesn't scare me."

"No, look at me." She held his face in her hands and his skin felt warm and smooth. "I don't want there to be any trouble, and I've told him so. Just please be careful. I don't want anything to happen to you."

"He's the one who should be careful," Johnny insisted.

"Johnny, please, you don't need to take on the mafia over me."

Johnny kissed her and his lips felt hot and moist on hers. She traced her fingers through his thick, dark hair and he smiled under her touch. Camille maneuvered onto his lap and took off her jacket and pressed her body into his.

Camille's revelation of their fathers' friendship had bonded them enough to make love in the car that night. Afterwards Johnny drove her home and kissed her goodnight. Camille knew that things were moving too fast, but she didn't mind. She already felt closer to Johnny than she had to Billy at that stage of their relationship and she sensed that there was something special about him. He seemed like the kind of man who would be trustworthy and committed to her, which Billy had been in his own way, but he'd been distant too, and Johnny seemed more receptive. Now, if only she could figure out a way to get her mother to like him.

13

Violet waited inside the pub for Sam to pick her up for their date. She knew they were going to a fancy restaurant, but she didn't know which one and she realized she should have asked him if he'd be meeting her in a car or on foot.

A couple of the regulars asked her why she was so dressed up and Catherine told them about Violet's date. She hadn't bought a new dress, she wore one of the ones she used to wear when Kevin had taken her out at night.

Violet's mother could have gone to her own apartment, where Tommy waited, but Violet figured she wanted to meet Sam. They had planned for Catherine to take Tommy back to Violet's apartment after Catherine was done at the pub for the night so that he could sleep in his own bed.

Violet sat at a table by the window and waited. One of the regular customers, a woman, told her she looked great and her date should consider himself lucky, and Violet smiled at her.

Catherine, who had been helping to tend to the bar, approached her as the time neared for Sam to arrive.

"I hope he's not going to be late," Catherine said.

"He isn't," Violet said. "He'll be here."

"I bet he drives a nice car," Catherine commented.

"We might be walking to where we're going," Violet replied.

"You don't know where you're going to eat?"

Violet shook her head.

"He didn't tell you or you don't remember?" her mother asked.

"He said it would be a surprise."

"How mysterious," Catherine said with a smile.

Violet considered leaving the bar and meeting Sam outside, but the rain prevented that.

"He'll be here," Catherine said and rubbed Violet's shoulders.

"I know," she said. "I'm not worried." But she was a little.

A sleek black sports car stopped in the street and parked by the pub. A tall man in a suit and tie got out of the car and she recognized Sam's handsome face.

"Is that him?" Catherine asked.

"Yeah, that's Sam."

"He's cute," Catherine said.

"Yeah, and he's nice, too."

"I don't think I've ever seen him in our pub before."

"He recently moved to the neighborhood," Violet said.

Sam locked his car door and walked to the sidewalk. Violet saw that he carried an umbrella. He entered the pub and she sat up as some of the patrons surrounded her, for a look at Sam and eager to meet him. Not enjoying being the center of attention, Violet braced herself and hoped Sam knew what he was in for. Half of everyone in the place wanted to meet him. She waved to Sam and he smiled at her. His hair was damp from the rain and looked darker than it had before.

Before Violet could say anything, her mother stepped in front of her and started speaking to Sam.

"I'm Catherine, Violet's mother."

Sam handled the situation well. "I'm Sam. It's great to meet you," he said and shook her mother's hand.

Sam seemed experienced at meeting and dealing with his dates' mothers, and her own mother seemed to like him a lot, and she imagined the other mothers did as well. The pub was like a community, and Violet rose from her chair before a patron could approach Sam and begin talking to him.

Sam hadn't moved far from the doorway because Catherine blocked him, and Violet arrived in time to hear her mother telling him about Tommy, and she was relieved that she'd already told him herself.

"He knows I have a son," Violet told her mother.

"And he's a true gentleman for being so kind about it," Catherine said to both as she beamed.

Her mother was right in a way, as a lot of the guys Violet met bolted once they found out she had a son.

More than one patron came up to Sam and introduced themselves and Violet wanted to get out of there before one of them could start telling him stories about her youth, how she'd been chubby and awkward as a teenager, or how her grandfather, if he'd been there, would have pulled a gun on Sam if he dared to try anything with Violet. That could lead to Sam asking questions about her family that she didn't want to answer.

Max came downstairs to say hello. He patted Sam's back.

"You be nice to her," he lectured Sam.

"We have to go now," Violet told her mother quickly. "Don't let Tommy stay up too late."

"I'll try not to but remember I'm 'fun grandma'." Catherine winked at her.

Violet grabbed Sam's hand and they left as one of the patrons called out for them to "Have a good time!"

"Everyone's so welcoming," Sam said to her as he opened the

umbrella and held it over her so she wouldn't get wet on the walk to his car. "And here I thought we newcomers weren't welcome."

"Don't let them fool you," Violet said. "They just want to know everything so they can gossip about it later. A lot of the old timers in this neighborhood are like that. They have to know everyone else's business."

"Really? They seem so nice."

"That's just so they can get information," she told him with a smile.

"I'll be careful, then," Sam said to her with a wink. He opened the door for her, and she got inside and then watched him as he walked around the front of the car and closed the umbrella and entered the driver's seat.

"You never told me where we're going," she said as he shut his door and started the car.

"This steakhouse called *Anthony's*, it's nearby," he replied.

Violet became quiet as she debated what to tell him, but on the inside she panicked a little. "I know where that is," she finally said. "My ex, Tommy's father, is there a lot because he works for the owner."

"He works at the restaurant?"

"Not exactly." It was way too early to introduce Sam to Kevin and his lifestyle.

"I don't think he'll be there tonight, though," she realized with relief.

If Sam was relieved, he wasn't showing it, but she imagined he was, as no one wanted to meet their date's ex on the first date. She looked back at the pub as Sam drove away and saw her mother and some of the patrons watching them from the window.

"We can go somewhere else if you'd like," Sam offered.

"No, that's okay. I'm sure you have a reservation."

"We do but I don't want you to be uncomfortable."

"I won't be uncomfortable," she clarified. "Some of the staff there are a bit nosey and they might report back to him, but it's all right, he won't care."

"What's his name, if you don't mind my asking?"

"Kevin Carmine."

"Carmine, is that Italian?"

"Yep."

"Does he live in the neighborhood?" Sam asked.

Violet found his questioning charming; it was as though he was concerned that she'd go back to Kevin.

"No, he lives in another part of the city."

"How did you meet him?" Sam paused. "I'm sorry, I'm not trying to pry, I'm just curious."

"It's okay. I met him through a friend." Which was a lie. She'd met Kevin because, starting with her grandfather, her family had done business with the Alfonsi crime family, who Kevin worked for.

"How long were you together?" he asked her as he drove.

The steakhouse was close by but not that close, and Violet couldn't wait to get there because maybe when they were eating, he wouldn't ask her as many questions. But she also knew that they were on a date, something she hadn't done for a long time, and that part of the dating process was getting to know the other person, something Violet wasn't comfortable with since Sam wasn't a mob guy.

"A long time. Years, starting when I was a teenager, and up until Tommy was eight. Kevin was older than me and more experienced and I think I fell for him because of that." Violet found herself telling Sam things she had never told Anton during the long time they'd been together.

"He took advantage of you?" Sam asked with concern in his voice.

Violet focused on the traffic light where they were stopped. "No, never. I might have been young, but I knew what I was doing."

Sam touched her shoulder—the first time he ever touched her—and warmth filled her body. "Good. I wouldn't want anyone to do that to you."

"You're sweet," Violet told him.

She hadn't been paying attention to the passing scenery, because if she had she would have recognized the neighborhood. She glanced at the brightly lit restaurant, which looked filled with customers despite the poor weather.

"We're here," Sam told her. "I don't think they have a parking garage, so we'll have to find a space and then walk. I hope that's okay."

"They don't have one. Sure, that's fine. We can just use your umbrella." She wouldn't mind being near him under the umbrella.

They had to park rather far away, and Sam exited first and opened the umbrella and then opened the door for her. The rain continued to pour. He angled the umbrella so she wouldn't get wet as she stepped outside.

"Thanks," she said, and he locked the car doors and they hurried to the restaurant with the rain pounding down on them.

The hostess, Gina, a beautiful, curvaceous young woman who Violet knew during the years she'd been with Kevin, greeted them when they entered. Violet hadn't been to the restaurant since she and Kevin broke up.

"Violet!" Gina smiled and gave her a hug.

"Hi, Gina. How are you?" Violet asked, standing somewhat awkwardly in her arms.

Sam waited patiently for her to introduce them.

"Gina, this is Sam. Sam, this is Gina, she's the restaurant's hostess and we've known each other for a long time."

Violet watched as the two shook hands.

"He's cute," Gina whispered to her when Sam wasn't paying attention.

Violet figured Gina would tell Kevin about Violet's date when she saw him, not that Kevin would mind, he wasn't the jealous type.

"You know, Kevin was in here earlier for a meeting with Vito and Billy," Gina told her.

"Really?" Violet said, though she wasn't too surprised since Kevin and his gang held 'meetings' there quite often.

Gina didn't know better than to not talk about the mob guys' business with Violet, which Violet had come to appreciate after she and Kevin broke up because that way, she always knew what was going on with Kevin.

"Yeah, it was strange because a woman met them," Gina told her. "It wasn't Kevin alone, though, so it wasn't a date or anything. He was here with some of the other guys, which is why I thought it was a meeting."

"What did she look like?" Violet realized that with Sam there it wasn't the appropriate time to discuss the meeting, but she had a reason for asking. Camille.

"She was on the younger side. Tall, attractive. She didn't stay long."

That sounded a lot like Camille.

Violet wanted to ask Gina if the meeting was out front or in the backroom because the latter meant that it was serious, but couldn't ask in front of Sam. Besides, Gina didn't know Camille, so she wouldn't be able to confirm she was there. Violet knew Camille's stepfather worked for the Alfonsis, but it had never occurred to her that they wouldn't be loyal to her and her mother since she was the mother of Kevin's child.

"Interesting," Violet said to Gina because she didn't know what else to say. But she didn't really find it interesting, her stomach tightened, and she felt unnerved about the situation. She felt like running home and telling her mother but knew that Sam would probably never speak to her again if she did.

Sam waited patiently for the women to finish talking.

"We have a reservation," Sam told Gina when he saw they were done.

"Name?"

"Paul."

"Yes, I see it. Right this way." Gina smiled at Violet and Sam.

"Who are those guys she was talking about? You mentioned Kevin was your ex, but Vito and Billy, I think she said?" Sam asked her once Gina had seated them at a lovely table by the window with a view of the street, one of the best tables in the restaurant.

"They're Kevin's business associates," Violet told him, which was sort of the truth.

She couldn't stop her mind from wandering and thinking about that meeting, and she debated whether to excuse herself right then to call her mother and inform her what Gina had said, but knew it would be rude to leave the table so soon after they'd sat down. She planned to tell her mother when she arrived home.

Sam placed the wine list between them so they could both read it.

"Gina seems nice," he said.

"Yeah, she is." Violet sensed he wanted to know more but she didn't want to give too much away about the nature of Kevin's business.

"You've known her for a long time?"

"Just from visiting Kevin here."

"Is he here now?" Sam asked, looking around.

"God, no," Violet said with a laugh, and Sam chuckled. "Kevin's boss owns this place, and Kevin comes here sometimes to help out but not often. He used to come more years ago, when we were together, but now he's higher up at the company." Higher up at the company. Violet smiled to herself. That was one way to put it.

She opened her menu although she already knew what she wanted to order. *Anthony's* might have been known locally for its steaks but as far as she was concerned, they made the best cheese ravioli in the city. Sam opened his menu after she did and then closed it quickly.

"I think I have to get a steak," he said, "How about you?"

Violet shook her head. She liked Sam. A lot. She found him charming and funny and handsome, and she wanted this to work out. But she also knew that she'd never be able to fully be herself around him if he didn't know the truth about what she and her mother really did for a living, and she didn't know whether Sam would accept the truth once she told him.

"They have fantastic ravioli," she said.

"Okay, then that's what I'll get."

"I thought you wanted a steak."

"I changed my mind," he said with a smile.

The waiter came over and recognized Violet and she went through a similar song and dance as she'd had with Gina. They ordered a bottle of red wine.

"I enjoyed meeting your mother," Sam said as they waited for their food to arrive. They had been served their wine right away.

Violet smiled. "You're too polite, Sam. You don't have to like my mother. It's okay. Even I don't like her sometimes."

"But I do. She reminds me of you. She has that same toughness to her."

"Toughness?" Violet asked as though he'd insulted her a little.

"Yes, you know, you're a New Yorker. We don't have women

like you in Ohio. I like that about you," he said when she frowned. "You're strong. I admire that."

Violet relaxed when she understood he was complimenting her. She took a sip of wine. She realized that in many ways she and Camille were similar, and in that way, she was frightened because she sensed how far Camille was capable of taking things.

"Everyone at your pub is like a family, that's really nice," he said. "They're quite a welcoming bunch for New York."

Violet couldn't tell him that the patrons of their pub feared them as much as they respected them and that was part of the reason they wanted to please Violet and her mother. As far as Sam knew she and her mother were pub owners with a loyal clientele. "They really are," she said.

"Have many of them known you since you were young?"

"Yeah, I was practically raised there, and a lot of them knew my grandfather, who, as I mentioned, started the place."

"That guy who patted me on the back and basically warned me to treat you well," Sam said with a smile, "who is he?"

"His name is Max."

"Is he your . . . uncle?" Sam seemed to be keen on guessing Max's relation to her.

Violet shook her head. "He's an old family friend. I've known him my whole life. He is like an uncle to me in a way."

"I can tell that he cares about you," Sam said.

Violet had trouble hearing him above the noise in the restaurant.

Sam raised his voice. "What does he do at the pub? I'm assuming he works there since he came down from upstairs."

"He does. He's the bookkeeper," she said, because it was true in a way.

Violet found herself sitting there in a dress she hadn't worn since she was with Kevin and thought how everything about

Sam was the opposite of Kevin. Kevin had been a good man to her and to Tommy when he was around but Sam had a real job and was a lawful man, but while she could be honest with Kevin about who she was and what she and her mother did because he shared her lifestyle, she'd never be able to be honest with Sam. Violet wondered if she should just leave right then since she and Sam would never go anywhere and what was the point? She sat there, filled with anger, anger at how she couldn't have the happiness she felt she and Sam were capable of having, how she couldn't be honest with him without risking losing him.

"You can ask me questions, too, you know," Sam said, bringing her back to reality, but she couldn't respond with the truth, that she'd been avoiding asking him questions because she didn't want him to ask her too many.

"What do you think of me, really?" she asked him. "Why are we even here?"

"What do you mean? I think you're great."

"Yeah, but we're so different from each other. I mean, I can't help but wonder why a banker like you would be interested in someone me. Are you just looking to have some fun with one of the locals?"

"Absolutely not. I like you, Violet. Honestly. I don't judge people based on what they do. My parents weren't wealthy. They were working class. Some of the guys I work with might be like that, but I'm not. I take it a lot of the new people in the neighborhood treat you that way?"

Violet nodded. "Although we haven't exactly been welcoming of them either."

"Why do you think there's so much resentment on both sides?" he asked her.

"The people who have lived in this neighborhood for a long time don't like how the new people, people like yourself, are changing the neighborhood and making the rents go up. I'm not sure why the new people don't like us, but it's probably because they can tell some of us resent them. This was a tightknit neighborhood before it started changing. People like things to stay the way they were."

"But we're not like any of them," Sam said to her with a smile. "We get along."

Their food arrived and they had a light conversation as they ate. After they finished eating, including dessert, Sam wanted to pay for the meal and wine, but Violet insisted on paying for half of it because she didn't want to feel like she owed Sam anything.

"I'd like to see you again," Sam said to her outside the restaurant. By then it had stopped raining. Would he try to kiss her?

Violet wondered if he'd feel the same way if he knew the truth, that she and her mother ran the Irish mob and Camille O'Brien was now after them. And that cop was hounding them for a murder. But she did wish to see him again and she wasn't going to deny herself some enjoyment even if it wouldn't ever become serious because she couldn't be sincere with him.

"Yeah, let's do this again soon," she said.

"Great. And I'd love to meet your son, when he's ready."

Violet found Sam's eagerness and acceptance of Tommy sweet, but she didn't want to introduce Tommy to a man who might not be in her life for very long.

They walked to his car and Sam drove her home. There were no spaces in front of the building, so he pulled up alongside some parked cars and stopped.

"Would now be a good time for me to meet your son?" he asked. He seemed eager for Tommy to like him, as though he needed Tommy's permission to continue to see Violet, which she figured in a way he did.

Violet checked the time. "It's a little late," she said, but even if it had been earlier, she would have come up with an excuse to say no. It was simply too soon for them to meet each other.

"You're right. Sorry," Sam said, looking at the car's clock. He leaned over and gave her a quick kiss on the cheek, and she found his inhibition endearing.

She looked straight at him and placed her hands at the back of his head, weaved her fingers through his soft hair, drew his face close to hers and kissed him. Sam blushed when she pulled away.

"That was nice," he said with a grin.

"I like you," Violet said. "I needed to show you that. Goodnight, Sam." She started to exit the car and he touched her sleeve and she stopped.

She looked back at him and he gave her a more assertive kiss.

"Goodnight, Violet," he whispered.

Sam waited to leave until she went inside, and from the street, she could see that the light was on in her apartment and assumed her mother was up watching TV, but she hoped that Tommy would be in bed. Sometimes her mother allowed him to stay up past his bedtime, and Violet let it slide because she had a hard time standing up to her mother.

She heard Sam driving away as she closed the entrance door to her building and entered the hallway. She went up to her apartment and unlocked the door herself instead of knocking in case her mother had drifted off to sleep in front of the television.

"How was your date?" Catherine asked her as soon as she stepped inside, clearly not tired, before Violet had time to shut the door.

Violet closed the door. She was somewhat relieved to find her mother sober, but Catherine was reliable when it came to Tommy. "It went well. He took me to *Anthony's*."

Catherine was sitting up on the couch, watching what

looked like the news. She turned off the TV. "Oh, no," she said. "I hope you didn't run into Kevin there."

"No, thank goodness. But of course, I had to explain why everyone knew me there."

"I hope you didn't tell him the truth," Catherine said.

"No, I didn't. I don't think I'll ever be able to be honest with him, that's part of the problem. How's Tommy?"

"He should be asleep. He didn't want to go to bed but I told him you'd be happy if he did, so he went."

"Thanks," Violet said.

"That's part of the problem with dating a regular guy," Catherine said about Sam. "You don't know if they'll accept who we are until we tell them and find out, and it could go badly. You can't trust them like you can trust another gangster, and you don't know if they'll run to the police as soon as you tell them."

"I know. I like him but I might not be able to be honest with him. And what kind of relationship would that be? He thinks we run the pub, he doesn't know the whole truth, and I don't think I'll ever be able to tell him the truth."

"You don't trust him?" Catherine asked.

"Not in the same way I could trust Kevin," Violet replied. "That's why I almost never date guys who aren't in the 'business'."

"You never know, he might be different, you might be able to trust him eventually. When the time is right maybe you can tell him."

"Yeah, but what if he goes to the police?"

"If he does that, nothing will happen. The police can't just arrest you because they suspect you're a mob member, they have to charge you with a crime. Speaking of that, I asked Max to see if one of his police contacts could give us information on our Detective Seale friend."

"And?"

"Max's contact told him the guy is serious and we should be careful. Seale is a straightforward cop. He's not going to go away and trying to bribe him would be risky because he would probably charge us for bribery."

"We have no choice but to wait and see?" Violet asked. "Shouldn't we do something?"

"Like what, have O'Rourke taken out? If we do that, it'll only draw more attention to ourselves. O'Rourke isn't reliable and I just have this feeling that the district attorney won't bother charging either of us. I just know that Seale's going to end up being disappointed."

"Yeah, it could work out that way. But it might not. Then what happens? This thing goes to trial and we're screwed? You know as well as I do that you don't need a wholesome witness for a jury to convict someone. Anyway, I can't think about this right now, because I think we have a bigger problem on our hands. Gina, you remember her from the restaurant?"

"Yeah, I do. What about her?"

"When I went there with Sam, I talked with her and she told me that Kevin had a meeting there earlier that day."

"That's not unusual."

"Yeah, but it was who the meeting was with that was unusual. Vito Russo and Billy were there also. A woman met them."

"A woman?"

"Yeah, and I think it was Camille."

"The leader of the Russians is a woman, her husband is in prison," Catherine stated.

"Gina didn't mention anything about an accent."

"You really think they would meet with Camille?" Catherine asked.

"Sure. Why not? Her stepfather is one of them."

"You're the mother of Kevin's child. He'd never betray you."

"He'd never betray Tommy, but me? We aren't together anymore. Besides, Vito is Camille's stepfather and she used to date Billy."

"She ended things badly with Billy, I doubt he likes her," Catherine said.

"Vito's going to be loyal to her because of her mother."

They were getting louder and Catherine motioned for them to quiet because Tommy was in the other room.

"I can't imagine them ever working with Camille. What does she have to offer them?" Catherine asked Violet.

"I'd ask Kevin, but he'd never tell me. You know how secretive he can be about business."

There was an unspoken rule amongst men like Kevin that you kept details of a meeting private between only those who needed to know, even lovers were excluded, and so even if she and Kevin had still been together, she doubted he would have told her what happened during that meeting.

"She doesn't have any guys on her side, as far as we know," Catherine seemed to muse aloud. "It'd just be her against us. She'll never win."

"Who knows what she has planned. I wouldn't be so dismissive of her, sometimes all it takes is one person to ruin something."

"What are we going to do about it, then?"

"Are you suggesting we eliminate her? I thought you liked her."

"I'm fond of her, sure, but if she's going to be a problem then we can't take that risk."

"I don't know," Violet said. "With that Detective Seale onto us, I think we should lie low for a while. We shouldn't do anything that draws too much attention to ourselves and getting rid of Camille would do just that. Besides, her mother would be devastated, and her stepfather would be angry, and we don't want to upset the Alfonsis. We could lose them in the process."

"We might end up losing them anyway," Catherine replied. "Who knows what Camille has planned?"

The phone rang, and since in their line of work there was no hour that was too late or too early, Violet answered it without so much as a thought.

"Hello?"

"Violet? It's Simone."

Simone was Kevin's mother, who often called to check on Tommy, but it was odd for her to ring Violet at the late hour.

"Hi. Is everything all right?" Violet asked her.

Catherine got up from the couch and asked her who it was and Violet mouthed, "It's Simone." The look on Catherine's face intensified, for she, too, knew it was unusual for Kevin's mother to call at that hour.

"Violet," Simone said on the phone. "I hate to do this over the phone. It's Kevin. The police came by my house."

"He was arrested?" Violet asked.

"God, I wish that's all it was. Kevin's dead, sweetie."

14

Violet clutched the phone and felt like all the life had been drained from her. "How?" she asked, her voice faint.

"He was shot. In the head. Billy's here now. He told me that there was an altercation with a rival family and Kevin ended up on the wrong end of it. It was an argument over something trivial, and now Kevin's dead. It happened in a pub of all places, and you know how Kevin hardly drank. Yet he died in a pub."

Simone started sobbing and Violet did her best to comfort her over the phone. No one from the restaurant must have known about Kevin yet. Violet stood there, listening to Simone wailing over her son and thought about how she would tell Tommy his father had died. Kevin hadn't been in Tommy's life much after he and Violet ended things, but he was still Tommy's father and Tommy would be very distraught. Violet had lost her own father young, but she had never really known him like Tommy knew his father.

Simone and her husband still saw Tommy regularly, and Simone put Kevin's father on the phone and Violet spoke to him and offered her condolences. By the time she hung up, Catherine had figured out what happened.

"I don't know how I'll tell Tommy," Violet whispered to her mother.

"I'll help you," Catherine offered.

"Do we wake him up now and tell him or wait until he gets up? I don't think he should go to school after he finds out. He should be with us."

Catherine nodded in agreement. "Let's wait until he wakes up, so he can sleep for a little longer."

Catherine suggested they try to get some rest, but Violet didn't think she would be able to sleep. She changed out of her evening clothes and waited on the couch for the sun to rise while her mother slept in her bedroom. A few hours later, she felt the warmth of the sunlight coming in through the window-blinds and turned to see the morning beginning in the city outside. She checked the time and decided to make coffee. She'd turned off Tommy's alarm clock earlier so that he could wake up on his own since he wasn't going to school.

Violet went into the kitchen and heard her mother rising in the other room.

"Should I make him a special breakfast or would that be strange?" she asked her mother.

Catherine rubbed her eyes. "I would just give him what he usually has."

"Cereal," Violet said, pouring some into a bowl and taking the milk out of the refrigerator.

She and her mother had coffee, and after a while she heard Tommy stirring in his bedroom. Catherine followed her into his room.

"Good morning," Violet said to her son, opening the curtain to let the light in.

He rolled away from her and grumbled. "Can I sleep a little more?"

"Tommy, honey," she said gently. "Grandma's here."

Tommy looked over at Catherine, who sat on his bed. "Grandma, what are you still doing here?"

"Tommy, sweetheart, your mother and I have to tell you something."

"What is it?" he asked, sitting up in bed. He didn't seem alarmed, and why should he be? He was only a child, after all. When she didn't respond right away, he seemed to sense something could be going on. "Mom?" he asked.

"Your father," Violet started to say, touching his arm and looking him in the eye.

"What's happened with Dad?"

"He died, sweetie," she said quickly. "I'm sorry."

Tommy collapsed into her arms and cried, and Violet hugged him, and Catherine embraced them both.

"It's going to be okay. We're all going to be okay," Catherine told them both, and while Violet wanted to believe her mother, she sensed that a storm was brewing and that what awaited them ahead would be anything but calm.

Tommy stayed home from school and Violet called them to explain why. They offered to have Tommy see a grief counsellor. Max took care of things at the pub, and Catherine spent the entire day at Violet's apartment, helping out with Tommy. Tommy had stopped crying after the initial grief and Violet worried about him because she knew what it was like to hold in your pain, what it could do to you over time, the toll it could take on you.

A few days later a wake, which Kevin's mother and father had planned, was held at a funeral home, and Violet and Tommy attended with Catherine. They arrived and parked across the street and outside found a long line of people waiting to pay their respects. On the other side of the street, Violet noticed that every other car was black. They started to wait in the line, but Kevin's father came out and spotted them and had them cut the line. They met Simone, a plump, attractive woman with tears in her eyes, inside and Violet embraced her. Simone kissed Tommy's cheek and shook Catherine's hand.

"Catherine, I haven't seen you in ages. How are you?" she asked her.

"I'm well, thanks. I'm so sorry for your loss."

"You're strong just like your father was at your age," Simone said to Tommy as she smiled at him. "You'll be okay."

Violet knew that Simone was trying to make herself feel better, but she also wanted Tommy to know that it was okay for him to show emotion, so she squeezed his shoulder.

"Joe, Vito, and Billy are already inside," Simone told Violet. "They're staying far from the windows because of the photographers outside."

Joe was the name of the boss of the Alfonsi crime family. The 'photographers' was a codeword for the FBI, who often watched mafia funerals to see who attended them and who the current players might be. Violet thought of the black cars parked outside.

Simone and her husband went to greet an older couple who'd entered, and Violet walked with her mother and Tommy into the room where Kevin's closed coffin rested behind rows of colorful flowers. It looked like a reception would be held in an adjacent room afterwards. The three of them sat down near Camille's stepfather, Vito, and her ex, Billy, and Violet saw the boss and his wife seated in the row opposite them.

Vito and Billy nodded at her and she smiled, but the boss didn't see her. After a moment, Violet took a deep breath and took Tommy's hand and led him to Kevin's coffin. Catherine followed behind them.

Tommy refused to look despite the coffin being closed and Violet held him as he cried, which she knew wasn't easy for him because he wasn't a little boy anymore and public hugs embarrassed him. Violet dried her eyes because seeing Tommy so upset made her emotional. Catherine had brought a red rose with her and she placed it on Kevin's coffin then put her arms around Tommy and Violet and the three retreated to their seats. Tommy was too young to say a few words in his father's honor, but Kevin's father gave a short speech while Kevin's mother sobbed.

The three went to the reception in the adjacent room after the viewing where many people came up to her and Tommy to offer their condolences. Joe, a large, heavy man in a dark, fine Italian suit and tie, sat with his lovely young wife at the head of the room, a sign that he was a man of true importance, and gestured for Violet to come over.

Violet assumed he meant alone so she asked her mother to watch Tommy then went to him. The boss's wife smiled at her and asked her how she was. And then she said how sorry she was about Tommy's father. Violet thanked her. Joe gestured for Violet to sit next to him and his wife left to give them privacy.

"I have to tell you how sorry I am about this whole mess," he told her in his deep, calm voice. His leather shoes shone in the light of the room.

"Thank you," Violet told him. She and her mother had spoken with the boss a few times, but she'd never done so alone before and her neck stiffened and her brow dampened.

"I want you to know that I'm here for you and Tommy if you ever need anything. Kevin was like a brother to all of us. You won't be forgotten."

His words should have assured Violet of his loyalty, but she still had doubts. But the Italians were all about a code system and Violet knew this, and she knew that he would have to bring up the matter of Camille first, she couldn't outright ask him.

"Would you like some coffee?" he asked her as he sipped his.

Violet nodded and the boss had the man who tended to his

needs get her one. He set it down on the table by Violet and she drank some.

"I believe you are thinking about the same thing I am thinking about," Joe told her. "Camille O'Brien," he said, confirming her suspicion.

Violet felt relieved he wanted to discuss the matter, but she also dreaded what he would say.

"As I'm sure you know, Vito is her stepfather, and he has been good to me. He has asked me to consider her offer. Billy, who used to be with her, has told me she is a smart woman and I know he still cares about her, but at the moment he wishes our partnership would remain with you and your mother out of loyalty to his dear friend Kevin. As you can see, I am a bit conflicted."

"I appreciate your honesty," Violet said, putting her coffee cup down.

"The thing is," the boss said, "Camille has offered us a better deal than the one you and your mother give us. If things were a different way, I wouldn't even have to consider it."

Violet sensed she knew where this was going: the boss would try to persuade her and her mother to give him a better offer, but she knew her mother wouldn't want to decrease their percentage.

"The percentage we give you dates back to my grandfather, who brokered the deal with your organization," Violet told him.

"Yes, but times have changed," the boss replied.

"I understand, but from a business point of view this percentage has worked for so many years so why change it now?" She asserted herself in a way that she wouldn't have imagined when speaking alone to him. The situation with Camille made her tense. "Sorry if that was too blunt," she added.

"No, no, you're right, of course," he said, the reasonable man that he was. "But now that Camille has come to us with this offer, I can't forget it. She proposed something I hadn't considered before. It made me realize that I wasn't happy with what you give us."

Violet clenched her fists at the thought of Camille ruining things for them. How dare she. She smiled at the boss when she really wanted to scream at the idea of him accepting Camille's offer.

"What exactly has she offered you?" Violet asked him. "Did she ask you to help her get rid of us?"

"We declined to do that. But she offered us seventy percent if she can gain control from you, and we promised to let her operate in the neighborhood if she did."

"She's confident," Violet said with displeasure. "But, boss, she's got no one on her side. She's on her own, there's no way she's getting control from us."

The boss thought for a moment. "Perhaps she can join you?" he proposed.

Violet shook her head. "No. I'm afraid she'd never consider that. Not after what my grandfather and mother did to her father. You're aware of the history?"

The boss nodded. "A little, yes."

"Then you know that she's out for revenge. This isn't just about money or power for her. It's personal."

"Personal. That's the worst kind of motivation to deal with," the boss said, "because the person won't give up easily."

"Yeah, I know she's not going away anytime soon."

The boss sat back in his chair and touched his chin. People stared at him admiringly but didn't come up to say hello. "I'm surprised you haven't considered dealing with her," he told Violet.

"We can't. Not now. We have a dilemma," Violet said but she didn't elaborate.

"What is it?" the boss asked her.

"There's this detective, he's paying close attention to me and my mother. There's a guy who used to work for us, and now he's implicated us in the death of this union guy."

"Yes, I remember that death. Unfortunate, but sometimes these things are needed, and I trust you and your mother's judgement."

"We thank you for that. Anyway, this detective has said that he is keeping a close eye on us. He could be outside right now for all we know. Acting on Camille isn't a possibility at the moment, not when we're under watch. We can't get rid of the guy who implicated us for the same reason. We have no choice but to sweat it out."

"I'm sorry to hear that, but I don't think there's anything I can do."

The Italians didn't 'deal with' cops, and she already knew that.

"My mother isn't as concerned as I am," Violet told the boss.

"Everyone handles these things differently."

Violet didn't want to delay the inevitable so she said, "I want you to know that we appreciate your working with us, but I think that an increase from fifty percent to seventy would be too much for my mother to accept."

"You've told me how your mother would feel, but what's your opinion?"

He'd put her on the spot, but she didn't want to disagree with her mother and create conflict between them. "I agree with her," she said.

"All right," the boss replied, not sounding satisfied. "You leave me no choice but to either betray Kevin or keep things as they are."

"Please," Violet practically begged. "In Kevin's honor I ask you to remain with us."

"Perhaps your mother would consider matching Camille's offer," the boss asked again.

But Violet knew that her mother wouldn't want to accept less than what she already had. "I don't think Camille O'Brien will succeed," Violet said, although she had her doubts.

"If that is true then perhaps, we have nothing to discuss. I still think you should ask your mother. In the meantime, you have nothing to worry about. Tommy is Kevin's son and so he is like a son to me. I'll reject Camille's offer."

Violet wanted to hug the big gangster, but she merely smiled and thanked him.

"What's going to happen with the guys who killed Kevin?" she asked him.

"Nothing," he answered. "Their boss has informed me that they took care of the guy who did him in, so we are even. I think they wanted to avoid a war."

She said goodbye and left. The boss's wife, who had been chatting with a couple nearby, returned to sit with him.

Catherine had been watching them and she approached Violet as Tommy played with some other children nearby.

"What was that all about?" Catherine asked her.

"He confirmed my suspicions about Camille," Violet told her mother. "She did meet with them, and she promised them a better offer than we have with the Alfonsis."

"What did she promise them?"

"Seventy percent."

Catherine shook her head in anger. "Is he going to accept her offer?"

"No, but he did consider it, and it would only have happened if she managed to take control from us, which she won't. The boss says he's loyal to us because of Kevin, but unfortunately, Camille has planted the idea of a larger percentage in his mind and he wants us to consider raising their percentage."

"She's going to squeeze us out," Catherine said. "The nerve of her even thinking of trying something like that, and to think that at one time I liked her, considered her like a daughter in a way."

Violet gulped, because her mother had never admitted that out loud before, although Violet had suspected it.

"Just Camille circling about them could cause trouble. We should consider raising their percentage," Violet told her mother. "That way, we can secure their loyalty if anything else should happen with Camille."

"The split has been fifty-fifty ever since your grandfather organized the partnership with them all those years ago. Why should we raise it?"

"I explained that to the boss, but Camille's put the idea of a better percentage in his head. We might not have a choice."

"No," Catherine said. "We're not giving in. Next thing we know they'll want eighty percent then ninety, or they'll move in on the neighborhood and take everything from us. We've always operated with their permission, and I don't see why things should change, especially since Kevin was one of them."

"Kevin's dead," Violet said. "They could forget about him and that loyalty after a while and we'll end up with nothing or dead ourselves. I know you're proud, but with Camille in the picture, everything has changed. If we agree to giving them a higher percentage then, maybe, we secure their loyalty forever and their help with dealing with Camille when the time comes."

The boss hadn't offered to eliminate Camille for them, but Violet sensed that if they continued to work together and Camille became a genuine problem then he might help them.

"I still think Camille could just go away. She'll realize she can't win and then she'll forget about it. And the boss will forget about her offer once she's gone. Everything will be like it once was." Catherine spoke with confidence, but Violet found her mother's reasoning a bit deranged.

"I have to say I don't agree with you," Violet said, although she knew that if she went behind her mother's back and gave the Alfonsi family a larger percentage her mother would never forgive her. Dating back to Violet's grandfather, the Irish had a thing about not giving into the more powerful Italian mob, and it was symbolic more than anything. The two groups were once traditional rivals but over the years had formed an unsteady alliance, where the Italians often had the upper hand much to the chagrin of the Irish.

Tommy ran up to them and asked if he could go outside with some of the other children to play. Catherine told him it was okay, but Violet didn't like him playing outside in the city without an adult watching.

"When you're a teenager, you can do that, but you have another year until you are one, so, no," she said to Tommy.

Tommy frowned and wouldn't look at her. It wasn't easy for Violet to be sensitive to his needs all the time, especially at a time like this, and with everything that was going on in her life.

"I'm sorry, kid," she said, touching Tommy's face, and he allowed her to keep her hand there.

"You should have let him go," Catherine told her as Tommy returned to the other children.

"He's my son," Violet stated, not looking at her mother, but she imagined her expression.

Violet let Tommy stay home from school to mourn for a while, and a few days later there was a church service and burial for Kevin which Violet attended with Tommy and her mother. Despite the sudden death, Violet had a little more happiness in her life from knowing that the Alfonsi family wouldn't be collaborating with Camille any time soon. Just picturing the look on Camille's face when she found out made her smile.

15

About a week after her meeting with the Alfonsi crew, Vito phoned Camille and asked her to meet him at the café he frequented in the mornings. Vito had told Camille's mother what Camille was trying to set up and her mother had encouraged her to pursue it. Vito had said he had some news he needed to tell her, and Camille didn't know whether that was a good thing or a bad thing. Would he have been more likely to give her bad news over the phone or in person? Camille had known Vito for many years, but she didn't really *know* him. She had kept her distance.

She had some money saved, but now she was using it for daily expenses until she got her life sorted out. Part of her felt she was crazy for believing she could take the Irish mob from the McCarthys, and that she'd either end up dead, broke, or both. But she had little to lose except for Johnny.

Camille walked to the café from her apartment in her father's favorite leather jacket despite the heat. She moved with grace as she walked, confident that her stepfather would tell her yes and that she'd secure the Alfonsis' cooperation. After all, her stepfather would lose her mother if she told her the truth about that night when Camille was a teenager.

She arrived at the café, removed her jacket and threw it over her shoulder. Her stepfather wasn't there so she found a table and sat down and waited for him. Camille hadn't eaten any breakfast before she left the house and she considered waiting for Vito to arrive before she ordered but decided to go ahead.

She ordered coffee and a bagel and Vito showed up as her food arrived. Vito waited, standing, and acted as though he expected her to rise and embrace him.

"That's never going to happen," she told him with a smile.

"You know, Camille ever since I got together with your mother, I've tried to be like a father to you," he said as he sat down.

"Fathers don't hurt their daughters," she snapped at him.

"Camille, that was a long time ago. I said I was sorry. I wasn't thinking straight. I'm a changed man now. I haven't done anything since then."

"There's no excuse for what you did. You weren't even drunk when you did it. You're a creep and you better hope that your boss agrees to my offer."

They were quiet when the waiter stopped by their table to take Vito's order. When he left, Vito said to Camille, "Why don't we eat first and then talk business. Okay?"

Camille could tell he wanted to control the conversation, which she also wished to control.

"You better have good news for me when we're finished eating," she told him.

They ate in silence, with Camille rebuffing Vito's attempts at conversation. She didn't like him, and even if he'd helped her, she still wouldn't like him, and she wanted to show him that. But at the same time, she knew that without his help the Alfonsi family wouldn't even be talking with her.

"Listen, Camille," he said as he put down his fork. "I've been sitting here thinking of a way to try to tell you this."

Camille couldn't stand the suspense and leaned forward in her seat across from him, but still far enough away from him. "It's bad news? Is that why you asked me to meet you here? You make me wait until you eat and then you—"

"The boss will be declining your offer," he interrupted her.

"I knew it," Camille said. "You didn't try hard enough!" She rose from her seat and yelled at him and the people seated nearby stared at them.

"Camille, please, you're making a scene." Vito gestured for her to sit.

Camille sat down and stared at him. "Was it Billy, was he behind it?" she demanded.

"No. It's about loyalty. Violet McCarthy is the mother of Kevin's child. Kevin was killed recently; did you know that?"

Camille watched him quietly in shock. "I didn't know. She must be devastated. They were together a long time."

"Yeah, and they had a son together, so the boss is going to be loyal to her because it's Kevin's son. They know them, they don't know you. It's just how things are."

"They know you, and Billy. Did he say something to discourage them? You can tell me," she said in a way that seemed gentle, reasoning it wouldn't hurt to use a different approach. "I won't tell him what you said."

"It doesn't matter if he said anything, the boss made up his mind as soon as he talked to Violet at the wake. She asked him to remain loyal and he agreed to."

"She knows I met with you guys?"

"Yeah, she went to *Anthony's* for dinner and one of the employees let it slip. Violet's got a connection to the place so they're friendly with her."

"She probably was livid," Camille thought out loud and

smiled at the idea of Violet's anger, although she wasn't a monster and did feel genuine compassion for Violet's son, who had just lost his father. "Did you talk to her at the wake? I'm assuming you were there."

"Of course, I was there. I saw her, yeah, but we didn't speak. The boss talked to me afterwards in private. I all but begged him to agree to your proposal, but he wouldn't because of Kevin's involvement with the McCarthys. Kevin was one of us. You have to believe I tried; I really did."

Disappointment overcame her, and she said, "I'm sorry but I can't accept that," pushing her plate with the half-eaten food away from her and crossing her arms. "I don't think you tried hard enough, Vito. You should've begged. Do you understand what's at stake for you? I'm not going to let you get away with what you did if you don't get them to reconsider."

"Please don't tell your mother. I did what you asked me to, there was never any guarantee they'd agree."

"No," Camille said. "You're wrong. I agreed to not say anything to her as long as you convinced them to work with me. Now that they're not, I have no reason not to tell her."

"I don't believe you would," Vito said arrogantly. "All these years have passed, and you never said anything. Why would you go and do it now?"

"Because I have nothing to lose. I'm not a girl anymore." Emotions overcame her and she resisted drying her eyes in front of him for as long as she could.

"You don't have a job anymore," Vito said in desperation. "You'll need us to support you. What are you going to do? Think about it."

"Don't worry about me, I'll think of something. You better get them to change their minds."

"How? I pleaded with the boss, more so than he probably liked. But there's only so much I can do. He's gonna get angry if I keep pushing him. My hands are tied." Vito held out his hands for emphasis.

"I don't believe you," Camille said. "You're high up enough in the organization that what you say to him means something. Do you know what I think? I think you don't like the idea of me running this neighborhood, you don't want me to have that kind of power, knowing what I do."

The waiter approached them.

"Is there anything else I can get for you?" he asked.

Vito ordered another cup of coffee.

"How can you drink coffee at a time like this?" Camille asked him when the waiter left.

"What do you mean?" Vito asked.

"I'm going to leave here and tell my mother what you did. She's home, right? I take it you'll be getting the check?" Camille stood up and Vito reached out and grabbed her arm, almost dropping his cup in the process.

"I'm not going to let you do that," he told her.

Camille shook him off her. "Let go of me or else I'll scream." She looked around and their waiter watched them from a distance. Camille indicated to Vito that they were being watched and he let go of her arm.

Then he tried a lighter approach.

"Camille," he said, his voice thickening with emotion. "I love your mother; I couldn't bear it if I lost her. Please don't do this to me. You don't have to do this. I'm sure we can work something out."

"Like what?" Camille sat down again. "You haven't given me what I want, so what could you possibly have to offer me?"

"I'll try again. I'll ask him."

"Good, that's what I want to hear. But no nonsense, do you hear me? You have to do what you say you will. And you better get them to change their minds. I don't want to have to return here in another week and hear that you failed again."

"I never knew you were like this," Vito said quietly.

"Like what?"

"Like a gangster," he said. "You were so quiet as a girl."

"I grew up," she stated. "You better get used to it. I'm not going to be quiet anymore."

"Please don't say anything to your mother. You know as well as I do that she'd be devastated. Do you want to hurt her?"

"Leave my mother out of this, this isn't about her, it's about you and me. I'm done here. The next thing I want to hear from you is that you've gotten me what I want."

"I said I'll try. I can't force the boss's hand. It doesn't work that way. I'm surprised you don't understand that. If you're going to be working with us, you need to know these things."

"I know it," Camille replied. "I also know that someone who's clever enough can get things done."

"I'm clever," Vito said.

"We'll see if you are."

16

Sam had invited Violet over to his apartment so he could cook them dinner. She had never been involved with a man who could cook before. Kevin had been very traditional, and she had always cooked for him. She and Sam weren't officially a couple, but Violet felt they were getting closer to becoming one.

Violet had bought a bottle of white wine at the liquor shop to bring with her. She hoped she'd chosen a good one, the shop owner said she had, but she didn't know much about wine, and Sam seemed like the kind of person who would know a lot about it.

Sam's apartment was a merely a street away from the pub, so Violet walked there quickly after work. Once again, her mother had agreed to watch Tommy, who was getting suspicious of where she was going to. She had dated men before, before Anton, but Tommy hadn't liked any of the guys as much as he liked Anton, so Violet didn't know how he would react to Sam and didn't believe they should meet yet.

She arrived at Sam's apartment and had to wait for him to let her in downstairs. She heard his voice on the intercom.

"Violet?"

"It's me," she said as she waited outside.

"One moment, I'll let you in."

Violet heard the buzzer and opened the door. She stepped inside the lobby and heard someone walking down the stairs and then Sam appeared, greeting her.

"I'm so glad you're here," he said, beaming.

"I brought you this," Violet said, holding up the wine bottle.

Sam took it from her and thanked her. "A great choice," he said, holding up the bottle, and she smiled.

"Come upstairs," he said, gesturing for her to walk with him. "Dinner's all ready. I made two options because I realized I should have asked whether you eat meat."

"I do, but thanks." Sam seemed almost too good to be true and she wondered if she should pinch herself or be suspicious of him.

She walked with him upstairs and they entered his apartment. The inside of the building had been plain but inside Sam's apartment was a bit more decorated, with bright furniture, and colorful artwork on the walls, which she didn't know anything about but imagined was quite expensive.

"I like your art," she said as Sam shut the door.

"Thanks." He smiled, and she was relieved when he didn't ask her whether she knew about the artists.

He didn't appear to have a dining room, but Violet noticed that he had the table set in the living room with a black tablecloth, shining, uniquely shaped crystal glasses and fine, chunky silverware. He already had a bottle of wine on the table and Violet felt foolish she'd brought one. Sam set her bottle next to his and Violet wondered which one she should drink.

"There's pasta with a red sauce and a side of steak or grilled eggplant," he told her.

"Sounds delicious," she said.

He pulled out a chair for her. "Have a seat."

Violet sat down and then wondered as he disappeared into the kitchen, if she should have offered to help, but, no, he seemed intent on going out of his way to make her feel comfortable.

"Steak, right?" he asked her from the kitchen, where the doorway was just outside the living room.

"Yes, please," she said. "But I'll take some eggplant, too," she said to be polite, figuring that it might not get eaten if she declined.

He returned with two plates filled with food and set one of them in front of her and the other at his place opposite her.

"Looks great," she said, and it really did.

"I can't wait to try some of the wine you brought," he said as he sat down. "Would you like some?" He picked up the bottle.

She nodded. "Yeah, thanks."

He uncorked it and poured some into her wineglass and then into his.

"I bet we'll go through both bottles," he said with a smile.

Violet had told him about Kevin over the phone and they had met for a quiet walk in the park once after. Sam had been comforting to her, and the situation had made them closer.

"This was a good idea, us having dinner here, I'm glad we decided to do it," she said.

"I am as well. It's good to see you getting out after what happened."

They began to eat, and it tasted quite good. "Kevin and I didn't see each other much after we split up, and he didn't see Tommy all that much either, but I'm worried about how Tommy's handling everything. My mother's been great helping out with Tommy, and he's also been seeing Kevin's parents more lately. But he's confused about everything."

"How did Kevin pass, if you don't mind my asking?"

She hadn't told him at the park and he hadn't asked then. "It was unexpected," Violet said now, reluctant to tell him the truth. She paused. "The truth is, Sam, he was murdered."

Sam's face went pale. "Murdered? That's awful," he said quietly. "I'm sorry, I had no idea. I knew the city was dangerous, but—"

"It was a long time coming," she said honestly.

He looked at her, puzzled.

"Tommy's father was involved with some shady characters," she explained. "I can't say I'm surprised he was killed." After she spoke the words, she realized how harsh they sounded. "Not that he deserved it, of course."

"Right," Sam said, seeming shocked.

"I think I've just ruined our dinner," she said during the awkward silence and put down her fork.

"No, you haven't," Sam reassured her. "I'm just a little surprised, that's all. I didn't know that about you. It must have been difficult being with someone who lived that kind of lifestyle and not knowing it."

If only he knew the whole truth.

"I knew what he did," Violet said. "I just didn't think about it." She didn't know how he would judge her if she told him she was used to that lifestyle because she lived it herself. "My grandfather was the same way as Kevin," she said after a pause. "He was a gangster."

Sam laughed. Then he said, "You're joking?" when she didn't join him.

Violet shook her head. Could she trust him? She couldn't stand lying to him because she knew that for things to really work between them, she would have to be honest with him.

"I like you, so I want to be honest with you," she told him.

"Okay," he said, setting his fork down. "I appreciate your honesty. I like you also. But I'll admit I'm a little confused by all of this."

"I know," she said. "And I didn't want it to happen this way. I wanted to wait until the right time to tell you, and now isn't the right time but I'm telling you anyway."

"There's more?" he asked, and she wondered whether he'd be able to handle it.

She braced herself to have to walk straight out the door and leave. "My mother and I, our pub, we run what's left of my grandfather's business from there," she said, looking at him.

"What do you mean, his 'business'?" Sam seemed genuinely confused. "I know you mentioned he owned the pub before you and your mother ran it."

"We now run all of his businesses," Violet clarified, "including the semi-illegal or illegal ones."

Sam stared at her in silence. "But you work at a pub with your mother."

"The pub is where our operations are based out of, it's a front of sorts. I'm telling you this because if I'm not honest with you we can't really be together, and I wanted to give you a way out. I understand if you want me to leave. Just say the word and I'll go. As a rule, I typically don't date guys outside of my lifestyle—"

"I don't want you to leave," Sam said calmly. "You've only dated . . . men outside the law?"

Violet smiled at his gentle phrasing and nodded. "I didn't plan to tell you all this today but knew that the longer I waited the harder it would be, and I didn't want our relationship to have lies. I'm not dangerous, and neither is my mother," she said, and felt guilty for lying to him about the last things.

Sam got quiet and seemed to be thinking, and Violet prepared herself to exit.

"Please, stay," Sam said, gesturing to her. "I appreciate your honesty. I have to say, I'm a bit shocked, being from Ohio and all, and I really do like you."

She waited for the *but*, but none came.

"Let's not allow this to ruin our dinner," Sam said after a moment, and she figured that either he truly planned to overlook it or once she left his apartment that night, she'd never see him again.

They had a pleasant dinner with good conversation and drank coffee and watched television afterwards and Sam didn't try to get her into his bedroom, which either meant that he was too polite to suggest it or what Violet had told him had turned him off. She didn't want anyone to pity her so after he kissed her goodnight and she left his apartment she planned to never see him again and not return his calls if he called. She figured that he wouldn't want to see her again after what she told him and wanted to cut him off before he could hurt her so soon after Anton had. But Sam didn't seem bothered by what she had told him, in fact it was almost as though the revelation made him more interested in her, as though it made her more intriguing somehow.

Still, she didn't pick up the phone at home if she thought it was him, and at the pub she had her mother say she was either absent or busy. The more she avoided Sam, the more he called. But Violet wouldn't give in, because she felt that in the end, he would leave her because of who she was. Catherine had praised Sam but agreed that it was probably for the best, and she expressed worry that Sam could use what Violet told him against them, that perhaps he could go to the police.

"He isn't like that," Violet told her mother one day when she had picked Tommy up from school and took him to the pub to see his grandmother.

Their new bartender had prepared Tommy a lemonade and he sat at the bar drinking it with his back turned to Violet and Catherine.

"Even if he did," Catherine said, "He hasn't got any proof, right?"

"Doesn't matter," Violet told her. "He just isn't like that. He won't do anything. I'm sure I'll never see or hear from him again once he stops calling me."

"He must have really liked you," Catherine said with a wistful smile. "Imagine, you could've been married to a banker."

"I only just started seeing him. We were nowhere close to that."

Catherine gestured to Tommy at the bar. His feet didn't touch the floor from his seat. "How's he doing?" she whispered to Violet.

"I'm worried about him. I'm glad I didn't introduce him to Sam before I ended things with him because I don't think he could have handled more loss."

"It's good you didn't," Catherine agreed. "About Sam, have you ever considered just calling him back and telling him you don't want to see him again? Some guys need you to be blunt, they won't get the hint. Maybe he just doesn't understand why you're avoiding him."

"I know it sounds terrible, but I don't want to deal with that right now, not after everything that's happened. He'll stop calling eventually. He won't understand my reasons for not wishing to continue. He didn't seem to care what we do for a living, but over time he will care, as any guy not involved in this business would. I need to focus on Tommy."

"All right," Catherine said. "I don't agree but I know you aren't a kid anymore and make your own decisions. I'm glad we're close enough to talk about it. Some women couldn't stand having their mothers around all the time, but the two of us are in business, and that keeps us close, and that's a beautiful thing."

Violet smiled at her mother's enthusiasm. Max came over and asked them what was going on.

"She wants to end things with the guy who took her out—

remember, the nice, good-looking one?—but she won't tell him and he won't stop calling her," Catherine said.

"The poor guy," Max chuckled. "What did he do to deserve that? He didn't hurt you, did he?" His gaze darkened.

"No, nothing like that," Violet told him. "I just can't be with someone who isn't involved in our lifestyle. It'll never work out. I can only see gang guys."

"Maybe you should aim higher. What was this Sam guy's job anyway? Wasn't he a banker?"

Violet nodded.

"Why shouldn't you date a guy like that?" Max said.

"There's nothing wrong with seeing a gangster," Violet countered. "After all, you're one yourself."

"That's true, but there's no rule you have to be with one."

Loud rock music played on the jukebox and the pub started to fill with patrons coming in after work. Catherine left them to assist the bartender with the crowd then Sam walked in.

Violet turned to Max because her mother wasn't there. "He's here. What do I do?" she asked him.

"Talk to the guy. See what he has to say. Tell him what you want to say."

Violet nodded and prepared herself as Sam approached. He looked clean-shaven and handsome and smelled good.

"Violet," he said. "I've been desperate to speak with you, but we can't seem to connect."

Max stepped away to give them some privacy.

"I know," Violet told Sam. "I've been avoiding you."

"Why? Did I do something?"

"No. Not yet."

Sam looked at her thoughtfully and touched her arm. "What do you mean? I'd never hurt you."

"Are you sure? You wouldn't leave me after what I told you? After what I told you I was so convinced that I'd lose you so I left you before you could leave me. And it's all right, Sam, if you want to not see me anymore. I understand. Most regular guys wouldn't want to be involved with someone like me."

"What are you talking about?" he said. "I'm here now. Of course, I still want to see you." He smiled. "I've been calling you like crazy trying to get in touch with you."

Violet looked at him skeptically. "After everything you know about me, why would you still want to be with me?"

"Because I like you, Violet."

"Someone like you, what could you possibly see in me? We're so different from each other."

"I see a caring, beautiful, fantastic woman," Sam answered.

"I used to be a drug addict," Violet told him, as though adding that to the mix would frighten him away further.

"I don't care," Sam said.

"Listen to the man," said Max, who had overheard.

Sam opened his arms for a hug and Violet embraced him. The people in the pub, many whom she knew, and who had been watching their exchange play out, clapped and whistled and Violet and Sam laughed. Her mother stopped working and smiled at her from the bar. Max patted Sam on the back.

"Now that you got her back, you better treat her good," he told him, seriously.

"I will, sir," Sam replied.

"Sir?" Max grinned. "I like this guy," he told Violet.

Violet hadn't been paying attention, but her mother signaled to her to look at Tommy, who she now saw had turned in his seat and was watching them from the bar with a frown on his face. It had been a mistake not to tell him about Sam.

"There's someone I want you to meet," she told Sam when the crowd had settled down. She took Sam's hand and led him over to Tommy, who stared at them approaching, still frowning.

"He looks like a great kid," Sam whispered to Violet as they strode.

"He is. Tommy's the one thing I've always done right, no matter what else was happening in my life."

"I can't wait to meet him."

"Tommy," Violet said as they stood alongside him, still holding hands. She wanted to give Tommy a signal that Sam meant something important to her. "I want to introduce you to Sam."

Tommy didn't say anything and looked at both of them. "Who are you?" he asked Sam, his tone not quite friendly.

Sam moved to shake his hand, as though he didn't know any better not to. "It's great to meet you, buddy. I'm Sam."

Tommy looked down at his hand then held it limply. "Okay," he said. Then he let go of Sam's hand and looked at Violet. "Who is he?" he asked her.

"Sam and I have been seeing each other," Violet explained to him.

"Like you saw Anton?"

Violet nodded.

"Okay," Tommy said quietly, but he wouldn't smile or even look at Sam, who stood there awkwardly and smiled at them, as though he was trying to make the best of the situation.

Catherine poured Violet and Sam each a beer and they sat at the bar next to Tommy, who rebuffed Sam's attempts to get to know him.

Tommy looked at Violet, who sat alongside him, and Sam was next to her. "I'm hungry," Tommy said.

Violet nodded at him. She waited for Catherine to finish a drink order and then gestured to her. "Can we fix Tommy something to eat?" she asked, although she knew the kitchen didn't open for another hour for dinner.

"Sure," Catherine said, smiling at Tommy. "What do you want, handsome?" She winked.

"A hamburger," Tommy said to her and finally smiled, but at his grandmother

"Thanks," Violet said to her mother, who left the bar for the kitchen.

Sam sat there patiently, tapping his finger on his beer mug. Then he made another attempt to win Tommy over. "How do you like school, Tommy? I loved school at you age."

Tommy didn't look at him, but Violet saw him roll his eyes. "I don't like it," he mumbled.

"Tommy, you're being rude," Violet scolded him.

She liked Sam and had hoped Tommy would as well, like he had liked Anton. But Tommy, like a lot of boys his age, could be finicky about the men in his mother's life. Violet wondered, did because Tommy didn't like him mean that her relationship with Sam was doomed?

"It's okay," Sam told her.

"No, it isn't," Violet replied. "You could make more of an effort," she said to Tommy. "Sam's being very nice to you." She nudged his foot with her and tilted her head toward Sam.

Tommy looked at Sam and apologized in a begrudging way.

"No problem," Sam said to Tommy.

"He's upset about his dad," Violet whispered to Sam, who nodded. Although she was concerned that Tommy didn't seem to like him. He hadn't liked Anton straight away either, but he had taken more of a shine to him than he had to Sam.

"It's all right, I understand," Sam said to Violet.

Catherine exited the kitchen and walked over to them with a hamburger on a plate for Tommy. She went behind the bar and set it and a bottle of ketchup down in front of Tommy.

Tommy thanked his grandmother and started eating.

"That looks good," Sam said to Tommy, but Tommy ignored him.

Violet shook her head. She didn't want Sam to think she couldn't control her son. "Tommy," she said, "Sam's speaking to you."

Tommy looked straight ahead at his food and ignored her. He mumbled something she couldn't decipher.

Violet looked at Sam and apologized for Tommy's behavior. Deep down inside she wondered if it might be about something more than Kevin. Tommy genuinely seemed to dislike Sam. Regardless, she smiled at Sam and tried to seem upbeat.

Reggae music played on the jukebox and a man and woman began to dance while holding their drinks in their hands. People gathered to watch them and clapped, and Violet and Sam watched them while Tommy ate.

"Makes me feel like dancing," Sam told her.

Violet had never considered herself a good dancer and was embarrassed by that. "I don't think so," she told Sam, her face burning.

"Come on, why not?" Sam grinned at her.

"Because I can't dance for the life of me and I don't want to make a fool of myself in front of all these people, that's why."

"But you're a tough girl," Sam said, "Why not give it a try? I'll help you."

She smiled at him then nodded, and they rose holding hands. Sam pulled her over to the area where the other couple was dancing and held her close, and using his movements as a guide, they swayed to the music. She rested her head on Sam's shoulder and tried not to step on his feet. When she glanced at Tommy at the bar, she saw that he wasn't watching them, as though he refused to, but her mother was.

The door opened and Detective Seale walked in.

17

Violet held on more tightly to Sam as she watched Seale enter. When the detective approached the bar and spoke to Catherine, who seemed distraught, Violet let go of Sam and went to see what was happening.

"You can't do this," Catherine told Detective Seale. "Not in front of my grandson."

"Maybe you should have considered that before doing what you did," the detective replied.

"Grandma, what's going on?" Tommy asked Catherine, his voice filled with a nervous energy.

"It's okay, Tommy," Catherine told him. She walked out from behind the bar to speak with the detective away from Tommy and Violet approached them.

"What the hell are you doing here?" Violet asked Detective Seale, unable to mask her anger.

"I've already explained to your mother that I'm here to arrest her in connection with the murder of Robert Shane, and I can either do it quietly or make a scene if that's what you wish," he replied with an arrogant smile.

"You can't," Violet said, at a loss for words.

"Oh, I can," Seale replied smartly. "You've messed with the wrong guy."

Max came over and looked at Seale then at Violet and her mother. He told Catherine, "It's going to be okay." Then the detective started to take out handcuffs.

"Please don't cuff me in front of my grandkid," Catherine begged Seale.

"I have to, it's protocol," he replied.

"You're really going to arrest her?" Max asked in anger.

"I am," the detective said bluntly. "Who are you?"

Max introduced himself.

"I know who you are," Seale sneered.

"Do you have a warrant?" Max asked him calmly.

"I don't need a warrant to arrest her," the detective stated. "But, no, I won't be searching the premises."

Some good fortune at last, Violet thought. She considered asking Seale if they would be searching the pub at some point but didn't want to seem suspicious.

"If you're going to put handcuffs on her, I think you ought to do it outside," Max told the detective. "You'll upset her grandson."

"She should have thought of that before doing what she did," Detective Seale replied to him and asked Catherine to turn around.

She sighed and complied, and he read her her rights. Max started to inject on her behalf again, but Catherine stopped him. "It's okay, Max," she told him. "I'll go with him."

Max seethed but obeyed.

Tommy left the bar and ran over to Catherine. "Grandma!" His eyes glistened with tears.

Violet hurried to him and pulled him away from her mother. Sam appeared at her side and whispered, "Violet, what's going on?"

"Remember when I told you who we are?" she replied in a whisper also. "These things happen all the time to us. My mother is innocent." Her face burned at telling him the lie.

Tommy kept crying and Violet reached out and comforted him. Sam tried to help as well but Tommy swatted him away.

"Leave me alone, I don't know you!" he said.

Sam quickly backed away as though Tommy had bit him.

Catherine looked at Violet and held her gaze and said, "You're in charge now. Take care of things. I trust you. Let my mother know what happened."

"I will, and I'll call our lawyer," Violet shouted to her mother as Detective Seale led her in handcuffs out of the pub.

Her mother didn't look at her again, but Detective Seale turned to Violet and mouthed, "You're next."

Violet shuddered at his remark but wouldn't let him scare her. When they were gone, Sam asked her if she was all right. He didn't seem to have seen what the detective told her.

"I'm not sure," she replied, and he touched her shoulder tenderly. "I think you should go," she said, embracing Tommy.

The people in the pub whispered to one another about what had happened and asked Violet if she needed anything and she thanked them.

"I want to be here for you," Sam told her. "What can I do?"

Violet didn't answer him. "I'm sorry but I need to be with just my family right now," she said, and that included Max.

Sam looked at her and nodded then he quietly left.

Still holding Tommy by his shoulders, Violet spoke to Max at her right. "We should close the pub and move things out. They could be back with a warrant at any time."

"Good idea," Max replied, then he began to speak to the patrons, who had been watching the action unfold, collectively, and explained that they had to leave so that he and Violet could sort things out.

Once the pub had been vacated and the last customer left, Violet wondered what she should do with Tommy while she and Max cleared out the pub.

Tommy, who was getting taller each day, looked at her. "Why did that cop take Grandma away?" he asked. "Did she do something bad?"

Tommy was innocent about their lifestyle and Violet wanted to keep it that way. Although he had seen the police in the pub before and Violet wondered how much he really knew.

"No," she told him. "He's just mistaken, that's all."

"But why would he put handcuffs on her, and why did Grandma go with him?" the astute Tommy asked.

"Because that's what they always do. Remember when they came and took Great-Grandpa away and then he was back the next day because it was a misunderstanding?" Violet said, recalling the incident that had happened shortly before her grandfather's death.

Tommy nodded. "Grandma will be back tomorrow?" he asked.

Violet didn't want to lie to him in case that didn't happen, so she said, "I hope so."

Then she called her mother's lawyer and explained what had happened. She and Max couldn't clear anything out until it was darker outside, and in the end she returned home to her apartment with Tommy and asked the elderly Polish woman who lived downstairs if she could keep an eye on him overnight. The woman agreed and didn't ask any questions because Violet would pay her. Tommy complained about having a babysitter and Violet didn't like leaving him alone after what happened with his grandmother, but she had to help out Max and so had little choice.

By the time she returned to the pub, night had fully arrived. Max only had one light on in the place, which she could see from outside. He had the front door locked and Violet had forgotten her key and had to knock to be let inside. The street was quiet.

"Is Tommy all right?" Max asked her inside the pub.

"Yeah, I left him with a neighbor. I don't like leaving him alone after everything that has happened, but I don't want him involved in any of this. I'm worried about what comes next, Max, and how Tommy will be affected. That detective threatened me."

"When? Earlier?"

"No, when he arrested my mother, he looked at me and said, 'You're next'."

"It might mean nothing," Max reasoned. "They threaten people like that all the time and nothing comes of it."

"That guy has it in for us. I don't think he's going away any time soon. We better use the back entrance to move things out, in case they're watching."

"I don't see anybody on the street," Max said, looking out the big window that faced the sidewalk.

"You know better than anyone that doesn't mean they're not watching."

"True," Max said. "All right, we'll take things out the back. You want a drink first?" He gestured at the bar.

Violet shook her head. "Nah, I need my head clear."

"Me too," he said. "I parked my car in the back just in case, so we can load the stuff in there."

Violet nodded.

It took them a few hours to clear the pub, Max's office, and Catherine's upstairs apartment of anything that could be used as evidence, mostly paperwork and weapons, and put it into boxes from the kitchen and stow it in Max's car. Violet knew that she would have to gather their men for a meeting to tell them the news of her mother's arrest, if they hadn't heard already. Word spread fast in the neighborhood.

While they were working, the phone rang in the kitchen and Violet ran to answer it. It was her mother's lawyer, informing her that her mother had been denied bail. Violet hung up and muttered a quiet curse to herself. Max came in to see what was going on.

"That was the lawyer. They won't allow my mother bail," she told him. "She's considered a flight risk because of her dual Irish citizenship."

"I'm sorry, Violet."

"What will I tell Tommy? He won't understand why she didn't come back."

"He's a good kid, he'll understand."

"I don't know if I want him to have that reality," she said. "Up until now, I've managed to protect him from everything we do."

"That's the reason I never got married or had kids, too many people to depend on your morality," Max reflected.

"Tommy happened unexpectantly but I'm grateful to have him," she said.

"I know how much he means to you," Max said. "I can help you talk to him if you'd like."

"Thanks, but I think this is something that I need to do by myself." With her mother gone, she couldn't depend on others to always help her. "I just wish all of this wasn't happening so soon after Kevin's death."

"He's a strong kid," Max said, patting her shoulder. "He'll be okay."

They turned out the light and then went out back to Max's car. Violet locked up the pub and then they drove to an apartment a couple of streets away that they used as a secret safehouse.

"Are you going to go home after?" Max asked her as they sat parked outside on the street.

Violet shook her head. "I can't sleep. As soon as we know

they're not going to come to the pub with a warrant tonight, I want to call a meeting with all the guys."

Violet exited the car first and checked the street for signs that they had been followed. Given the late hour, there were just a few homeless people out for the night as well as a handful of couples and singles enjoying the warm evening.

They moved the boxes into the first-floor apartment, and despite the late hour, they knew no one would complain due to their fierce local reputation. Once everything was secured in the empty apartment, Violet locked the door and they left to return to the pub.

McBurney's was ablaze with police lights, red and blue, which illuminated the side of the building. Max braked and stopped the car in front of the place.

"What the hell is going on?" he whispered to Violet.

"Looks like they came back with their warrant," she replied. "We got out just in time."

They parked on the street and exited. Violet spotted Detective Seale standing by one of the cop cars, speaking to a police officer. He waved and smirked when he saw her.

"Here you go, as promised," he said, handing a piece of paper to her.

She read the warrant then threw it on the ground. She wanted to tell him to go to hell but used restraint.

"I hope you didn't already clear everything out," the detective remarked to Max at her side.

Max shrugged and didn't answer him.

"Doesn't matter," Seale said. "We already have everything we need to charge Catherine McCarthy. This is just a matter of formality."

Violet didn't want to see the pub being picked through, so she and Max waited outside for the police to finish.

"They tried to get your grandfather too," Max told her as

they waited, "but never could. I think they view this is payback."

"I'm glad Tommy isn't here to see this," she told him. "Camille O'Brien will be delighted once she finds out."

"Your mother told me all about that. I'm not surprised she has it in for you," Max said. "I knew her father. He was a tough, smart guy. She's like him."

"How worried should I be about her?" Violet asked him.

"I'd be very worried," he replied solemnly. "I wish I had taken this thing with the police and your mother more seriously. I'm sorry I didn't. But I know you'll do well in her place."

The police finished their work after a few hours and left the pub in disarray.

"It's an odd hour but I should call that meeting now," Violet said to Max as they stood inside the pub and cleaned up. The police had left most of the lights on and Violet went around turning all but one of them off. "The guys need to know what's going on, if they don't already."

"Shouldn't we wait to see what your mother says first?" Max replied, suddenly seeming to shift his attitude.

"She's in jail, she doesn't get a say," Violet said.

"We can still communicate with her," Max said, seeming surprised at her blunt words. "We know guys on the inside."

"You were there when my mother was hauled away, she told me I was in charge now."

"I'm sure she wants you to oversee things in her absence, but I don't think she meant you would lead."

"She did," Violet retorted.

"Violet, you have experience but not like your mother has."

"Are you saying I don't know what I'm doing?" She disliked arguing with Max, she considered him to be like family, but business was business.

"No, not at all. But we owe your mother the respect of being our leader until as long as she wants to."

"She gave me control," Violet stated calmly. "I don't want to talk about this anymore. We should take your car to collect the guys in case the police are listening in on the phones."

Max looked at her and nodded.

Violet wondered whether the other guys would resist her leadership as much as Max seemed to. She loved her mother but saw her arrest as an opportunity for herself to lead, whereas before the unspoken rule had been her mother led because she was the elder.

They went outside and entered Max's car, with Violet sitting in the passenger seat and Max driving. Jake and Pat lived together, so they drove to collect them first. Derrick lived with his girlfriend farther away.

At Jake and Pat's apartment building, with the car parked outside, Violet followed Max upstairs. Max knocked and they waited for one of them to answer.

Jake opened the door halfway and stared at them.

"What's going on?" he asked, shirtless and unshaven, and rubbing the sleep out of his eyes.

"There's a problem," Violet said.

"What is it?" Jake asked, with fear thick in his voice.

"Don't worry, it's not you," Max said.

"My mother was arrested, and the police just searched the pub," Violet told Jake.

"I heard something about that but didn't know if it was true."

"It is," Max said. "Is Pat home?"

"He's sleeping," Jake said.

"Get him up and both of you get dressed. We're going to have a meeting."

"Is Derrick with you?" Jake asked.

Violet shook her head. "We're getting him next. We didn't want to ring you guys in case the police are listening in on the phones."

"Okay. Hold on a second." Jake closed the door and disappeared into the apartment.

Violet could hear Pat's voice and the sounds of them getting ready to leave. A few minutes later, both exited the apartment and met Violet and Max in the hallway.

Pat greeted them.

"I'm sorry about your mother," he told Violet, and she thanked him.

"Yeah, she's a great lady," Jake said. "Did she make bail?"

Violet shook her head. "She was denied it because of her dual citizenship."

Both men shook their heads in disbelief and then they walked downstairs and left the building with Violet and Max. They reached Max's car and Jake and Pat sat in the back while Violet rode up front with Max.

Derrick was a bit farther away and Max put on the radio as he drove to help the time go by.

Derrick and his girlfriend lived in a newer building than Pat and Jake. They were night owls and were up watching television when Violet went upstairs by herself to collect him.

"I'm calling a meeting," Violet told Derrick at his door. "My mother was arrested."

"I'm sorry, Vi, I hadn't heard. How's she doing?"

"I don't know. They denied her bail and I haven't been to see her."

"What did they get her on?"

"The Robert Shane thing."

"Does Tommy know?"

"Yeah, he was there at the pub when it happened."

"That's terrible. It must have been quite a shock for him. Where is he now?"

"A neighbor's watching him. He's just lost his father, so this event has double the impact."

Derrick shook his head in dismay. His girlfriend, a pretty blonde woman, appeared at the door behind him to see who he was talking with. Violet had met her a few times before and they each asked one another how the other was, but Violet knew that Derrick didn't discuss business with her, so that was the extent of their greeting. Derrick turned to his girlfriend and explained he had to leave and then walked to Violet out in the hall as his girlfriend shut the door behind him.

"Max is waiting with Jake and Pat in his car outside," Violet told Derrick.

"You're worried the police are listening in on your phones?" he asked her.

"They might be. They had a warrant and searched the pub."

They drove to an isolated location by the pier and Max turned off the car and lights so they could hold their meeting there in secret, away from the police's watch and where nobody would bother them. Violet didn't trust the cops wouldn't be watching the pub or listening in.

"As you all know," Violet told the men, "my mother was arrested today, and she's been denied bail. I've been threatened by the detective in charge of her case, so if anything should happen to me, Max will be in charge."

The men nodded. Then Derrick asked her, "Is your mother calling the shots from jail?"

Violet shook her head. "She left me in charge."

Derrick looked at Jake and Pat.

"Is that going to be a problem?" Violet asked them.

"I just assumed Catherine would be controlling everything from jail. We have ways to communicate with her," Derrick said.

"When my mother was arrested, she told me I was in charge," Violet said to them. "Max heard her say it. Didn't you, Max?" She looked at him.

"I did," Max said, "But I get what the fellows are saying," he added quietly.

"What is this, gang up on the girl time? You all have a problem with me leading because I'm younger than you?" she demanded.

The men flinched at her wrath and quickly shook their heads, except for Max.

"I've known you for your whole life," Max replied in an even tone, "and I respect you a great deal. But you've never been the leader before, Catherine always called the shots."

"You don't think I have enough experience?" she asked him.

"I think that a lot is going on, with your mother's arrest, and Camille O'Brien intentions to get rid of you. I think your mother would know how to handle things better, even from jail."

"She didn't think she'd be arrested, she said we had nothing to worry about. She doesn't think Camille will be a problem; how do you think that'll turn out?"

"I think this O'Brien girl is angry but will cool off eventually," Derrick interjected.

"Listen to what Max thinks. He knew her father," Violet said.

"Her father wasn't the type of man you ignored," Max told them. "If she's anything like him, we have something to worry about."

"She's got nobody," Derrick said. "We have a whole group. One against many. What could she possibly do?"

"She had enough brass to reach out to the Italians," Violet responded. "Her stepfather is one of them, and her ex. Thankfully, the boss turned her down. But the boss is getting on in his years and he won't be around forever. We could have trouble on our hands if he's gone. The Italians cooperation has been vital to our success, and, as you know, dates back to my grandfather."

"If they turned her down then we have nothing to worry

about," Pat said.

"I'm not sure, remember what Max said," Violet replied. She looked at Jake and Pat. "Keep an eye on her for me, but don't let her know you're watching her. I want to know where she goes, who she talks to."

"All right," Jake said.

"You can count on us," Pat said.

Then Violet looked at Derrick. "What about you?" she asked him. "Can I count on you?"

Derrick eyed Max as though waiting for his reaction before he responded to Violet.

"Yes," he finally said when Max remained quiet.

Now that she had the three under her control, she turned to Max. "It's my right to lead," Violet told him.

Seeing that he was outnumbered, Max sighed and said, "All right, Vi. You win."

"I'm glad that's settled," Violet replied. "Of course, my mother will still have a say. We aren't going to forget about her. You should all be aware that this Robert Shane thing isn't going to go away," Violet told them.

"We ought to bump off O'Rourke," Pat said. "I'll volunteer to do it." He grinned at her.

"Yeah, and I'll help," Jake said.

"Thanks, but that will just make us look even more guilty. We need to stay off their radar," Violet said.

"What do you think, Max?" Derrick asked him

Violet scowled. Just when she thought she had finally gotten them to listen to her...

"Whatever Violet thinks," Max muttered.

"Max, you said you didn't have an issue with me calling the shots. But, do you?" She held his gaze.

"No, Violet, I don't."

"Good. After what happened to my mother, everyone needs

to be more careful. The police could be watching us at any time. You need to be vigilant. We can't have Camille O'Brien use this as an opportunity to move in on us." Then Violet added, "I know how much you all love my mother, and I'm grateful for that, and I know she is also. I appreciate you all respecting her wishes to have me lead." She really wanted the message to sink in.

By the time they finished the meeting it was the early morning. Max drove the guys home and then took Violet to her apartment. She had been up all night.

"We shouldn't be seen together too much," she told Max as he dropped her off by her apartment building. "Any of us."

Max nodded. "I'll tell the others."

She said goodbye to Max and went into her building. She stopped on the Polish woman's floor to collect Tommy and get him ready for school. She also had to tell him the news about his grandmother still being away.

Violet knocked on the woman's door.

"Come inside," the white-haired woman, wearing a black housedress, answered the door.

Violet entered and found Tommy still asleep on the couch. She paid the woman for watching Tommy, and the woman thanked her. She didn't know about Catherine's arrest and didn't ask questions, one of the reasons Violet liked her.

"How was he?" Violet asked the woman.

"He was a very good boy. You've done a good job with him."

The woman smiled, showing the few teeth she still had left, and Violet filled with pride at her words. Tommy was the one thing she had always done right.

The woman went to the couch and woke Tommy up. He stirred and opened his eyes, looking up at her.

"Hey, kid," Violet said with a smile. "How are you?"

"Where's grandma?" he asked.

Violet didn't want to discuss Catherine's arrest in front of the woman, so she said to Tommy, "We'll talk about that when we get home."

Tommy nodded and sat up. He'd fallen asleep in his day clothes, so they were able to leave straight away. Violet thanked the woman again. Inside their apartment, Violet told Tommy to take a bath and put on fresh clothes while she made him breakfast. He'd kept asking about his grandmother and Violet kept responding, "I'll tell you when you're ready for school." She felt negligent that she had let him sleep in his clothes overnight and that she hadn't been there for him. Catherine would normally have watched him, and Violet cursed Detective Seale for taking her mother away.

Tommy appeared in the kitchen, bathed and changed. His damp hair glistened in the sunlight that came through the windows.

"Where's Grandma?" Tommy asked. "You said you'd tell me when I was ready, and I'm ready."

Violet sat down at the kitchen table and patted the empty seat next to her. "Sit with me," she told Tommy.

Tommy sat down.

"Eat," she told him, gesturing to the breakfast on the table.

"What happened to Grandma? Is she in prison?" Tommy crossed his arms and looked down at his stomach.

Seeing that Tommy wouldn't eat unless she told him something, she said, "They still have your grandmother, but they're mistaken. She didn't do anything." Telling the lie hurt but she told it anyway; she needed to shield Tommy, for as long as she could, from the world she and her mother lived in.

Tommy looked over at her. "Why do they still have her then?"

"It's a misunderstanding. We'll have it cleared up very soon." Violet doubted that would be the case, but she still had to have hope.

"Will she be home tonight?" Tommy's eyes brightened at the possibility.

"I'm not sure."

"Where were you last night? Why did you leave me with that lady?"

"I had something important I needed to do," Violet replied.

"For Grandma?"

"Yes, something like that."

"Wasn't the lady nice to you?" she asked him.

"She was but I don't need a babysitter. I can just be on my own when you're not around."

"You're not old enough," Violet replied.

"I'm twelve."

"Twelve is too young to be left alone overnight. When you're a teenager, an older teenager, then you can start doing that. Okay?"

Tommy seemed to be thinking then nodded. "What did they arrest Grandma for?"

Violet didn't want to tell him the truth of course, so she had to think of something to say fast.

"A parking ticket," she said.

"They arrested her because of a parking ticket?" Tommy asked in astonishment.

"Yes, because she had a couple of unpaid ones." Violet knew that the more of the lie she told the harder it would be to unravel. "If anybody in the neighborhood tells you otherwise, don't you listen to them." She touched his chin and looked at him. "Okay?"

Tommy nodded. "Can she make, what's it called, bail?"

Violet hesitated then answered, "They wouldn't give it to her."

"All because of some parking tickets? That doesn't make sense. Can they really do that?"

Violet nodded. "Yes, they can."

"Wow. I better remember to pay them when I start driving," Tommy said, and Violet felt relieved that he believed her.

"I hope you won't get any," Violet said with a smile, and Tommy laughed.

Seeing his mood improve warmed her soul.

She and Tommy ate breakfast and then after she cleaned up, she planned to walk with him to school, but Tommy protested.

"It's too dangerous to be alone in the city at your age," she told him.

"When then, when I'm a teenager?"

"When you're an older teenager," she said.

"You're too overprotective," Tommy complained. "I know you were allowed to walk to school alone when you were my age. Grandma told me."

"That was a different time, when the city was safer, and I always went with a group of friends."

"Can I go alone if I go with my friends?" Tommy asked her.

Violet shook her head. "Besides, Grandma wouldn't want you to go alone. She'd be worried about you, and you don't want her to be worried, now do you?"

Tommy shook his head. "Is she okay? I mean, it must be hard for her. Are you going to see her?"

"Yes, as soon as they allow her visitors. I'm sure it is difficult for her, but she's very strong."

"Is she going to be away for a long time?"

"I hope not," Violet said. She didn't want to think of the possibility that there would be a trial, although she knew it was likely, or that her mother could be sent away to prison for many years, but that could happen. She didn't want to frighten Tommy, so she chose not to elaborate.

They both left to walk Tommy to school.

18

Camille had heard what had happened to Catherine McCarthy, and she believed it meant that, finally, she had some luck. One had fallen. One more to go—Violet. The arrest, which everyone in the neighborhood gossiped about, had surely weakened Violet, and it propelled Camille to move faster. She reached out to a Russian gang in Brooklyn, a traditional rival of the McCarthys, to propose working together. Their leader was in prison and his wife was now in charge, and she responded to Camille's invitation that she was intrigued by Camille's boldness. She knew of Camille's father's street reputation and wanted to meet the woman who would dare ask to see her.

Camille arranged to meet with them at a nightclub they owned in Brooklyn. Despite the heat, she wore her father's beloved leather jacket during the train ride there. She had arranged to meet the Russians when the nightclub was closed so it was the early morning. The train crowded with commuters going to and from work, and Camille had to stand during the trip. She exited at her stop and walked to the nightclub, a short distance away. She enjoyed the feeling of the morning warmth on her face as she strode through the neighborhood where most of the shops had Russian writing and most of the people on the streets spoke Russian. She arrived at the nightclub in a few minutes and outside there were a few brightly colored sports cars parked in front, which Camille assumed belonged to the gangsters.

She spoke to the two obviously secretly armed guards at the front entrance, two hulking men with Russian accents, and they seemed to be expecting her. They searched her for weapons and didn't find any—she had left her gun behind at home, which she knew was a risk, but she didn't want to come across as threatening to the Russians. Then they opened the gold door of the dark-red building and gestured for her to enter. Above the door, a neon sign displayed the name *Valeria's*.

Camille went inside and was greeted by a tall, unsmiling young man.

"I'm here to see Mrs. Valeria," she said, for that was how the female boss was known on the streets.

"Yes, I know," the young man said, offering to shake her hand.

"Camille O'Brien," she said, shaking his.

"I'm Demetri," the young man said. "Follow me, please."

There was a large dance floor inside the dimly lit club with a silver disco ball glittering above it, and an area for the DJ. Tables with chairs were gathered around the floor, and there was a long black-marble bar in the back of the room where a solitary bartender stood polishing glasses. Camille didn't see anyone else in the club.

"Everyone's in the backroom, waiting for you," Demetri said, as though reading her mind.

She followed him down a short hallway. Before they entered the backroom, Demetri checked her for weapons.

"I promise I don't have any," she told him with a smile. "Your men outside already searched me."

"I still have to," Demetri said with a shrug. He patted her less vigorously then the men had outside, as though he was a bit shy. He mumbled, "All right," when he had finished.

He opened the tall black door with a silver handle and there were a group of people inside the softly lit room, sitting at a card table. Camille heard the door closing behind her then looked at the table. Two men, one of whom she recognized as Violet's ex-boyfriend, Anton, a large, tall man with a trimmed beard, and another she didn't know, a shorter, bald guy, sat across from an older woman who she knew was Mrs. Valeria, a curvy, heavily-made-up blonde with stylish eyeglasses. The two men, unsmiling like Demetri had been, nodded at Camille then rose. Mrs. Valeria said hello but didn't get up from her seat. Anton and the other man shook her hand then indicated for Camille to sit down to the right of Mrs. Valeria, who finally reached across the card table and shook Camille's hand once she'd sat.

She looked at Camille over her eyeglasses. "Camille O'Brien, it's wonderful to meet you. You're just as I pictured you," she said warmly. "My husband, who I'm afraid is not here to meet you today, and I, met your father once. You look so much like him."

"It's good to meet you, ma'am," she said.

"Please, call me Valeria."

"Valeria."

Anton and the other man, who had both sat down, looked at her. "How's Violet?" Anton asked Camille with a smirk. "Did you know that crazy woman pulled a gun on me?"

Camille thought that Anton probably deserved it but didn't tell him that, of course. "No, I didn't know she did that."

"She did," Anton said. He seemed on edge, looked thinner, and had dark circles under his eyes, and Camille figured he might be using drugs again. Violet had told her about his history with them. "I still love her son, but I hope I never see that crazy woman again," he told Camille.

"Can't say I like her much myself these days," Camille replied.

"I thought you two were friends," Anton said.

Camille shook her head.

Valeria looked at her to explain.

"She and I were friends until I found out the truth about her family. They helped kill my father, her mother did. Max did the actual killing. Do you know him?"

"I'm familiar with him," Valeria said. "You must want blood," she told Camille. "I know I would."

"I want what they have. I believe it would have been mine and my father's if they hadn't killed him."

"I understand, but why should I help you? The Italians have a pact with the McCarthys. If we work with you against the McCarthys then we work against the Italians also."

"I've spoken to the Alfonsis," Camille told her.

The woman smiled at her as though she admired her. "And what did they say?" she asked, as if she doubted they would go against the McCarthys.

"They responded as you might expect them to, they said no. But I came close," Camille said, because she believed she had. "And I haven't given up. I have an in with them because my stepfather is one of them, and my ex is as well. I guess my ex being one of them could be a good or a bad thing," she said with a nervous laugh. She didn't tell Valeria that while they were still considering her plan, the Italians had only agreed to allow her to operate in the neighborhood if she gained control; they had not offered to help her get control, because she didn't know if Valeria would view that as a failure.

"What is your experience? What did you do before this?" Valeria asked her after a moment.

"I used to be a bartender."

Valeria leaned back in her chair and looked at Camille, who couldn't tell what she was thinking.

There was a knock on the door and then a young woman entered with a tray of what looked like tea and set it on the table. Valeria thanked her then the woman exited.

The man who sat with Anton, who hadn't introduced himself, poured the tea into the cups and handed one to Valeria first then to Camille and Anton then himself.

"Russian tea, the best," Valeria said. "Irish tea is good also," she added with a smile.

"My stepfather," Camille suddenly said. "I have something over him," she said, without elaborating.

"You believe he can convince the others?"

Camille nodded. "In time, yes. The thing I have over him is pretty big."

Valeria smiled at her. "You are a smart girl, I admire that. You remind me of myself when I was younger."

Camille thanked her. "Catherine McCarthy was arrested; did you know that?" she asked after a moment.

"I had heard, yes. She and I are certainly not friends, but I don't believe she has ever been in prison. She will find it difficult, I'm sure. My husband is currently serving time, but at his age he's used to it by now."

"I doubt she'll be comfortable," Camille said. "But she's a hard woman. Anyway, I believe that now is the perfect time for someone like myself to move in. Their influence is slipping in the neighborhood."

"You would like my cooperation," Valeria said, in a way that was more of a statement than a question.

Camille nodded.

"I'm sure you're aware that historically we don't work with the Irish," Valeria said. "We don't usually fight, but we aren't friends either."

"I want to change that," Camille replied.

Valeria looked at her and smiled. "I admire your ambition. But I have to ask, what can you offer us? You are only one woman."

Camille calculated in her head how much she was willing to give them. If she managed to win over the Italians with Vito's help then that would leave her with thirty percent, which basically meant they owned her, which she didn't love, but that's how it always went with the Italians: The Irish might have controlled the neighborhood but the Italians controlled the whole city.

"We can work together when needed," Camille offered.

"You seem confident the Italians will eventually work with you. What is the percentage they would want?" Valeria asked her. "If we are going to work together, we will have to agree to a regular percentage each of us will get from the other."

Anton grunted in agreement with Valeria.

"They've asked me for seventy percent," Camille replied.

"And you've agreed to it?"

Camille nodded.

"Of course, you did. We also are allowed to operate with the cooperation of the Italians and give them a slightly lower percentage. They are ruthless negotiators, but not as good as us Russians," Valeria said with a wink. "What do you think we should give each other, then?"

"All right," Camille said, thinking. "How about we each give the other five percent of what we make?"

"What are you making now?" Valeria asked.

Camille was ashamed to admit the answer was 'nothing' so instead she said, "I'd rather not say." She took a sip of her tea.

"You are all alone, you are probably not making much. Am I correct?"

"I'm alone, yeah, but not for long. The Italians—"

"What if they say no in the end?"

"I'll make it work."

"The Italians' cooperation is crucial to controlling your neighborhood, like it is crucial to mine. The only reason the McCarthys can operate there is because the Italians let them. If the Italians say no to you then you can't operate there even if you are able to gain control from the McCarthys."

"I'll get them to say yes," Camille spoke with confidence.

"Whatever you have over your stepfather, it must be terrible," Valeria said admiringly.

"It is."

"You know, when you first reached out to us—where did you get my phone number anyhow? I don't believe you ever said."

"From an old friend," Camille said, even though Vito had given her Valeria's number.

"When you first reached out to us, I thought to myself, who is this Irish girl that she is so brave to ask to meet with me? I wanted to see what you looked like. Then when I realized you were Colin O'Brien's daughter I knew where you got your spirit from. I'm hesitant because you are on your own, but because of your confidence, I am willing to take a chance on you. I never liked Catherine McCarthy or her daughter much, I always felt they thought they were too good for everyone else. So, all right, Camille O'Brien, if you need anything, let me know, and when you start making some money, then we will discuss a percentage." Valeria smiled.

19

Camille wasn't alone anymore, and Violet felt that could spell trouble. She had heard that Camille had made a pact with Mrs. Valeria and her Russians, who included Anton.

Sam had stayed with her despite witnessing her mother being taken away to jail, and Violet felt relieved because he offered stability in her life, although Tommy still didn't like him. She knew that seeing her mother arrested must have made both Sam and Tommy think about how it could have been Violet being taken away instead.

But Catherine's arrest put a lot of pressure on Violet and when she heard the news from Max about Camille's partnership with the Russians, she went searching for her while Tommy was playing at his friend's home. The most obvious place to find Camille would have been her apartment but when Violet checked, she wasn't there. She knew Camille was close to her mother, so she went to Sheila's apartment to see if she knew Camille's whereabouts. She also wanted to speak with Sheila to see if she could get Sheila's assistance with defusing Camille and making her stop this madness. If she could get Camille's mother to see Camille's plan for what it really was, lunacy, then maybe

Sheila would talk with Camille and discourage her, and Camille would go away.

Sheila answered the door with a frown. From the way she acted, Violet didn't think Vito was home.

"I heard about your mother, Violet. I'm sorry," Sheila said, as though she knew she had to be polite to Violet because of the working relationship Violet and Catherine had with Vito.

"Thanks," Violet said, to play along. "I know Camille is out for revenge," she said to cut to the chase.

"Do you want to come inside?" Sheila asked.

"No, thanks. I'm fine here."

Sheila stared at her. "After what your mother and that Max did to my late husband, Camille's father, is it any surprise she wants revenge?"

"That was a long time ago. I had nothing to do with it."

"Your mother did."

"She's not around anymore."

"She was denied bail?"

Violet nodded. "And if this thing goes to trial, she could be locked away for a long time since it's a murder charge."

"What will you do without her?" Sheila asked coolly.

"I'll manage. I have Max's help."

"I'm sure you do, that bastard."

"I've always found Max to be a decent guy."

"That's because he didn't kill your husband."

"Look, whatever Max did all those years ago is in the past." Then she considered saying, 'I'm sure he had his reasons' or 'He's sorry' but knew that would outrage Sheila.

"I live with my husband's death every day. It was because of Max and your mother that Camille never had a father."

"I'm sorry for what they did," Violet said, trying to smooth things over. "But it had nothing to do with me. Are you sure it was even them?"

Anger flickered across Sheila's face. "As sure as I am that you are standing here."

Violet had her doubts, but she said, "You and I both know Camille will never win. She's only got herself," to try to reason with Sheila.

"Actually, she told me she's working with the Russians now, so she isn't alone. I'm proud of my girl."

Violet had wondered if Sheila knew about Camille's pact with them. "That doesn't matter. The Italians say we can control the neighborhood, so we control the neighborhood. If they don't want Camille in, then she's not in. That's how it always worked, and how it always will," she said resolutely.

"That could change," Sheila said.

"I doubt it. My son Tommy's got Kevin Carmine's blood in him, and you must know how old man Alfonsi loved Kevin."

"Kevin. I was sorry to hear he died. Genuinely," Sheila said, with sympathy in her eyes, and an honest affection passed between them.

"Thanks," Violet replied to her in the doorway. "I've always admired you, your strength."

Sheila leaned against the doorframe and looked at her like she knew Violet wanted something. "We can't be friends," she said. "I'm loyal to my daughter. If Camille doesn't like you, I don't like you. I'm sorry, but that's just how it is."

Violet tried a different approach. "This whole thing that's going on here, all of this turmoil, it isn't good for Camille."

Sheila straightened and glared at her. "Are you threatening my daughter? You're the one who should watch your back, Violet McCarthy. You never knew my husband, but my daughter has his blood."

"I don't believe you," Violet said. "What could she do to someone like me? She doesn't even have a gun." She gave a nervous laugh.

A look appeared on Sheila's face that made Violet realize Camille had a gun. But she told Sheila, "In the end, she's the one who will be getting hurt. We McCarthys always win."

"You sound just like your grandfather. After my husband died, do you know how he treated me? He ordered my husband killed and then gave me nothing. I had to learn to survive. Camille has my strength." Sheila started to close the door in her face, but Violet stopped her.

"Do you want some money now? If I give you some money will you get Camille off my back?"

Sheila looked at her and her eyes darkened. "You don't understand, do you? It's not about money. This is about loyalty and about blood. I encouraged Camille to push you and your mother out. I love my daughter, but both she and I know the risks."

"Does she really? Have you ever talked with her about them?"

Sheila seemed to be weighing how much she should tell Violet. "Not directly. But she knows them through the stories I tell her about her father."

"And you're okay with her possibly dying over this?"

Sheila looked like she hadn't thought about that before. Then she gave Violet a sly look. "Are you?" she asked with an arched eyebrow.

"My mother and I never think about that. I don't know many of us who do. It's always a possibility, of course."

"My Camille is going to be fine. It's you who should be worried."

Violet felt that Sheila spoke that way to comfort herself.

"My mother and I have always been fine," Violet stated.

"If you're so fine then why is your mother in prison? You and your mother are slipping up." Sheila looked straight at her. "Now if you'll excuse me, I'd like to shut my door."

Violet held her gaze. "Where is your daughter now?" she asked.

"Why?" Suddenly, Sheila seemed nervous.

"Because I want to talk to her."

"About what?"

"About business."

"What could you possibly have to discuss with her? Unless you're going to give up now that your mother is gone because you don't think you can run things."

"Just tell me where she is," Violet said in disgust.

"No," Sheila snapped at her.

"Tell me," Violet shouted.

Sheila seemed to enjoy enraging her because she smiled and didn't say anything.

"Fine, I'll find out where she is myself," Violet said, and retreated down the hallway to leave the building.

"You leave her alone," Sheila shouted after her.

Violet wanted to reach Camille before her mother could notify her. She went outside to a payphone and called Pat at home.

"You've been keeping an eye on Camille," she said when he answered. "Where is she usually this time of the day?"

"Sometimes she eats at the restaurant near her mother's place," he said, after a pause.

"Which one?"

"The new one, the nice one."

"She's moved up in the world now that she's with the Russians," Violet said with sarcasm, and Pat chuckled. "It's a little early for dinner, isn't it?"

"Maybe she likes an early dinner."

"Is she usually with that Garcia guy?" Violet asked.

"No, I don't think so. She's usually alone."

Violet thanked him and trudged over to the restaurant Pat

mentioned, tracing the outline of her gun in her purse as she walked. She didn't have that long before she had to pick up Tommy at his friend's house, which her mother couldn't do anymore. She had arranged through her mother's lawyer to visit her mother in prison tomorrow while Tommy was at school. She longed to take the anger she felt towards her mother's situation out on Camille because she needed to take it out on someone. And although she felt like she could kill Camille, if given the right opportunity and setting, she also knew that it would be a grave mistake. If Camille ended up dead everyone in the neighborhood would think that Violet did it and eventually the police would also.

The restaurant was nice enough that Violet couldn't just barge in and rush to Camille's table. The maître d at the front asked her if she had a reservation as she stood waiting in the uncrowded restaurant, given the early evening hour.

"As you can see, we aren't very occupied, so it's fine if you don't have one," the man with a thin moustache told her.

"I don't have one," she replied. "Actually, I'm here to see someone."

He looked at her hands as she rubbed them anxiously, eager to reach Camille before Sheila could. "You're meeting them? They're expecting you?"

"Not exactly."

A touch of worry appeared on the man's face and he tensed. "I see," he said. Violet wondered if he thought that perhaps she might be insane.

"Her name is Camille O'Brien." She couldn't see into the rest of the restaurant from where she stood even if she craned her neck to look. "If I could just look to see if she's in here . . ."

"I'll go check. Please wait here," the man interrupted. "What's your name so that I can tell her?"

"It's a surprise," Violet said with a smile.

"Oh, okay. One moment, please." He watched Violet over his shoulder as he walked away as though he didn't quite trust leaving her alone there. When he left, a waiter walked past her then stopped and smiled at her.

"Do you need anything?" he asked her.

"No, that's all right, thank you, he's already helping me." She gestured at the maître d.

The man nodded and went on his way.

The maître d returned. "I'm sorry but she told me she isn't expecting anyone and doesn't want to be disturbed. Perhaps you could try her at another time, somewhere else."

"But it's very important that I be able to speak with her. It's an emergency," she spoke with a sense of urgency because she knew that could persuade him. She could have very well slipped him some money, but he didn't seem like the type of person to accept such an offer.

"All right," he said uncertainly, "Let me show you to her table."

Violet thanked the man and followed him. As Violet walked toward Camille's table, she could see Camille looking in her direction to see who was there to see her. When she saw that it was Violet her face paled and her expression darkened. If looks could actually kill, then Camille's would have.

She stood up and gestured at Violet. "What is she doing here?" she demanded to the maître d.

"She said it was an emergency," he replied quickly.

"She's lying," Camille said loudly.

"Madam, please lower your voice."

"You want me to lower my voice? I wouldn't be this angry if you hadn't let this person, who I don't want to see, come to my table."

"I'm sorry, I didn't know that, she said—"

"I don't care what she said, it isn't true," Camille cut him short. She glared at Violet. "How did you know I was here anyway?"

"Your mother told me," Violet lied, looking down at Camille's half-eaten spaghetti.

"You talked to her?" Camille said, aghast.

Violet nodded. "I went to her apartment."

"Leave her out of this."

"I didn't do anything to her. We talked, that's all."

"I can't believe she talked to you, and I can't believe you went there."

"She isn't to blame," Violet said, suddenly feeling the need to protect Sheila from her daughter's wrath because she, too, knew mother-daughter relationships. "I would have found you anyway."

"You need to leave now, madam. Please," the maître d told Violet.

"Not so fast," she replied, and looked at Camille. "I need to speak with you. How dare you work with Anton behind my back. You know my history with him."

Camille looked at the maître d as though she didn't want to discuss the matter in front of him. Then she looked at Violet.

"Let's talk about this outside."

Violet nodded.

"Excuse me, madam, you need to pay first," the maître d told Camille.

"Of course," she said, going through her purse on the table. She took out her wallet and handed him some money. "This should more than cover it. But I'll be back to finish my food when I'm done. Can you reheat it when I return?"

The maître d nodded. "Of course, madam."

Camille looked at Violet. "Let's go."

Camille grabbed her purse and Violet walked slightly behind her as she followed her outside.

"You made this even more personal by bringing my mother into this," Camille said over her shoulder.

"It already was personal," Violet replied.

They exited the restaurant and Camille stopped in the street. The fading sunlight cast a glow on her face and with her classic beauty, made her look almost angelic, and Violet smiled at the irony.

"What do you want?" Camille asked her.

"I can't believe you had the nerve to work with Anton."

"I didn't seek to work with him directly. He works with Valeria."

"Valeria," Violet said in exasperation. "Everyone knows the Russians traditionally don't work with the Irish. Anton only worked for me and my mother because he was sweet on me."

"I'm changing that," Camille said.

"You're willing to work with a junkie like Anton," Violet emphasized.

"You should talk," Camille said coolly. "You used to be one yourself."

"How dare you bring my past into this. This has nothing to do with that."

"Does your son know his mommy used to be a druggie?" Camille said with a cruel smile.

Rage coursed through Violet's body and she tensed. "Damn you!" Violet reached into her purse and before she knew it, she had her gun out in the open street.

Camille quickly pulled hers out of her own purse and pointed it at Violet before Violet could point hers at her.

"Don't even think about it, Violet. You've really gone mad."

"You're pointing a gun at me," Violet said. "What am I supposed to do?"

It was the early evening and the street was quite crowded, but in the kind of neighborhood theirs was most wouldn't bother to call the police. Most people ignored them because the sight was common in the neighborhood. Still, a few people stopped walking to stare at them, with Camille pointing her gun at Violet in the daylight, and the part of the street where they stood became quiet. One man shouted that they were "cowgirls."

Violet held her gun firmly in her hand. She couldn't resist telling Camille, "How's Johnny doing? It'd be a shame if something happened to him."

"Don't you threaten him."

"What are you doing, Camille? You're going to kill me with all these people watching?"

They stared at each other intensely in silence, and Violet didn't know what Camille would do but she wasn't about to yield. Then, seeming to sense the crowd forming around them, Camille said, "Put your gun away and I'll put mine away."

Violet didn't quite trust her, so it took her a while to agree. She nodded. Camille put her gun away in her purse after she did and then the small crowd around them dispersed.

Violet hadn't misjudged Camille's brashness, but Violet's mother certainly had. Then Violet thought of something crazy, but maybe it wasn't such a crazy idea after all. She and Camille were alike in many ways, and, once, they had been friendly.

"Maybe we can work together," Violet proposed. "We used to be practically friends."

20

Camille looked at her like she had ulterior motives. Then she laughed. "Are you joking?"

"No, I'm not."

"I'd never work with you, after what your people did to my father."

"That was a long time ago. It had nothing to do with me. My mother's in prison now, so it would be just you and me."

"And Max, don't forget about him. He was the one who pulled the trigger."

Camille must have really hated Max.

"You don't have to interact with him," Violet said.

"Let him go and I'll consider it."

"I can't just do that."

"Why not?"

"Max has worked for my family for a very long time. He's not going to just go away."

"He will if you tell him to."

"People don't just 'retire' from this business, Camille. Maybe you don't know that. So, no, he isn't going anywhere."

"Then we'll never be able to work together. That's my offer.

You get rid of Max and I'll think about what you said. I'm not asking you to kill him—I know you would never do that—I just wouldn't want him around."

"You wouldn't see him. You don't understand, my mother will never allow me to let Max go."

"I thought you were calling the shots now."

"I am, but what you're asking me to do, it's not possible. My mother will view it as a betrayal because she loves Max."

"Then we're done here."

"You'll work with anyone, Camille, even a lowlife like Anton," Violet said, unable to resist getting in one last punch. "That's no way to do business. It's no wonder the Alfonsis want nothing to do with you."

Camille seemed frozen in place as she stared at her. "That will change," she spoke with such defiance that even Violet herself believed her words. "Anyway, you should talk, you dated him."

"Now that I know he's a junkie again, I'd never do business with him. Did you know that about him?"

"I assumed he was," Camille admitted. "I'm not doing business with him. I'm working with Valeria. He works for her. It's not the same thing." She held Violet's gaze.

"You still have practically no one. I have the Alfonsis."

"I have to finish my meal. I really don't care what you think, Violet."

Violet watched Camille walk back into the restaurant and admired her resolve though she also despised her. It was Camille's confidence that made Violet think that she herself might lose their battle and that frightened her. Camille was a lot like her, but, Violet suspected, she was, in some ways, stronger.

Violet picked up Tommy at his friend's house and took him home. The next day after she walked him to school in the morning, she had coffee and went to the train station on her way to visit her mother in the city jail where she was being held. She'd left her gun at home, of course.

Violet couldn't find a seat in the crowded train, so she had to stand. She looked around at the other passengers and tried not to make eye contact, an unspoken city rule. A man stared at her and smiled but she didn't return the gesture, another city rule. Lots of people exited at the second stop and Violet finally could sit.

When she was a little girl her mother had taken her to visit her grandfather in jail, the same jail her mother was now in, and it had frightened her. She hadn't understood why he was in there and her mother had trouble explaining the reason to her. So Violet came to a conclusion about it on her own, and she decided that for her grandfather to be in jail it must have meant he'd done something bad, but she loved him anyway because he'd always been nothing but gentle with her. He was only in there for a few days until the charges were dropped because the witness decided to retract their statement, which now Violet figured probably had something to do with Max threatening them.

Violet sat staring ahead with her purse in her lap. When she'd visited her grandfather in jail as a child, she and her mother had taken the train there. As an adult, Violet knew that, logically, her mother being in jail didn't mean that she wasn't a good person, it just meant she had made a mistake. But she also now had inside knowledge about her mother's transgression, because she had helped her commit it. Did that make her a bad person?

Sometimes, as she entered and exited her apartment or the pub, she felt as though she was being watched, and it was entirely possible that Detective Seale and his team were watching her. She had told Max and her other men to be careful, and perhaps she should have listened to her own advice. Had he seen her arguing with Camille? And if so, what did he think about it? Would Camille soon be watched by them also? Camille was naïve in the sense that she didn't know what was ahead of her like Violet did. Camille wanted to avenge her father, but she wasn't thinking about the consequences of being a gangster. Then again, she didn't have a child like Violet had, and so maybe she had less to lose.

Perhaps Seale was getting closer to arresting Violet, and she wondered, would Tommy's great-grandmother take him on the train to visit her?

The train arrived at her stop and Violet exited, left the station and walked to the jail. She knew she had to sign in at the front gate. Her mother's lawyer, a top man, but Violet had come to doubt him somewhat after her mother had been denied bail, had arranged for her to visit so they would be expecting her.

She gave the guard her name and then stood in line with the other family members waiting to visit their relatives inside. One by one, they were allowed through the front doors inside and then made to give their names again to compare with a list and then they walked through metal detectors and had their belongings searched. Violet watched as a guard went through her purse. She received a visitor's pass from another guard and then she, along with a group, were escorted to the female wing of the prison. They were led through a large metal door and entered a room with tables and chairs spaced evenly throughout. The guards directed the visitors to the tables, but a few visitors were taken aside, including Violet.

"Families of violent offenders, come this way," the female guard said. She was a tall, strong-looking woman in a baggy beige uniform and had a clipboard with her.

Violet flinched at the word 'violent' being associated with her doting mother, but she knew her mother was in jail for her connection to a murder. Violet's group were led into an inner room with a glass partition separating the prisoners from their visitors. Violet could see her mother, in an orange jumpsuit, seated behind the partition farther down the line. The guard asked for her name then directed her over there, and Violet sat in front of her mother and smiled. She planned to act upbeat, although she didn't feel that way.

Her mother looked older than when Violet had last seen her, although it had been only a week.

Violet picked up the phone attached to the partition and could hear her mother's voice. She watched her mother's hands, shaking from withdrawal.

"Violet. You look beautiful. How are you? How's Tommy?" Catherine's eyes brightened at the mention of her grandson.

Violet imagined they were being recorded so she planned to be careful about what she said.

"He's doing well, considering," she told her mother. "He really misses you and doesn't understand why you can't come home."

Catherine's eyes watered and she dried them with her hands. Often it seemed like the only way Violet's mother would weep would be because of Tommy.

"Do you think we should get you a new lawyer?" Violet asked her mother.

Catherine's eyes widened. "What? No. David's a good man."

"You were denied bail. How good can he be?"

"It wasn't David's fault. They thought I was a flight risk. I never should've gotten dual citizenship."

"All right, fine, David stays," Violet replied, irked at her mother's obstinacy.

"Think that maybe I can escape from this place?" Catherine joked.

"Mom don't say that," Violet whispered. "They can hear you."

Catherine waved her off. "I was only kidding."

"Our favorite bartender got friendly with Mrs. V," Violet said to her mother in abbreviated fashion so as not to draw attention to their conversation.

The 'bartender' was Camille and 'Mrs. V' was the Russian, Valeria.

"How did she manage that?" Catherine replied incredulously.

"She doesn't follow the rules, and it seems to be working for her. She doesn't care that, traditionally, we have never gotten cozy with them. She reached out to them and they accepted her."

"The meeting with the big guy and now this. She's ambitious."

The 'big guy'—the Italian mob boss Joe Alfonsi.

"I know she's going to be trouble, so I tried talking with her," Violet told her mother.

"You *what*?"

"I tried having a conversation with her about she and I playing nice."

"Together?" Catherine almost laughed at the absurdity.

Violet nodded.

Seeing that she was serious, Catherine asked, "What did she say?" Her mother seemed more receptive than Violet had thought she would be.

"She didn't say no."

"That can't be possible. She must have some kind of plan."

"No, she wanted something."

"What did she want?"

"Us to ditch M. I only think she'd play with me, though. Not you."

'M' was Max.

"Probably better as I might not be getting out of here," Catherine said.

Her mother seemed quite defeated and not in her normal high spirits, which wasn't unusual given the circumstances she found herself in.

"Don't say that," Violet replied. "Tommy needs you. I need you."

"It's probably better me being in here. It's stopped me from drinking and might be the only way for me to get sober. You seem to be handling things fine on your own." She held up her hand when Violet started to protest. "And I'm fine with that. I think it's good. I always wanted you be to more independent."

"You seem positive," Violet said. "That surprises me."

"It helps me get through the day."

"I told her no about M, by the way," Violet said.

"Maybe you ought to say yes. We might not have a choice. If it would get her to back off, you should consider it."

"M has been like a father and grandfather to us both ever since grandpa passed on. We could never do that to him."

"He understands that sometimes tough decisions have to be made in business."

"M isn't 'business'," Violet replied. "He's like family."

"Sometimes you're going to have to make hard decisions, Violet," her mother said.

"How could you even consider it? I'm not doing that to him."

"So, you're going to tell her no?"

"I'm not going to tell her anything. I'm going to make her wonder what I'm thinking. I hope it drives her crazy. But she already is crazy."

Violet's comment piqued Catherine's interest and her eyes lit up. "What do you mean?" she asked.

"She's got depression or something like that."

"How do you know that?"

"She told me when we were on friendlier terms."

"That's her weakness, then. Do you think we could use it against her?"

"How? If her mind isn't right, maybe she'll crack and mess up, right?"

"One can only hope."

They were silent for a while then her mother asked, "How are things going otherwise?"

"The boys didn't want to listen to me at first, even M, and you know how the others follow his lead, but now everything is settled."

"I'm disappointed to hear they resisted, and especially to hear that about M. Maybe it means it's time for him to bon voyage."

"No," Violet said. "Everything is fine now. There's no need to shake things up. If he's gone, it will only hurt the morale. M stays because I want him to."

"All right, I understand. I love him like family."

"I know you do. You just have a funny way of showing it sometimes. Our favorite bartender's not going anywhere, and her getting chummy with Mrs. V means that she's serious and knows what she's doing. I'm glad the big guy remains with us but there is the connection he has to her. That could be a problem for us someday."

"The big guy loves you and Tommy. He's not going anywhere."

Violet felt that her mother's confidence was unwise, but perhaps she needed to remain positive to cope with her circumstances.

"There is one way to make you fly," she told her mother, meaning 'set you free'.

Catherine waited for her to explain.

"Have the rat go for a swim," Violet said, meaning that they should eliminate Frank O'Rourke. "I could have someone in there give you the details."

"No," Catherine said sharply. "Nobody is going for a swim. I'm just glad you're all right, and that's the way it must stay. Tommy needs you. You don't take any risks for me. Do you hear me?"

Violet looked at her and nodded, because like she was right about a lot of things, her mother was right about this.

21

Camille loved Johnny Garcia Jr. in a way that she hadn't loved anyone else before, not even her mother or Billy. And he had told her he loved her as well.

She wasn't expecting a visitor one morning when someone knocked on her door. Camille got out of bed and put on her bathrobe and tied her hair. Who could be calling at this hour? Was it Johnny? Filled with excitement, she peered through the eyehole at the visitor on the other side and didn't recognize the woman, who appeared around her mother's age, and was attractive and well-dressed. Not feeling wary, she opened the door, a little disappointed it wasn't Johnny.

"Can I help you?" she asked the light-haired woman, who was around her height.

"Camille O'Brien?" the woman asked uncertainly.

"That's me. Who are you?" Camille became more on edge. Had Violet sent the woman?

"My name is Lucille Byrne. I was a friend of your father's."

Camille had never heard of her before, but she became less tense. "My mother never mentioned you," she said. The last time she spoke to Sheila, she'd found out that Violet had lied about Sheila telling her Camille's whereabouts, which wasn't too surprising.

"I don't believe your father talked about me with your mother," Lucille said.

"Were you lovers?" Camille asked.

Lucille shook her head. "We were very close friends."

"He's dead, my father is," Camille said.

"I know." Lucille looked down at her purse in her hands. Then she looked at Camille again. "It devastated me when I heard about it."

"I was very young when it happened. I never really knew him." Camille paused. She changed the subject to something less grim. "Do you live in the neighborhood? I don't think I've ever seen you around before."

"No, I live in the suburbs, with my husband. Our daughter is around your age."

"Did your husband know my father as well?"

"Not personally, no."

"He just knew of his reputation?" Camille asked with a smile.

Lucille nodded.

"Come in," Camille said, extending her hand to the doorway, feeling at ease because of the woman's connection to her father. She shut the door behind Lucille after she entered. "I was just about to make coffee. Would you like some?"

"That would be very nice, thank you."

Camille pointed to the red couch in her living room and Lucille sat. Camille walked into the kitchen and could see Lucille from the doorway. They spoke as she made coffee.

"Do you want a muffin or something?" Camille asked her. She checked the cupboards and the refrigerator. "No, wait, I don't have any," she told her. "Sorry about that."

"It's all right, I'm not hungry."

"Do you work in the city?" Camille asked her from the kitchen as she prepared the coffee.

"No, I was just a mom up until my daughter left for university."

"How does she like school?" Camille asked as though she knew the girl. "I never went myself."

"She likes it very much." Lucille paused. "You remind me so much of your father," she said, looking at Camille in a pensive way.

The idea filled Camille with sorrow. "What does your husband do?" she asked, to talk about something else.

"He was a policeman," Lucille said. "Now he's retired."

"Pretty ironic my father being friends with you," Camille said.

"What do you mean?" Lucille sounded hurt.

"I didn't mean anything by it. You do know what my father did for a living?"

"Yes, I do, and I never judged him for it."

"You were a good friend to him," Camille concluded. "Why didn't he want to tell my mother about you? Was she jealous? I could see her being jealous of you."

"I'm not sure, but, yes, that might have been the reason."

Camille finished making the coffee and came out and set it on the table in front of the couch.

"I wasn't sure if you liked cream or sugar, or both, so I brought out both," she said.

"This looks great, thanks. I appreciate you inviting me inside, since you don't even know me."

"You looked trustworthy, and I can take care of myself," Camille said with a smile.

There was a sparkle in Lucille's eyes, and she smiled as well. "Just like your father. You look just like him, you know. He was a beautiful looking man."

Camille sat down on the couch, a seat down from Lucille. "I've seen pictures of him, but I look like my mother as well. I'm like her also, in a lot of ways. I'm sorry, but why did you come here? How do you know where I live?"

"An old acquaintance in the neighborhood told me you live here, but I used to live downtown, where your father did for a long time. I came here because I've always wanted to meet you. Your father talked about you."

"I understand," Camille said. "I'm glad you came. I enjoy meeting people connected to my father because it makes me feel closer to him."

"I'm so sorry about what happened to your father. He was gone much too soon." Tears formed in Lucille's eyes and Camille offered her a tissue from the table.

"Thanks," Lucille said, plucking one from the box.

Camille put sugar in her coffee and told Lucille about her plans for those who took her father's life. "I don't know why I'm telling you all this. But for some reason, I trust you, because I assume my father trusted you, despite who your husband is. Do you know my father's secrets?"

"Some of them, I'm sure."

"Tell me one," Camille said as she stirred her coffee. "I want to know him better." She lifted the cup and drank from it.

"I don't think that would be right," Lucille said, putting cream into her coffee cup and then sipping.

"I promise I'll never tell anyone else. It will help me feel closer to him. My mother will tell me about his family, but not his secrets."

"You already know what he did for a living, so that's not a secret. But the only thing I can tell you is what your father suffered a lot early on in his life and had a lot of sadness."

"I know that from what my mother said."

"He survived sexual abuse as a boy."

Camille put her cup down and stared at Lucille. For a while she didn't say anything; she just absorbed what she'd heard. She had trouble breathing as she filled with sorrow, and her hands trembled. "I never knew that," she said quietly after she'd composed herself. "Did he talk to you about it? What happened to him?"

"It was someone close to him who did it."

"It wasn't his father, was it?"

Lucille shook her head. "No, it wasn't him. He didn't say much about it, just that it happened."

"Are most of his secrets like that, sad?" Camille asked, trying to decide whether she wanted to hear more of them.

"Not all of them," Lucille said.

"He must have told you secrets about my mother, about their relationship. What was it like? She's never told me. Did they get on? From how she talks about him, I'm assuming they did, but who knows?"

"He loved your mother very much," Lucille said, but Camille sensed she was holding something back.

"But he loved you more," Camille said. "Isn't that what you're trying to say?" When Lucille hesitated, Camille said, "It's all right. I always sensed that about my mother and father's relationship, but I never told my mother that. You were the love of his life. Why weren't you ever together?"

"It was complicated. I was older than him."

"And then my mother became pregnant, right?"

Lucille nodded.

"I'm planning to avenge his death, you know," Camille said.

Lucille set her cup down on the table and had a worried look on her face. "You mentioned that. But how do you plan to do it?"

"By taking over the Irish mob," Camille said casually.

Lucille looked at her with a stunned expression. "How do you plan to do that?"

"I guess I can trust you, because my father trusted you with his secrets, even though you're married to a policeman." Camille told Lucille a little bit more about her plans.

"The McCarthys are dangerous people," Lucille cautioned her. Camille's cat came up to them and rubbed against Lucille's legs and Lucille stroked her shiny fur. "They killed your father."

"I know they did, that's why I want them gone. Can you imagine what his final moments were like? He must have been so afraid. They deserve what's coming to them."

"Does your mother know your plans?" Lucille looked concerned.

"She does. In fact, she was the one who convinced me that my rightful place would be as the leader of their gang. I would have led with my dad, had he lived. My mother is helping me."

Lucille didn't seem surprised to hear that about Camille's mother. "You don't want that kind of life," Lucille told her. "Your father wouldn't have lived it if he'd had a choice. He would want something better for you."

"I was working as a bartender up until recently, for the McCarthys, actually."

"Your mother never told you what they did?"

"That they killed my father? No. I didn't know until recently."

"She was protecting you from them," Lucille said.

"I was sort of friends with Catherine McCarthy's daughter— she and her mother ran the mob until Catherine got sent to jail. Now it's just her daughter Violet running things. I started working at their pub, and by then my mother thought it was too late to tell me the truth. Now that I know the truth, I know what I must do. I don't have a choice."

Lucille touched her hand and the kind gestured startled Camille because she didn't know her well. "You always have a choice," Lucille said, looking her in the eye.

"Is that what you told my father?" she asked, not rudely.

"Yes, as a matter of fact, it is."

"But he didn't heed your advice?" Camille said.

"No, obviously, he didn't."

"Thanks, but I can take care of myself."

"I know you can, but you should know that you don't have to go through with anything."

"My mother thinks I should."

"You don't have to listen to her, you're all grown up."

"Are you saying my mother is wrong?" Camille asked her, pulling her hand away from Lucille's.

"I'm not saying that, I'm just saying it's okay to be your own person," Lucille said gently.

"My mother must have not liked you." Camille paused when Lucille looked at her. "It's all right, I know she can be difficult."

"I never met your mother, but your father talked about her."

"I'm not surprised, my mother's the jealous type. How did my father talk about her? I already figured out that they got married after she was pregnant with me. Did he marry her just because of that? Did he love her?"

"Those kinds of questions are better discussed with your mother," Lucille told her.

"You don't want to tell me, I understand. Did you really just come here to get a look at me?"

Lucille nodded.

"I wish I'd known him," Camille said.

"I wish you had as well," Lucille said.

Camille asked her if she wanted more coffee and Lucille declined, but Camille got up to pour more for herself. She returned to the couch.

"Are you hungry?" she asked Lucille again. "I just realized I haven't eaten breakfast."

"I'm fine but please eat if you are."

Camille didn't want to abandon her guest again, so she decided to wait. "That's okay, I'll wait," she told Lucille.

"Are you married?" Lucille asked, looking around the apartment for signs of a man. "I didn't see a ring, but some young people don't wear them these days."

Camille shook her head.

"Are you seeing anyone?" Lucille asked her.

Camille nodded. "You might find this interesting, actually. You must know about my father's friend, Johnny Garcia?"

"Yes, I do," Lucille said quietly.

"I'm dating his son."

Lucille looked at her and didn't say anything and her face blanched. Then she looked away.

"What's the matter?" Camille asked, internally searching for a reason for Lucille's behavior.

Lucille had a difficult time looking her in the eye. "You don't know about your father and Johnny."

"You knew Johnny also?"

"Yes, I did."

"They were friends. What else is there for me to know?"

"Johnny died before your father did," Lucille said.

"I know, my mother told me."

"Your father, he had something to do with Johnny's death."

The revelation hit Camille like a cold splash of water in winter. At first, she considered that Lucille might be lying because she didn't want to believe her.

"That isn't true," said a stunned Camille.

"I'm afraid it is," Lucille said quietly.

Camille rose from the couch and paced in the room. "Why are you telling me this?" she asked Lucille. "Is that why you came here?"

"No, no, I don't want to upset you."

"You have. You've told me my father is a monster."

"He wasn't, but he made mistakes."

"He killed his best friend, that's the worst kind of 'mistake'."

"He didn't kill him, but he was there when it happened, and he didn't stop it. It tore him up inside afterwards and he was never the same person. Johnny was in a rival gang, and your father made a choice, and it was the wrong one. But you, Camille, you have the opportunity to say no."

"You're telling me not to become like him?"

"In a way, yes. You're at a crossroads, and you have a choice."

"Why did you tell me about my father and his friend? Why should I believe you, when I don't even know you?" She spoke as though Lucille must have had a motive for revealing it.

"I'm telling you the truth. I cared about your father very much, and so I care about you. I don't want you to get hurt."

"Why, because Johnny would leave me if he knew? He's told me he wants to kill the people responsible for his father's death, and because that means my father and because my father isn't around any longer, does that mean he wants to kill me? He just told me he loved me," Camille said to Lucille. "And now I have to tell him that what we had was based on lies."

"You don't have to tell him anything," Lucille said.

Camille sat down on the couch and looked at her. "No, I should. If I don't, then what kind of relationship would that be? I can't lie to him, although I know it will be over for us once I tell him."

"You shouldn't have to be punished for your father's mistakes. Don't tell him. I'm sure it won't ever come up, so don't bring it up."

"It doesn't matter, now that I know, I should tell him. I love Johnny. I can't lie to him, even if that means losing him." Camille paused. "That's why my mother didn't want me seeing Johnny. She must've known what my father did. I wish she had told me, because then I would have never gotten involved with him."

"But then you would've missed out on knowing love," Lucille said, as though she was trying to lighten the mood.

"Then I never would have gotten hurt," Camille replied, unable to reciprocate her attempt at warmth at that moment. "You should leave. I'm not angry with you but you should go. I need to be alone for a while."

Lucille nodded. "I understand," she said. She thanked Camille for the coffee and rose from the couch.

Camille saw her to the door.

Lucille turned and looked at her before she exited. "Your mother didn't know about your father and me. I would appreciate if you wouldn't tell her about me and that I came here."

"Your secret's safe with me," Camille told her.

"I'd like to see you again," Lucille told her.

"I'm not sure if that's a good idea," Camille said, with her hand on the door. "I know you were my father's friend, and I respect that."

Lucille had brought Camille's father's secrets with her, some of which had devastated Camille, and Camille didn't want to learn any more. She realized that for her entire life her mother had told her some truths about her father, but she'd also told her many lies.

Lucille looked down at her hands and nodded. She left and Camille closed the door behind her.

Camille loved Johnny and her love made her selfish, so in the end she decided not to tell Johnny what Lucille had told her.

22

With the help of Mrs. Valeria and with Catherine McCarthy still in jail, Camille gradually began to take control of some of the neighborhood with her mother's guidance. She started with moving in on the jukebox leasing and servicing business that the McCarthys had let slide, which included providing local establishments with the latest records.

Then something happened.

Rafael, Johnny's second in command, was beaten outside a local restaurant when he was alone, and Johnny's gang blamed Violet's men. One night afterwards, the gang set *McBurney's* on fire when it was closed for the night. Camille could hear the fire engines from her street and could see and smell the thick smoke.

Camille disliked Violet and her mother but *McBurney's* had meant something special to the entire neighborhood, so in turn, that meant it meant something to Camille. She confronted Johnny about it when he took her for a ride in his car one day in the late morning during a holiday when the city was quieter and the traffic less difficult to navigate. Ever since learning what Lucille had told her, Camille found it difficult to be around

Johnny, but she had been unable to avoid him when he showed up at her apartment with his car.

"I knew about it, but I didn't participate," Johnny told her as he drove. "Besides, I thought you hated them."

"I don't like either of them, but the pub meant something to the neighborhood. It's been there for a long time. It's a landmark."

"They put Rafael in the hospital. It was payback."

"There might have been another way to go about it," Camille suggested.

"Like beat them up? That would start a war with them, and we'd probably lose."

"Torching their pub is almost as awful. And you wouldn't lose if you joined me and the Russians. Or do you have something against them as well?"

"No, but Cuban gangs don't work with Irish ones, at least not in this neighborhood. It was an Irish gang who beat Rafael."

"I have nothing to do with them," Camille said. "I dislike them, too. We used to say the same thing about the Russians, we used to not work with them, but I changed that. You have no problem dating an Irish girl."

"I love Irish girls, and I love you, I just can't work with your group." Johnny looked at her and winked. "You know how I feel about Irish gangs, after what they did to my father," he added in a more somber tone.

"Do you feel that way about me?"

"Of course not. It's a symbolic thing for me, that's all, like their pub was for you. I love you." He reached down for her hand and squeezed.

"Is Rafael going to be okay?" Camille asked.

"The doctors say he was badly hurt, but he'll survive. He might have permanent damage to his hand, though."

"Should we stop by the hospital to visit him?" Camille asked.

"I'm not sure," Johnny said.

"What do you mean?"

"Rafael doesn't like that I'm seeing you," Johnny said softly.

"You never told me that. I thought your guys were fine with us being together."

"The others are fine with it. Pedro especially, he loves you. But Rafael, he's very old school, and in his way of thinking Cuban men should date Cuban women."

"We're just supposed to avoid him? How's that going to work if he's close to you and I am also?"

"We don't have to avoid him, but he's in the hospital so I thought it best to respect his wishes."

"He wants to act like I don't exist? And you're all right with that?" The revelation had offended Camille, although she wasn't entirely surprised to hear it.

"I'm not okay with it." Johnny took his eyes off the road to look at her then quickly braked at a red light.

Camille was jolted forward in the car, then she wouldn't look at Johnny.

"Rafael and I have argued a lot about it," he said. "He's one of my closet friends and he's hardly speaking to me. But I don't care because I love you. Camille, look at me. I love you."

Camille held his gaze and saw honesty in his eyes.

"I'm sorry I was angry with you about *McBurney's*," she told him.

"You don't have to apologize," he said with a smile. "But does this mean you forgive me?"

His apprehensive expression was like a boy's, and she said, "Yes."

Then something happened again that evening, and everything changed.

Camille was at home, getting ready for bed and making herself a cup of tea. There was a persistent knock on her door.

She wasn't expecting anyone, not even Johnny, so, startled, she grabbed her gun and went to the door. She peered out the eyehole, and somewhat expected to see Lucille again, but it was Johnny. She put the gun on the hallway table and unlocked and opened the door.

"You scared me," she said to him. "I didn't know who you were."

Johnny seemed distraught. His hair looked wild and his eyes red-rimmed. He stood there, not speaking, and didn't seem to know what to do.

"Are you all right?" Camille asked him in concern.

Johnny shook his head. "They killed him, they killed Pedro. I've just come from the hospital. He's dead."

Camille felt as if her legs would give in and she started to fall, and Johnny steadied her in his arms. She didn't know Pedro well, but she'd liked him, and the news shocked her.

"Who did? What happened?" Camille asked him weakly as he held her. "Was it the father of the girl he was seeing? I think her name was Fiona. Pedro told me her father disliked him a lot."

"No, it was one of Violet's men, this guy named Jake, he killed Pedro."

"Jake. I know him from the pub, but not well. Did Violet ask him to do it?"

"I'm not sure."

"How did Pedro die, did Jake shoot him?"

"No, he beat him to death, like they almost did to Rafael."

"My God, poor Pedro. That's horrific. He was such a good kid."

"He was," Johnny said, coughing back tears.

They'd been talking with Johnny standing in the hallway, and then he came in all the way and Camille shut the door.

"Violet must have asked Jake to do it, since it was her pub

that was torched," Camille told Johnny in her living room as she held him.

Johnny gradually moved out of her arms and sat down on the couch, but Camille didn't feel like sitting; she felt like doing something about what had happened. Then the reality of what happened to Pedro sunk in and her eyes filled with tears. Johnny got up from the couch to console her and dried her eyes with his sleeve.

"Pedro really admired you," Johnny told her. "He thought the world of you."

"I can't believe he's gone. He was just a kid. He had his whole life ahead of him."

"I know, it's unimaginable," Johnny said, stroking her face.

"We have to do something about it," Camille spoke with determination.

"I don't disagree, but I can't start a war with them. We'd lose. They have the Italians on their side."

"We can help you," Camille insisted. "I can help you."

"You'd need the Italians' help."

Camille cursed her stepfather for failing to bring the Alfonsi family over to her side. She would give him a little more time and then tell her mother his secret.

"I think I can convince them," Camille told Johnny.

"Because of your stepfather?"

She nodded. "They said no initially, because of Violet, but there's something that I have against my stepfather that is an incentive for him to convince them." She nestled deeper into Johnny's strong chest.

"It must be something big, for you to have such confidence."

"It is," she said.

"Now, I'm curious. Tell me."

Internally, Camille debated whether to tell him and how

much to tell him. So, she just said, "He did something to me when I was younger."

Johnny peered at her with concern deep in his eyes. "Camille, what did he do to you? You have me worried."

"He attacked me when I was a teenager," she whispered. She didn't know why she felt ashamed, as it wasn't her fault, but she was.

"That bastard, I'll kill him," Johnny said, seething with rage. He held onto Camille's body more tightly, as if to protect her.

"No, you're not going to do anything about it," Camille instructed him. "I'm using it against him to get what I want. Don't worry, he'll be punished."

"Your mother doesn't know, right? That's what you threatened to do, tell your mother?"

Camille nodded.

"How will he be punished, then, since you won't tell her if he does what you want?" Johnny asked as he held onto her. His body rocked and she moved with him.

"Men like him don't get punished, he's with the Alfonsis. But he is afraid of what my mother thinks. The best revenge is him being terrified I'll tell, knowing that I have that power, and making him do what I want. Trust me, this way is best."

"But what if he can't bring them over to your side?"

"Then I'll tell my mother," Camille said, stepping out of his arms.

She walked into the kitchen and he followed her.

"I'd been in the middle of making tea when you arrived," she told him. "Would you like some?"

"I've never tried tea," he said.

His words made her smile. "Are you kidding me?"

"Iced tea, but not hot tea. My mother likes it, though."

"You don't know what you're missing. Let me make you a

cup," she insisted, seeking some comfort in the tumultuous moment.

"All right, thanks," Johnny said.

"I meant it when I said we have to do something about what happened to Pedro," Camille told him as she reheated the water. Then she concluded, firmly, "I'm going to call Violet. She thinks she can do something like this and there won't be consequences? Nobody's that powerful."

"We don't call the cops, no matter what happens," Johnny said.

"I know that, but I need to talk with her."

"What's that going to get you?"

"She needs to know someone cares. She needs to know she made a huge mistake and that I'm certainly not going anywhere now. What she did has made me dig my heels in deeper."

The water came to a boil and the kettle whistled and Camille got two mugs out of the cupboard.

"You're already upset, calling her will only anger you further," Johnny replied in a gentle way. "I don't want to see you become more upset."

"I appreciate your concern, but I'm going to give her a call after I've made the tea."

She brought the mugs of tea into the living room and set them on the coffee table in front of the couch.

"I would like to attend his funeral," Camille said.

"We can go together," Johnny said.

"Rafael won't mind?"

Johnny stroked her arm. "I don't care what he thinks."

Johnny sat down on the couch and Camille went into the kitchen again, where the phone was. Given the hour, and because Violet had no pub to tend to, she figured that Violet would be at home with Tommy.

233

"I wouldn't call her," Johnny spoke to Camille from the living room. "She'll upset you."

"I can handle it. She needs to know what she did was wrong," Camille replied.

The phone rang a few times before Violet answered.

"Hello?" she said.

"It's Camille."

There was a pause on the other end. "Why are you calling me? I'm not getting rid of Max, if that's what you wanted to ask. I'm sure you know what your boyfriend and his friends did to my pub."

"Johnny had nothing to do with that. And my offer is off the table. I don't disagree that it's a shame about *McBurney's*, and I'm sorry it happened."

"You're apologizing to me? What changed?"

"Nothing's changed between you and me. The pub was a symbol in the neighborhood, that's all, and I recognize that."

"Tell that to your boyfriend."

"I already said Johnny didn't participate in what happened."

"But he must have known about it."

Camille didn't want to agree so she stayed silent. "What you did to Pedro was wrong. I knew him, and he was a good kid."

"Pedro—who is that?"

"You know who he is, he's the kid you ordered your man Jake to kill to avenge what happened to your pub."

"No, the guys beat up some other guy—I don't know his name—and I had nothing to do with it. They were drunk and saw him alone outside a restaurant. I never ordered them to do anything, and they didn't kill anyone, they just beat him. I've already had a word with them because they're not supposed to be drinking and they do senseless things when they drink."

"They killed someone tonight, his name was Pedro. He died

at the hospital. I knew him. He was just a kid. You've done a terrible thing."

"Wait, who killed him?"

"Jake killed him," Camille said in exasperation. "Because you told him to."

"I never did such a thing."

"Yes, you did, you asked him to kill Pedro because it was your pub that was torched."

"No, I didn't. I never asked him to do anything. If he did something, then it was his own fault, I had nothing to do with it. I'm just as shocked as you are."

"You're lying," Camille stated firmly.

"No, I'm telling you the truth. I had nothing to do with what you're talking about. Unlike your boyfriend and his friends, I can control myself."

"Your men beat up Rafael, that's why Johnny's guys torched your pub. Then one of your guys killed Pedro. Of course, I think that what happened to your pub is a shame, despite our hatred for each other. Your pub has been a part of the neighborhood for a long time, and you know how I care about the neighborhood. Don't forget, your men started it."

"I didn't ask them to do any of it," Violet replied.

Camille didn't know whether she believed her. "You need to control your crew better," she said, because she knew her words would hurt Violet.

"Are you done here?" Violet said quietly. "Because I am. Goodbye, Camille." She hung up.

Camille turned around to find Johnny staring at her.

"Did you overhear?" she asked him with the phone still in her hand and the sound of the dial tone droning in the kitchen.

"Parts of it, yeah." Johnny leaned in the doorway and smiled at her, and he had such a beautiful smile.

"She denies ordering her men to kill Pedro. I'm not sure if I believe her. But hurting Rafael seems to have been their own decision. They started this whole thing."

"Still, I'm sorry about what my guys did to the pub, I know that place meant something special to you."

"Not to me in particular," Camille clarified. "To the neighborhood. It's been here forever. It's symbolic. It's hard to explain," she said quietly, feeling silly. She put the phone on the receiver.

Johnny approached her and rubbed her shoulders and she relaxed into his touch. "It's not silly," he said. "I don't think anything you believe is silly. I love you."

Camille looked back at him and smiled. "I love you, too." But the words pricked her like a little needle, for she felt that the vast secret she kept from him could unravel everything. "You're a good man, Johnny Garcia."

"And you're a good woman, Camille."

She felt as though she couldn't accept the compliment, because she wondered, would he say that if he knew the secret she kept from him?

Camille went to Pedro's funeral with Johnny. She gave Pedro's family her condolences and wondered if Fiona knew what had happened to him. She met Rafael while she was there, and he was quiet but polite to her, and she sensed that Johnny had asked him to be gentle.

The day afterwards she decided to stop by Johnny's apartment to surprise him. She had never been to his place and was curious about where he lived. Her heart was still heavy with the secret she kept, and she didn't plan to reveal it to him anytime soon because she knew that doing so would be the end of them and she couldn't bear that yet—or probably ever.

The day was gorgeous, and the sidewalks quiet with everyone at work, so she decided to walk to his apartment. Johnny had mentioned he would be home that morning.

Camille herself wondered if she'd have to get a day job. Being a gangster wasn't paying the bills just yet.

Keeping the secret from Johnny made her feel guilty, so she wanted to do something special for him and decided to bring him breakfast. She stopped at the bagel shop and bought bagels and coffee for them and walked the rest of the way to Johnny's place.

Camille discovered that she could enter the hallway of Johnny's apartment building without him letting her in, so she walked straight on through and went up the stairs. She knew he lived on the upper floor, in apartment twelve. She balanced the warm bag of bagels and the tray of coffee as she walked.

She walked down the hall to Johnny's apartment and when she arrived at his apartment, she found the door open and a woman leaving holding the hand of a young girl. Camille bumped into the woman in the hallway and apologized. The woman smiled at her then went on her way with the child. Johnny appeared in the doorway, calling goodbye to the woman. But who was she? A relative of his?

When Johnny saw her his face looked ashen. "Camille," he said, unsmiling. "What are you doing here?"

She showed him the breakfast she carried. "I wanted to bring you breakfast." She glanced back and could see the woman and child walking down the stairs. "Who were they?" she asked Johnny, although straightaway she could sense that he was uncomfortable.

"Camille," he started to say to her, and she sensed she wouldn't like what he was about to tell her. Johnny stood in the doorway, with her still out in the hall, and he hadn't invited her inside yet. "She's my ex-wife, and that's my daughter with her."

Camille was so startled she didn't know what to say so she said nothing. "How come you never told me about them? You kept them a secret from me." Camille had kept her own secrets from him, and guilt plagued her as she spoke the words, but she still spoke them loudly.

"I didn't want to scare you away," he told her, and his answer sounded honest. "I didn't want you to think I had too much baggage."

He invited her inside, but she wasn't ready to go in just yet. She didn't know whether she liked his answer.

"Here, take this." Camille shoved the bagels and coffee towards Johnny, and he took them from her.

Johnny looked at the food and drinks and thanked her.

"I wanted to do something nice for you," she told him. "I didn't mean to drop by unannounced. Sorry I ruined your secret," she said, not unsarcastically.

"No, it's my fault. I should have told you. I'm sorry, Camille. I didn't want to scare you away." He sounded sincere.

"I'm not scared," she said. "It doesn't scare me."

Johnny seemed relieved, but Camille was still hurt by what he'd done, although she knew it was hypocritical of her, considering the secret she kept from him.

"Your daughter looks like you," she said to break the tension, though she wasn't ready to tell him she forgave him. "I'm just disappointed you felt the need to hide her from me. Does your ex-wife know about us?"

Johnny nodded. "She didn't know it was you in the hallway, though. Otherwise, she would have said hello and introduced you to my daughter. I was just seeing them out. My daughter visits me every week."

"What's your daughter's name?"

"Phoebe," he said.

Camille felt funny standing out in the hallway, speaking to him in the doorway, but she didn't feel comfortable entering. "How long were you and your wife married?" she asked.

"Not for very long. Two years. It was when we were young, too young. We were just teenagers when we got married."

"What's your ex's name?" Camille asked.

"Irene," he said. He paused, then said, "Would you like to come inside? I can't wait to try what you brought with you." He nodded at the food in his hands.

"Johnny, I'd like to meet Phoebe someday, when she's ready to meet me. But I don't want to have breakfast with you this morning."

"You're angry with me?" He gave her a wistful look.

She nodded. "I am, but I'll forgive you, eventually."

"I understand," Johnny said quietly, but there was devastation in his eyes.

Camille left Johnny's apartment building that day and didn't see or speak to him for days, even though he rang her many times and left messages on her answering machine. She sensed that he knew she was upset with him and so he didn't stop by her apartment. Part of her felt that it was for the best because of what she knew about their fathers, what she could never tell Johnny without him despising her. But she knew she had to forgive him because she loved him, even if that meant, eventually, they couldn't be together because of her secret. Even if they were only together for a short while longer, it would be worth it because she received so much comfort from loving Johnny.

So, one day she answered the phone when he called and spoke to him, and the next thing she knew, Johnny was at her apartment and they were in bed together, and together again.

23

Then a couple of days later when Camille was alone, she received a surprising phone call.

She answered and heard Vito's voice.

"Camille?"

"Yeah. What do you want? You better have some good news for me," she told him.

"Actually, I do. That's why I'm calling."

"Tell me."

"Joe Alfonsi wants to help you," he said.

Camille couldn't believe what she was hearing, and she could barely stand. She wanted to scream for joy, instead she said, "You aren't kidding, me, are you?"

"Of course not, Camille."

"The Alfonsis are ditching the McCarthys for me?" she said, wanting to hear him say it again. She had the phone cord wrapped around her hand and toyed with it.

"Yeah, Camille."

"Does that mean they'll let me run the neighborhood *if* I get control or that they'll actually help me take over the neighborhood?" She remembered what had been said at the meeting, but she wanted to see if Vito had gotten them to change their minds, after all, a lot was at stake for him.

"No, they'll help you. They don't want a full out war with the McCarthys, but Joe wants to start bringing you into our fold and pushing them out. For instance, there's a gambling ring that, currently, Violet and Catherine run for us in your neighborhood, and now Joe wants you to run it. He's going to send them packing. The McCarthys will get the message they're not wanted."

"They're not going to just go away," Camille said.

"We'll take care of that if the time comes. But for now, I think they'll listen. Nobody wants to make a guy like Joe angry."

"What made them change their minds?" Camille asked him, wondering if there was a catch and what it might be. She didn't think he'd dare lie to her, but if he was desperate enough, who knew what he'd do?

"They're still loyal to Kevin, but his death changed things. He's no longer present so he's become more diminished in our minds. That sometimes happens over time."

"It didn't take long. I thought that Joe Alfonsi was loyal to the McCarthys because of their connection to Kevin. What did you do to convince him?"

"Joe just changed his mind. He does that sometimes. Consider yourself lucky. I didn't do anything that great."

"You should consider *yourself* lucky," Camille said.

"So, are we even, then?"

"Do you mean, am I going to tell my mother what you did? Where are you calling me from, anyway?" She pictured him at a payphone near the apartment he shared with her mother.

"I'm at a payphone."

She'd guessed right.

"You're not going to say anything to her, right?" Vito asked.

"Don't worry, your dirty little secret is safe." But Camille still planned to tell her mother about Vito someday, which would be a very unpleasant surprise for him.

"Thanks, Camille," Vito said, and sighed with relief. He waited for her to say something, and she didn't know what more he expected from her. "Aren't you going to thank me?"

"No," Camille said, and hung up the phone.

There was a knock on her door. She'd been getting dressed for the day and pulled her bathrobe tightly around her when she went to answer it. First, she checked through the eyehole, and saw Billy standing outside. What did he want? Had he come to tell her the news Vito already had told her, and had that news angered him? Camille didn't know what kind of a reaction he would have, so she said through the door, "Why are you here, Billy?"

"Did Vito tell you about Joe's decision?" Billy asked her through the door.

"He did."

"Can I come in?" Billy asked after a pause.

"Why are you here?"

"I wanted to see you."

He seemed harmless, so Camille opened the door. As soon as Billy saw her slinky bathrobe he stared at the shape of her figure and she wished she'd put on something more concealing. Standing in front of her, he looked as tall, fresh, and handsome as ever. He reached for her hand and she let him hold hers, and for a second it felt like the old times again.

"I've brought the Russians over to my side, too, did you know that?" she told him with pride.

"I didn't, but that's great."

Then something disturbing occurred to her, something she hadn't thought of until then. "Do you think that will be all right with Joe?"

"Yeah, sure. We work with them also."

Camille exhaled in relief.

"I know the name of the guy you're seeing," Billy said casually.

Camille let go of his hand because he suddenly seemed dangerous. "You leave him alone."

"His name's Johnny Garcia, and he's the gang leader of the Cubans. Rumor has it he's in love with you and that you love him. Is this true?"

Camille looked up into his eyes. "Yes, it is. Why are you here, Billy?"

"I came to say congratulations. I heard about the old man's decision to help you. You must be thrilled."

"I am."

"It did surprise me to hear he'd agreed. I did think he'd remain loyal to the McCarthys because of Tommy being Kevin's son. But Vito tried very hard to convince him, and he did. You must have had something big to hold over Vito to get him to work so hard on your behalf."

"It's none of your business," Camille replied, and nearly closed the door in his face, but he stuck his foot out and prevented her.

"I think it is, actually, as I am part of the Alfonsi crew."

"You don't need to know everything."

"Tell me what it is, Camille."

"I know something about him that he doesn't want anyone else to know," Camille told Billy because she felt it would be the only way to get him to go away.

Billy looked a little surprised and very intrigued. "It must be something big because it made him try so hard to convince Joe."

She'd met Billy when they both were in high school, and he'd been the only man she'd ever been with up until they separated, so she loved him like family. But Billy didn't know her secret about Vito.

"Tell me, Camille. You can trust me," he said when she gave him a look like she didn't.

"Come inside first," she said, which was something she had been avoiding.

Billy entered and she shut the door behind him. Standing close to him, he smelled of leather and expensive cologne and cigarette smoke, although he didn't smoke—he spent a lot of time in pubs with his friends, although he didn't drink much either.

"Are you going to see him today?" Billy asked her.

"Vito?"

"No, this Johnny Garcia guy?"

"Maybe. It's none of your business."

"I hate it when you say that, Camille."

"Why? We aren't together anymore. What I do *is* none of your concern."

"We were together for a long time, and I still care about you."

"If I tell you about Vito, you can't tell anyone else. Is that clear?" she said, to get him to stop.

Billy nodded and suddenly looked worried. She sat on the couch and he followed. She'd had the television on, with the news playing, and she used the remote to turn it off.

"As you know, Vito married my mother when I was in high school."

"Yeah," Billy said. "What are you about to tell me?"

Camille motioned for him to be patient. Then she had a few misgivings. If she told Billy what Vito did, would Billy confront Vito? Would he try to harm him? After all, Billy could be quite unpredictable. So, she said, "If I tell you, you have to promise me that you won't go crazy. Do you promise? Otherwise, I'm not telling you."

"I'm not sure if I can do that, Camille. What are you going to tell me? I'm getting concerned."

"Billy, you have to promise, or I won't say."

He sighed. "All right," he said after a moment.

"After Vito married my mother, soon after, he attacked me," she said quietly.

"You were just a kid," Billy said, distraught. "Did he...do anything to you?"

"He tried to. He was very aggressive."

"That's terrible," Billy said. "Makes me want to kill the bastard."

Camille sat near him on the couch and she looked at him and touched his arm. "Please, don't. That will only make things worse."

"I've known Vito forever, and I can't believe he'd do such a thing, but I believe you, Camille." He tried to hug her, but she stopped him because she wasn't sure if she'd be able to let go, and she didn't want him to get the wrong impression.

Instead, she thanked him for his support. That had been one of the things she'd liked most about Billy, that he'd always supported her, no matter what.

"Does your man know?" Billy asked her. "What's he going to do about it?" he said, as if Johnny had no other choice but to avenge her.

"That's not your business, Billy."

"All right." Billy paused and looked at her and touched his forehead. "Is he the type of guy to do something about it?"

"Yes, he is," she replied.

"I don't think I can ever look at Vito the same way," Billy said. "Are you sure you don't want me to do something about it?"

"I'm sure." She paused. "Do you want coffee?"

Billy shook his head. "I don't think I can drink right now after hearing what you just told me. My stomach doesn't feel good."

Camille nodded and decided she didn't really want any either.

"It wasn't just Vito who convinced the boss, you know," Billy suddenly said.

Camille looked at him earnestly. "What do you mean?"

"I helped convince him."

Camille started to rise from the couch then changed her mind. "But I thought you didn't want to work with me? You told me that."

"I didn't at first, then I decided that I had to help you."

"Why?"

"Because I'm still in love with you. You can't say you're surprised to hear that."

"Billy, I'm in love with Johnny," she said gently, because she could see that his heart was in the right place.

"I know about his father and yours," Billy said.

That made Camille rise. "How?"

"So, you already know," Billy said, as if he'd been testing her. "I found out while we were seeing each other."

"And you never said anything? How did you find out?"

"This guy, some old-time gangster, told me when he was drunk."

"How could you keep that from me?" Camille asked, and she didn't know whether she should slap him or cry.

"I wanted to protect you. You put your father on such a pedestal, and I didn't want to tarnish that. Besides, I didn't know whether the guy was talking nonsense, but now I can see that it is true. I must admit, after you told me you were seeing someone, and after I found out who he was, I thought about telling you that I would tell him the truth, to make you come back to me."

"You wouldn't dare," Camille said, unable to control her anger and shaking her finger at him.

"I know, it's terrible of me, but I thought about it."

Camille considered throwing him out, then Billy said, "I thought about doing it, but knew I never would because I'm not that kind of guy."

"I don't like that you kept such a secret from me. I'm disappointed in you," Camille said.

Billy apologized. "And I'm sorry I was against working with you at first."

"That's all right, you came around."

"And while we were seeing each other and you got sick," he said, and she knew he meant her depression. "I'm sorry I didn't handle it better. I should have."

"It's all right, Billy, that was a long time ago. I'd forgotten about it."

"Still, it was wrong of me. You needed me, and I wasn't there for you," he said, because emotionally he hadn't been. "I still love you, Camille. Go out with me." He rose and rubbed her hand.

"Billy," Camille said, pulling away, but she had to smile. "I can't. I already told you I'm seeing someone else, and I'm in love with him."

Billy looked at her and shrugged. "I know, but I had to try."

Then someone disturbing occurred to her. "Billy," she told him. "Now that you know who Johnny is, you have to promise me that you'll leave him alone," she said because she was well-versed in Billy's jealous streak.

"You really love him, don't you?" Billy said, looking at her. "I have to admit I'm disappointed. But, okay, I'll leave him alone. You don't have to worry."

"Thanks, Billy."

After a moment, he asked, "Does your mother know about what your stepfather did?"

Camille shook her head.

"Are you going to tell her?" Billy asked.

"I promised Vito I wouldn't if he helped me."

"You still have the power to do so if you want to, you know."

Initially, she had wanted to, but now she had second thoughts. She wanted to ask Billy his opinion but knew it was a decision she'd have to make for herself. Camille saw Billy out the door.

Less than an hour later, she'd made her decision. She would go see her mother and tell her the truth. She knew that she wouldn't be able to live with herself if she didn't.

The hour was perfect, since Vito would be at the café, and she would have her mother all alone. Camille knew that she didn't have much time, as Vito would go home from the café eventually, so she quickly showered and dressed, and left her apartment. She raced outside and toward her mother's building and saw Violet walking toward the still-smoldering ruins of *McBurney's* in the distance. She didn't feel like a confrontation with Violet right then, and besides, she didn't have the time for one, so she ducked out of the way and walked faster. She glanced over her shoulder once, and Violet didn't seem to have noticed her, and if she had, she was ignoring her.

24

Camille reached her mother's building, entered, and knocked on her mother's door. She heard her mother's footfall.

"Who is it?" her mother started to ask through the door then she must have looked through the eyehole because she opened the door. "Camille," she said. "What a surprise." She smiled. "Is everything all right? Not that you can't just stop by to see me, of course."

Not wanting to have the conversation out in the hallway, Camille said to her mother, "Actually, there's something I have to tell you."

"You have me worried, honey."

"Let's talk inside. Okay?" Camille said to her mother.

She wiped her feet on the doormat, entered and her mother closed the door.

"Vito isn't here, is he?" Camille suddenly asked, though she didn't believe he was.

"No, he's at the café, as usual. Did you want him to be here?"

"No, no," Camille said.

She walked with her mother into the kitchen and they sat at

the table. There was a vase with bright red flowers in the center, and Camille touched them, and they felt soft.

"I just made a fresh pot of coffee, if you'd like some," Sheila said.

"Thanks, I'll have a cup."

Her mother smiled as she rose and prepared the coffee. She seemed to enjoy doing things for Camille, and Camille didn't know if this was genuine or because her mother felt she had to act that way.

Sheila returned to the table and set a steaming cup in front of Camille. She'd already put a little milk in it, like she knew Camille preferred. She sat down across from her with her own cup and touched Camille's hand across the table.

"Whatever it is, sweetheart, you can tell me."

Camille decided to give her the good news first.

"I'm working with the Russians now," she told her mother. "They've agreed to a partnership."

"That's wonderful." Her mother squeezed her hand. "I'm so proud of you. If anyone could build a partnership with them, I knew it could be you. They're tough, and none of the other Irish have worked with them before. You have your father's sense for business." Then Sheila chuckled to herself. "That Violet must be very angry, with her pub in ruins, her mother in jail, and you in full bloom."

"Did Vito tell you the Alfonsis have agreed to work with me?" Camille asked.

"He might have mentioned it," Sheila said with a smile. She got up and hugged Camille. "Your father would have been proud of you as well. You're carrying on in his spirit."

Some daughters might have thought it odd that their mothers encouraged them to be gangsters, but in the O'Brien house that's just the way it was.

Sheila sat down and looked at her. "Now, what did you want to tell me?"

For a moment, Camille lost her courage and almost said, 'It's nothing, never mind.' Then she said, "It's about something that happened a long time ago." She paused. "This is hard for me to say," she said, searching for the right words to use to break her mother's heart. "It happened a long time ago, and I never told you."

"Camille, tell me," her mother urged, and she reached for and held Camille's hand.

"Not long after you married Vito," Camille began the story. "He attacked me one night when you were at your cousin's and he and I were watching television."

Her mother became silent and Camille was suddenly worried her mother wouldn't believe her.

She needn't have been concerned, however. "Oh my, Camille. I'm so sorry. I never knew. Why didn't you tell me?" Her mother spoke as though she couldn't believe what she was hearing, yet she believed it.

"I was just a teenager. I didn't want to upset you."

Sheila squeezed Camille's hand. "Honey, you should have told me. I wouldn't have been upset with you, it's him I'm upset with."

"I also didn't know if you'd believe me. You do, right?"

"I believe you because I know you, and I know you're an honest person. You're my daughter, and I trust you."

"And Vito?"

"I love Vito, but, this, I can't forgive. You must have been terrified." Her mother's voice shook with anger.

"I must admit that this secret is how I got him to help me win over the Alfonsis," Camille said.

"You blackmailed him?" Sheila asked, but she didn't seem shocked.

Camille nodded.

"You're a clever girl," her mother said.

"What's going to happen now?" Camille asked after a while.

"If I had known, I would have thrown him out and called the police. I wish you had told me."

"I didn't say anything because I didn't want to hurt you." Camille paused. "So, what's going to happen now?" she asked anxiously.

"I don't think I can live with him, but most of the money in our marriage belongs to him. Your father left me with not very much."

"I know that. You're really going to stay with him because he's got money?" Camille asked, hurt, but she wouldn't rush to judgement before she heard her mother's reply. "I can help you out financially, you know."

"I don't want you to have to do that, sweetheart. No, of course I won't stay with him. But I must figure out what I'm going to do. After what he did to you, he owes us something, both of us, and I'm going to make sure we get it."

"He helped me out with the Alfonsis, so I already got what I wanted."

"He still owes us money," Sheila said. "I'm going to make him give us half of everything he has, or else I'll smear him all over town."

It took a lot of gumption for Camille's mother to take on one of the city's most powerful mobsters, and she admired her mother.

"One of the reasons I didn't say anything was because of who he is," Camille told Sheila. "Back then, when I was just a kid, I was afraid of what he could do to me."

"Don't be afraid of him."

"I'm not anymore," Camille said with confidence. "Are you going to toss him out when he gets home?"

"I'm going to, yes, but I'm not sure when I'll do it."

"Are you going to tell him what I told you?" Camille asked, panicking. "I don't want to give him the chance to retaliate against me." She considered the consequences of her actions. Would Vito convince the Alfonsis to no longer work with her, so soon after she'd won them over? She hadn't thought about that before she told her mother because she'd been so overcome with emotion. Now, she almost wished she hadn't said anything. What good could come of it? Her mother's heart was broken, and the deal with the Alfonsi family might be off.

"He wouldn't dare," Sheila said.

"He might."

"If Joe Alfonsi wants to work with you, then he wants to work with you. Vito doesn't have enough power to outvote him."

"Yeah, but he might convince him not to work with me."

"Sweetheart, I can't stay with Vito and pretend like nothing happened, not after what you told me," Sheila said, as though she could tell what Camille was thinking.

"I know that," Camille said, then forcing herself to be numb because she somewhat regretted her decision to tell her mother, she said, "Whatever happens, happens. I'll just have to lose the Alfonsis, if that's what happens."

Sheila squeezed her hand again. "You won't lose them. If he dares to retaliate against you, then we'll tell the whole city, we'll ruin his reputation," she tried to reassure Camille.

Camille wasn't as confident as her mother. She finished her coffee and left the apartment before Vito returned, still not sure what her mother could ultimately do about Vito.

The next evening Camille had arranged to meet Johnny for a drink at a local bar, where she planned to tell him what Lucille had said about their fathers. She knew that it might mean the end of their love, but she couldn't really *be* with someone and be dishonest.

When she left her apartment, Vito confronted her in the street. He looked unshaven, his shirt was untucked, and he reeked of booze. Tears shone in his eyes, and the sight of them shocked Camille because she had never seen him cry before. She didn't feel like speaking to him, for she imagined her mother had thrown him out, and she tried crossing the street, but he wouldn't let her walk around him.

"You're a backstabbing bitch," he told her in a voice that wasn't loud enough to draw outside attention to them but was loud enough to make her jump.

Camille often used sarcasm to protect herself and did so in that situation. "Tell me something I don't already know."

"Your mother, she kicked me out of my home," Vito told her. "You promised me you wouldn't say nothing if I helped you. Well, guess what, little girl, I'm gonna make sure the boss stays away from you. You can kiss your chance to work with us goodbye."

Camille had already comprehended it could come to that, and although she cared deeply, she couldn't let him see that. "Fine, but just remember, my mother and I will tell everyone in the city what you did. Think about how your reputation will suffer. Everyone in this neighborhood thinks you're a gangster with a heart of gold, but if they know the truth, they'll think you're a creep."

"You wouldn't dare."

"Even if I wouldn't, do you really think that my mother wouldn't?" Camille asked him as they stood on the sidewalk, merely a step apart from each other.

Vito seemed to be recalling Sheila's aggression. "You bitch," he said. "Both you and your mother, you bitches!" He'd raised his voice, and people started to take notice and stared at them. "Your mother kicked me out," he repeated. "She's gonna get half of my money, maybe more. You ruined my life!" he yelled at her.

Camille simply shrugged. Then she looked straight at him. "You better stay the hell away from me and my mother. Your threats don't scare me. Old man Alfonsi does what he wants, so we'll see if he still wants to work with me, and if he wants to, then there's nothing you can do about it." She spoke so forcefully that spit flew out of her mouth and landed near Vito's eye.

He wiped the moisture away and glared at her, but he didn't say anything in reply, and Camille knew she'd won.

She left Vito standing in the street, and although he had delayed her in meeting Johnny, she went to a payphone instead of the bar.

She'd been given a number to use to reach Joe Alfonsi, and she rang him up. Despite believing that Vito wouldn't say anything to him because of her threat, she still needed to tell Joe what had happened so he wouldn't be surprised if he found out —she'd heard he disliked surprises.

One of Joe's handlers answered, and Camille explained who she was.

"One second," the man said, and then there was silence as she waited for the sound of the boss's voice.

She heard Joe Alfonsi's baritone. "Hello?"

"It's Camille O'Brien."

"Camille, it's wonderful to finally speak with you. Vito has told me a lot about you. I met your father once or twice and was very sorry when he died. He was a good man."

Camille thanked him.

"What's going on, Camille?" Joe asked, and straightaway she realized he wasn't the type of man to exchange unending pleasantries with her.

Camille breathed out then explained what Vito had done when she was a girl and what he had just threatened her with.

"I don't want this to change our relationship," she told the boss.

"You're worried that since you're on the outs with Vito, I'll listen to him and won't want to work with you?"

"Yes," she replied. Although she wasn't sure whether Vito would try to undermine her relationship with the Alfonsi family, she wanted to be the first to discuss it with the boss, just in case.

"I don't jump because Vito says so," the boss replied. "In fact, he's got to listen to me," he said with a chuckle. "I like your honesty, Camille, and I believe you are something special. Thank you for telling me these things. Someday you and I will meet, and I look forward to that moment."

She'd been a little surprised the boss hadn't wanted to meet her before, but she had assumed that Vito was high up enough in the organization that his word was good enough for the boss.

"You have nothing to worry about, Camille," the boss continued. "But I'm not going to get rid of Vito—unless he does come to me to try to convince me to disconnect my relationship with you and proves he's a no-good rat—but you won't be having any interaction with him from now on. I heard you know Billy; he can be your go-between."

Although Billy was a temptation she would probably never get over, he was better than dealing with Vito.

Camille thanked the boss and he told her to ring him 'anytime.' She left the payphone and ran to meet Johnny. She knew she was late, and by the time she arrived at the bar, she had perspired so much that when she touched her eyes, she could see her mascara had bled. From the outside window she spotted Johnny having a drink at the bar. All the time she'd been with Johnny, she'd rarely seen him touch a drink, and she'd been a little surprised when he asked her to meet him there, but he'd explained that the place was owned by a Cuban couple and popular with his friends.

Camille entered and kissed Johnny's cheek at the bar. Inside it was packed with customers and lively with music and the sounds of glasses clinking.

"Hi, beautiful," he said and embraced her from his seat.

"Sorry I'm late," she told him, and luckily, despite the bar being crowded, there was a place next to him, so she sat down.

"It's no problem at all," Johnny said. "I'm glad you're here."

Camille realized then that she didn't want to lose him. She wouldn't tell him the secret tonight, and she knew that the longer she put it off, the more likely she wouldn't tell him, but she couldn't risk losing him. Keeping the secret had started to weigh her down and as she sat at Johnny's side, her body rocked with guilt.

"What would you like to drink?" he asked her, snapping her out of it.

"Scotch and soda, thanks," Camille said with a forced smile.

Johnny was drinking a cola. He signaled the bartender and ordered Camille a drink.

She started to explain to him why she was late.

"I guess you could say I'm in with the Italians now," she told him. "They've chosen me over the McCarthys."

Johnny beamed at her. "That's great news," he said. "You're really good at this gangster stuff, better than me, I think." He gave her another smile.

"If you ever want to work with them, let me know. I can help you since I have an in with them."

To her surprise, Johnny said, "That would be great, thanks." Many men would have shirked the offer for help, but not Johnny.

"Though, I have to ask, because you've got me curious, and I know that they were with the McCarthys for a long time—how did you manage to accomplish all of this?" Johnny asked her.

"My stepfather helped me," Camille admitted, though she disliked giving Vito credit.

"Right, he does work for them," Johnny said.

The bartender set Camille's drink in front of her and she sipped. She noticed that Johnny didn't order another drink despite being finished with his first.

"And Billy helped me also," she told him when the bartender left to tend to another customer.

"Billy, your ex?" Johnny asked, and he seemed surprised.

Camille nodded. "That's right. I only found out that he had something to do with it when he came to see me and told me." She didn't want anyone telling her who she could and couldn't speak to, and so she hoped Johnny would be understanding.

Johnny's posture tensed and he stared at his empty glass. "He came to your apartment when you were alone?"

"Yes," Camille said.

"I thought you weren't friendly with him," Johnny said, looking at her now.

"I'm not. We aren't."

"But he feels entitled enough to go to your apartment. That's bold of him," Johnny said to her as though he disliked the thought.

"Are you jealous?" Camille asked, setting her drink on the bar. It was becoming difficult to hear Johnny over the noise.

"I am," Johnny admitted and then he smiled, and she knew they were okay.

"You have no need to be," Camille assured him. "What Billy and I had is gone. I didn't ask him to help orchestrate the deal with his boss, I just found out that he had when he stopped by. Nothing happened between us, and nothing will happen. I love you."

Johnny turned to her and held her hand. "And I love you."

Hearing the words gave her pleasure, but her guilt increased. *You might not love me if you knew the truth.*

"Are you worried about what the McCarthys will do?" Johnny asked her.

"There's only Violet now."

"But she's got men."

"I've thought about what she might do to me, yeah, but I'm not afraid of her."

"You should be," Johnny told her. "I'm worried about you. Violet and her mother are very dangerous."

"I know they are," Camille said. "But if I'm going to be in this business, I can't think about that."

"I don't want to lose you," Johnny said.

"You won't," Camille told him, but she thought of her mother losing her father and how her present situation reflected that. "I worry about you in the same way, but I've accepted who you are. I'm a trouble girl, Johnny, a gang girl, and if you're going to be with me, you'll have to accept that."

25

Violet stood outside the ruins of the pub with Max at her side. The fire and smoke had long since dissipated and all that remained was a burned-out skeleton of what had once been the lively *McBurney's*, and piles of ash around it. Violet had been at home with Tommy when the news broke of the fire and Max came by her apartment to tell her. Max had stayed with Tommy and she ran straight there in her bathrobe.

"I'm glad no one was inside when it happened," she told Max now. "Something could have happened to someone. Something could have happened to Tommy." Her voice shook with anger at the thought.

"Yeah, and it's a good thing your mother wasn't in the apartment." The apartment above the pub had also been destroyed.

"I'm glad she isn't here to see this."

"Will you tell her what happened?"

Violet nodded. "I'll have to, when I visit her again. She'll be devastated."

"Of course, she will be. It's been in her family for a long time. What did the police tell you?"

"You know how they don't like us, but they told me they were investigating it as arson. They also said that cases like this are very hard to prove so we shouldn't hold our breath. None of this would have happened if the guys had just left the Cubans alone. I asked them why they did it, and did they know the risk? You know what they told me? They said that they didn't like that guy hanging out in their section and that he gave them a funny look. Some of them are quite hot headed so I'm not surprised they beat a guy for giving them a funny look. But do you know who I am surprised at? Jake. He had to go and kill that guy and cause a huge headache for me."

Max murmured in agreement. "It's a good thing you kicked him out," he told her. "And thank God he is gone from this earth."

She'd removed Jake from the gang for killing Pedro. It wasn't easy to get pushed out of the McCarthy gang, but Jake had exceeded her limits. As far as Jake being gone from this earth, the night after Violet got rid of him, he had drunk himself to death and was found in front of a pub the next morning.

"The Cubans—do you think they'll retaliate?" Max asked her.

Violet shrugged. "I don't know. I would think that they wouldn't want to start a war. Jake's dead. Perhaps we're even now and nothing will happen. I can only hope, right?" She gave Max a smile and he patted her back.

"You have a lot of strength, Violet, just like your mother and your grandfather."

"You sound like you don't know how I can keep going after everything that's happened," Violet told him.

"I did wonder," Max said.

Camille was encroaching fast on her territory, and now had the Italians on her side and Violet had lost control of the neighborhood gambling ring to her.

"I did consider eliminating her after I found out," Violet told Max. "But I figured she would be expecting me to, and I'd rather strike her when she isn't prepared. Doing so would be risky, since the cops are watching us. If I get rid of her, they might catch me, and I don't want Tommy to lose me."

"I could do it," Max offered.

"Thanks, Max," she said, embracing him. "But they're watching you, too, and I don't want you to have to clean up after me. Camille's my problem, and if I take a risk and she dies, I'll be the one to do it."

"The police have to know about the drama in the neighborhood, perhaps they'll start paying attention to Camille."

"Maybe, but it would take years for them to do anything, like it took years for them to finally get my mother."

"She isn't going to stop, Violet. You're gonna have to deal with her sooner or later. She's like her father, once she digs in, she doesn't give up."

"She hates you more than me," she told Max. "Because of what you did to her father."

"I know that, and every time I'm out on the street, I'm always looking behind my shoulder."

"And to think that my mother wasn't that concerned about her. But I agree with you, she's dangerous. The new union leader of the dockworkers, is in her pocket now, thanks to the Italians."

"You still have me and the guys," Max said, patting her back again.

A woman stopped walking to ask Violet how she was.

"Hey," Max said when the woman left, "Lots of people in the neighborhood have been asking me how they can help you rebuild the pub," he said, as though to take her mind off the dire situation. "What should I tell them?"

"I'm not sure if there's enough money to rebuild. Camille's taking everything I have."

"Maybe we could raise money," Max suggested.

But Violet didn't want to think about that right then, all she could think about was Camille and how the law enforcement keeping a close eye on her meant she couldn't do anything yet—unless she wanted to risk it all. And maybe soon she would.

It distracted her so much that she hardly spoke to Sam when he took her out to dinner that evening while Max stayed with Tommy. Tommy still didn't like Sam, so she couldn't bring him with her, and she didn't know what she'd do without Max. Sam knew about the fire, and he had even offered to help her pay to rebuild the pub, but she couldn't accept that kind of money from a man she was merely dating, she didn't want to be tethered to him in that way, so she'd declined.

"Are you all right?" Sam asked her when they were halfway through sharing the chocolate dessert that he had eaten most of.

"How can you ask me that?" Violet replied in exasperation. Sam knew everything, he knew about the pub, and he knew about Camille taking control, because if Violet was going to be with Sam, she would have to be honest with him, and so far, he had accepted what she'd told him. Max had said that he must have really liked her not to have been frightened away by her gangster lifestyle.

"I'll get the check when the time comes," Sam said, as though he thought that was why she was concerned, because they usually split the check.

"No, you don't have to pay for everything, let me help."

"Are you sure?" he asked, as though she was broke, and while she wasn't, she was edging towards being that, thanks to Camille.

"I have to have some pride left," she said.

Sam nodded, though he looked unsure, and Violet sighed.

She would find a way to pay for everything, including her mother's expensive lawyer, but things had never been tight for her before and she didn't know what to do, really. It angered her because she imagined that Camille would have a plan if she was in the same situation, as Camille was more accustomed to the school of hard knocks. Violet's mother hadn't sheltered her from the gang lifestyle, but she had sheltered her from poverty.

"How's Tommy?" Sam asked after a moment, as though he disliked where their prior conversation was heading.

Tommy. Violet was preoccupied with much these days, but she thought of him often, whenever she wasn't around him. And, thank God, Max had stepped up to help her with Tommy in her mother's absence. He was like a father to her, and a grandfather to her son. What would happen to Tommy at the end of all of this? She knew that often it was the families who ended up being hurt the most in gang wars, because they were left to survive after everyone else was gone.

Sam hadn't seen Tommy since the day her mother had been arrested, and Tommy was perfectly fine with that as he'd been quite vocal about his dislike of Sam. He had loved Anton. But not Sam. It figured, because Violet really liked Sam, not quite loved him, but she liked him a lot.

"He's doing well," Violet said, when times had been tough for her son, with his father's death and then his grandmother imprisoned. And then the pub, which was like both of their second home, gone. "Considering," she added, "everything that's been happening."

"I meant it when I offered to help you rebuild the pub. I make all this money and it might as well be put to good use."

Violet knew he was trying to be kind, but his words rubbed her the wrong way, because she was tight on money and he wasn't, and she resented him for that.

"I don't need you to pay for everything for me, Sam." She

needed to take out her frustration on someone, and she couldn't take it out on Tommy or Max, or her crew, who needed her to convey optimism, so Sam was the easiest target.

"Okay," Sam said, a little blunter than she would have expected. "Do you have a plan for how you're going to rebuild? I'm assuming the pub was a large part of your income."

Suddenly, she imagined the kind of life that Sam wanted them to have: suburban and clean, with retirement savings, and a college fund for Tommy. He wanted them to be like an 'ordinary' couple, and a part of Violet wanted that as well, but she almost laughed at the table. Underneath the surface her life had always been chaotic and complicated, and that was all coming up now, because although her mother might have been able to shield her from the reality of the criminal life they led, she now faced it head on.

"The pub was a front for illegal activities," she told Sam in a raised voice. When people at the other tables turned to see who was shouting, her face heated and she lowered her voice. "It was used for that ever since my grandfather's day. It's not my main source of income. Camille O'Brien is taking my main sources of income. Remember when I mentioned that she is moving in on the neighborhood?"

Recently, after the pub fire, she had finally told him what Camille was doing, briefly, and she explained why the pub being gone wasn't her sole problem. But she didn't tell him the whole story, which was why Camille was doing it in the first place.

"Why is she doing this to you, anyway?" Sam asked her now, and Violet saw that it was her chance to explain, but she didn't want her family to appear more tainted or wicked in Sam's eyes, so she replied:

"I don't know why. We used to be on pretty friendly terms." Truthfully, she didn't want to entangle Sam any more than she already had, she wanted to protect him. "Believe me, the less you know, the better," she said when it seemed like Sam would ask her again.

"I'll admit I don't know much about your business," Sam said, and his endearing way made her smile. "But can't you ask her if she wants to work *with* you?"

Violet shook her head. Then she noticed Sam had finished the dessert, but she didn't want much of it anyway. "No, she doesn't want that. My mother's in prison, so she's out of the picture. Now Camille wants me gone. She wants to take over the neighborhood."

"Do you mean, she wants to start a war with you?" Sam asked, and his expression turned worried.

"Possibly, yes."

"That's serious," Sam said. "Maybe you should go to the police."

"The police? We don't go to the police. We handle it our own way."

"What do you mean, Violet?"

She didn't want to tell him what she meant, because she meant violence, if needed.

"This doesn't concern you, Sam. It shouldn't concern you. This is just the way things have always been, and always will be."

"I am concerned, because I care about you."

"You said you understood, Sam, when I explained what being with somebody like me meant."

"I'm trying to understand but I don't like what I'm hearing."

Violet shrugged. "It's the way it is." She'd grown up in the lifestyle, and Sam hadn't been exposed to it until he met her, and she knew she should have been patient with him, but she didn't have patience anymore.

"Why does this Camille woman dislike you so much?" Sam asked as he signaled the waiter for the check. "There must be a reason."

"She has one, but we shouldn't discuss it."

"Why not?"

"Because I don't want to at the moment." Violet paused and he frowned. "She has a vendetta of sorts," Violet said without elaborating, to get him to cease asking her.

"What does she look like?" Sam asked.

"Why?"

"I might have seen her around the neighborhood."

"She's younger than me, tall and pretty, but tough looking."

"I've probably seen her, but, of course, I wouldn't have known it was her." He paused for a moment. "So, what are you going to do about the pub?" he asked, as though he didn't wish to discuss Camille anymore, and neither did she.

"Max said people in the neighborhood offered to help me raise money to rebuild."

"That's great. Will you take them up on their offer? You should."

Violet shrugged. "I don't have time to think about that right now."

"This Camille has really gotten to you, hasn't she?"

Violet nodded. It had become where she couldn't think of anything else. Every day, every hour, every minute, Camille's encroachment plagued her.

26

That same evening, Camille left her apartment to meet Johnny at the movies. Things were going quite well for her, and Violet was quickly going down, so she was filled with ebullience as she walked and there was a little hop in her step. She and Johnny were set to see a romantic comedy and then go for a stroll afterwards and maybe get a cup of coffee. Johnny had joked that he ought to throw her a party, since she was doing do well, but Camille didn't want to make a big deal out of it, because she felt that doing so could bring her bad luck.

Camille arrived at the theatre and waited for Johnny outside. The queue for the new, popular film started to grow and soon stretched around the street and Camille knew that if she didn't get on queue soon enough that there would be no tickets left. As the time passed, and Johnny never showed up, Camille began to doubt he would come. She finally got on queue and waited, but when it was her turn there weren't any tickets left. Johnny still wasn't there. The queue began to dissipate as the news of the lack of tickets was announced. Camille stood on the sidewalk in the warm night, under the bright lights of the theatre, empty handed except for her purse, and realized Johnny wouldn't be there.

Furious, Camille raced to his apartment, then halfway there she felt that there must have been some sort of explanation for why Johnny hadn't shown up. Johnny wouldn't do that to her unless he had a very good reason. Perhaps something had happened with his daughter. Camille calmed herself down and walked the rest of the way to Johnny's building. She reached Johnny's apartment and knocked on his door.

Johnny opened straight away, without asking who it was, and there seemed something off about him, but Camille couldn't quite pinpoint what. Then she realized that he seemed drunk. His hair was disheveled, and his shirt unbuttoned, and he kept rocking back and forth on his heels as he stood in the doorway, staring at her with his red-lined eyes, drunken eyes.

"What do you want?" he asked in a way that was so cold she took a step back. This wasn't the Johnny she knew. Something had happened.

"Johnny are you all right?" she asked, though still uncertain and from afar. His imposing, rigid posture frightened her, when she had never been alarmed by him before. Something had changed between when she last saw Johnny and now. But, what?

Johnny laughed, a drunken laugh, and she realized that he was a wreck over whatever it was that had happened. "Am I all right?" he said. "Am I all right?" The smell of booze drifted off him and reminded her of her past. "Why don't you tell me, Camille?"

"Johnny, what are you talking about? You have me worried. What happened? You never came to the movies. I waited for you . . ." Then she grasped what was behind his behavior. The secret. Somehow, he had found out.

"I told my mother about us," he said. "I was waiting until I knew you were the one because I didn't want her to be disappointed. I finally tell my mother I'm dating this girl named Camille O'Brien and I'm in love with her, and she tells me that some guy named Colin O'Brien helped kill my father. She said he did it with his old gang he ran with before the McCarthys. Colin. That's your father's name, isn't it?"

She debated how she should react. She could lie and act shocked and pretend she hadn't known, or she could be honest. Either way, she grasped that she and Johnny were finished and that she would lose him. She knew she ought to act stunned, that was what he'd expect her to do, as though she hadn't known and it was news to her. But she didn't do any of those things. She nodded.

"My father was there when your father died, but he didn't actually kill him," she said.

"He didn't try to stop it. It's the same thing. You knew and you didn't tell me?" Now Johnny retreated slightly back inside his apartment, as though he couldn't bear being close to her. "I can't believe you. How could you? You knew this whole time and never said anything? How could you have pursued me, knowing what you did? What kind of person are you?"

Camille kept shaking her head. "No, no, I didn't know until this woman—she was a friend of my father's—told me."

"That happened while we were dating?"

Camille nodded and couldn't look at him.

"And you never said anything?" Johnny asked.

"I didn't want to lose you," she said, reaching for him, but he pushed her away.

"I don't know you," he shouted, and she thought he might slam the door in her face.

"I'm so sorry, Johnny. I wanted to tell you, but I was afraid you'd hate me."

"I do hate you. Do you know what I planned to do when I found out the names of the guys who killed my father?" Johnny's voice grew louder with emotion and his eyes turned fiery with passion. "I planned to kill a relative of each of the men involved in my father's death. In your father's case, that would mean you. But I can't hurt you, Camille."

Her spirits lifted with hope because she knew he still loved her. Then he said, "But I don't want to see you ever again," and it crushed her because she knew their fate was sealed. "My mother kept the details about my father's death a secret to protect me, that's what she said, because she knew I'd want justice. I knew it was Irishmen who killed him, but I didn't know their names. I know one now, though."

"I'm so sorry, Johnny, I didn't know what to do. I wanted to tell you, I really did, but I knew you'd hate me if you knew."

Johnny wouldn't accept her apology. "I can't hurt you, Camille, but I can't see you anymore. Please leave."

He looked at her and he had the most miserable expression on his face then he closed the door and she stood there, alone, trembling.

Now she'd never get to meet his daughter. She'd never get to share her life with him. Everything they had was gone, and it only took a moment. She started crying and once she started, she couldn't stop, still standing in front of his door. She thought Johnny might open the door and comfort her when he heard her, that he might even change his mind. But he never did, and she stood there, feeling very alone. Her body shook with the force of her sobbing. A minute or so passed and she stopped crying because she had nothing left inside her. He wasn't coming out. Johnny's neighbor opened her door and stared at Camille from the doorway for a moment, and their eyes met, briefly, then the woman shut the door.

It was getting late, and Camille knew it was time for her to leave even if she didn't want to. *Pull yourself together.* She didn't have a tissue or a handkerchief, so she used the corner of her shirt to dry her eyes, and then she left Johnny's apartment building. She walked outside and the hot city summer air made her feel ill. She had a lot of things besides Johnny these days, but she wanted Johnny to have been a part of that.

She wanted to go home and curl up in bed with her cat and call her mother and cry her heart out some more, but her mother hadn't wanted her dating Johnny in the first place and wouldn't understand her mourning. Seeking to distract herself, and feeling numb, Camille decided to conduct some business instead of going home. Something had been on her mind a lot lately, and that was the fact that in order to gain complete control of the neighborhood, she would have to find a way to win over the men who worked for Violet and her mother, and that included Max, whom she despised with everything she had. Camille had contemplated eliminating Max, but the other men respected him, and she needed to win them over and wouldn't do that by harming Max. At least not right away.

Ever since *McBurney's* had burned down, Violet's men had started spending time at another pub on the edge of the neighborhood, but Max wasn't a regular there. On most days he could be found in the basement of his friend's local butcher shop, where he now ran the bookmaking business. Camille decided she would visit Max in the morning and stop by the pub to see the other guys tonight.

She entered the crowded pub and pushed past people to get all the way inside. A few people looked at her as she walked by them, which didn't surprise her, as she must have been in a state. The pub was filled with people who had lived in the neighborhood for all their lives. Most of them recognized Camille and acknowledged her with a nod of respect. Many had come to see her as the new leader of the neighborhood and had started to go to her, asking for favors and her assistance with matters like borrowing money and dealing with those who gave them trouble. Camille had started to look into getting a 'office' to run her operation out of and had her eye on an old pub that was for sale in the neighborhood.

She spotted three of Violet's men, whom she recognized from around the neighborhood—everyone knew Violet and Catherine's guys—Derrick, Pat, and the third man she didn't know his name, at the pool table in the corner, drinking beers and laughing. What did they have to be so joyous about?

She didn't want them to know that she'd come there just to talk with them, so she ordered a beer at the bar before approaching them.

They stopped laughing when they saw Camille walking towards them. Each nudged the other, and they stared at her with somber expressions on their faces.

Camille stopped in front of them with her beer in her hand. "Derrick. Pat."

Derrick rested his beer on the side of the pool table. "What do you want?"

Camille drank some beer before speaking. "I have to want something to say hello?" She grinned. She didn't know them very well, but she knew them well enough from working at *McBurney's*, that it wasn't unusual for her to approach them.

Neither of the men returned her friendly gesture. The third man hung in the background and watched her.

"I know you've been watching me for Violet," Camille told them.

"We shouldn't talk to you," Pat said and resumed drinking.

"I think you should," Camille told both. "You should hear me out."

"Why should we?" Derrick asked her. She knew him and Max to be the most loyal to Violet and her mother of the group.

She could barely hear them over the music.

"I don't believe we've met," she said to the third man, a tall young guy in a black t-shirt with bulging muscles, piercing blue eyes and a dark mustache, handsome in a classic way.

"Danny," he said, shaking her hand.

"Right, Danny," she said, remembering she had seen him around *McBurney's* once or twice, and he was a newer member of Violet and Catherine's crew. Of the four men, Pat, Derrick, Max, and Danny, she reasoned Danny would be the easiest to win over since he hadn't had much time to become loyal to the McCarthys. Derrick would be the most difficult.

"What are you doing here, Camille?" Derrick asked her.

"Can we talk?" she said and gestured to the only vacant table in the place.

"Whatever you have to say, you can say it right here," Derrick replied, standing firmly in his place by the pool table.

"Come on, let's sit," Pat told him. He looked at Danny, who nodded in agreement.

Derrick glared at the other men, then grunted and went over to the table and they followed, carrying their drinks. Camille sat next to Danny, across from Derrick and Pat. She set her beer bottle on the table and began her plan.

"Have you thought about what would happen if Violet goes to jail after her mother?" she asked them.

"She's not going to jail," Derrick said.

"It's possible she could. I read about her mother's case in the newspaper, and it makes sense that she is also involved. If she goes down, too, then you guys would be on your own."

"Max would take over if that happened."

"Maybe not," Camille said.

"You want us to work for you," Derrick said, seeing right through her. His intense stare made her shiver.

"We couldn't do that to Violet," Pat spoke up, and Danny remained quiet, taking it all in.

Once again, she had difficulty hearing them because of the music and other conversations at the tables surrounding them.

Camille entwined her hands on the table and looked at them calmly. "I know how you feel about Violet and her mother; I've seen you with them. But you need to start thinking about yourselves. Things could get messy, and you need to decide if you want to be on the winning side."

Derrick scowled and sat up. "Are you threatening us?"

For a moment, Camille thought he would get up and leave, and that the other two would follow him.

"Not at all," Camille said. "I'm making you an offer."

"Too bad our friend Jake isn't here," Derrick said. "How's your boyfriend Johnny doing?"

Camille figured that Derrick blamed Johnny and his gang for Jake's demise.

"You guys beat up Rafael," she told Derrick.

Derrick shrugged and gave her a smile. "What can I say? He was hanging on the wrong street corner."

"They wouldn't have torched the pub if you hadn't done that, and perhaps Jake wouldn't be gone if he hadn't killed Pedro," she told him coolly.

"You're blaming Jake for his own death?" Derrick said, incensed. He rose a little in his seat.

"No. It was simply a chain of events that happened. I'm not blaming anyone," she said, though she despised Jake for murdering Pedro. "We can put that all behind us," she said after a while, "and talk business. Because that is what this is, business."

"Violet's not just business to us, she's like a sister to us," Derrick said, sitting down again, and Camille saw that he would be the spokesman of the group.

"I respect that, but this is a business decision. Come work with me. I'm winning, Violet's losing, it's as simple as that. She will lose everything in the end. You don't want to be there when she does."

"Maybe we don't want to work for a woman anymore," Derrick said, and she heard him loud and clear.

Camille smiled at him. "Yes, but us ladies seem to be doing most of the winning around here."

To her surprise, Danny and Pat laughed at her joke.

"Maybe we should see what she has to say," Pat told Derrick.

"Yeah, let's hear the lady out," Danny said.

Derrick raised his hand to silence them then he looked at Camille and drank his beer. "All right," he said after a moment and gave her a cool gaze. "We're listening."

"They'll be less rules when you work with me, like with drinking. You can drink as much as you want as long as you don't mess anything up. But no drugs, because I like that rule," Camille said.

Pat and Danny seemed satisfied at the idea and they nodded at each other. Derrick didn't react.

"What else?" he said, and it dawned on her that her plan might actually happen.

"More money. More power."

"What does your boyfriend think of all this?" Derrick asked her.

She'd forgotten about Johnny temporarily, and now he'd made her remember. "I'm my own woman. I'm not with him anymore, anyway."

"Sorry to hear that," Derrick said, but he didn't sound genuine. "We know what Max did to your father. Violet told us you'd found out. I'm assuming you plan to eliminate him and that if we were to work with you, we'd have to be fine with that."

"I have no plans like that," Camille responded.

"I don't believe you," Derrick said. "You don't just forget something like that."

"I can," Camille said firmly. "When it comes to business, I can do a lot of things."

"So, you're saying you'd work with Max after what he did to your father?"

"I have to say I don't believe you either," Danny suddenly said.

"Yeah, I don't see how you could do that," Pat said.

"It's simple," Camille replied. "I don't like what he did, of course, but I'm willing to move past it for the sake of my business."

"That's pretty cold," Derrick said, but he said it in a way that was more of a compliment than a criticism. He seemed to look at her in a new light, and Camille thought that maybe she could win him over. Then he said, "I don't know if I can work with someone who was sweet on Johnny Garcia. Jake was my friend."

"I'm no longer with him," she emphasized.

"Sorry to hear that," Pat said.

"Pat," Derrick scolded him.

She thought of Johnny, and her body ached from the weight of her grief. She was surrounded by people in the pub, but she felt entirely alone sitting among the sounds of their merriment, but when she'd had Johnny in her life, she'd always felt fulfilled, no matter where she was.

"That's good to hear," Derrick told her. "I still don't believe you about Max, though. I wouldn't want anything to happen to him."

Camille calmly drank her beer then set it down. "I can assure you that won't happen." It was a lie and Camille knew that eventually she'd have to think of a way around it, but for now it would have to do. Perhaps she could convince them of the need when the time came and they knew her better. Max walking the streets so freely enraged her but if she eliminated him now, she would lose the opportunity to pull Violet's other men over to her side.

"Good, because we like Max," Pat said.

Camille looked to Derrick because, clearly, he oversaw the others.

"All right," Derrick said. "Let's say that maybe I'm willing to believe you—when you said more money and more power, what did you mean by that?" His eyes lightened with interest and Camille saw she had him right where she wanted.

She didn't want to outspend herself but because of the men's longstanding relationship with Violet and Catherine, and their loyalty to them, she needed to somehow convince them to join her. "I'll pay you more than her, and I'll give you more say in what we do."

"How much more are we talking about?" Derrick asked, still appearing intrigued.

"Do they give you a steady salary? Do you get a bonus? Vacation time?" Camille asked the men. She planned to run her organization like a normal business.

"We get paid when we work," Derrick replied.

"But you're working all the time."

Derrick thought about it for a moment then frowned as if he realized she was right. "That's true," he said. "But they pay us well. Pat and I have worked for the McCarthys for a while now, and they've been good to us."

"I'll be even better to you," she insisted.

"We don't know you like we know them," Derrick, the spokesman, said.

"You know me from when I used to tend their bar."

"Yeah, but they're like family to us."

"I can give you a salary and a bonus, and vacation time, gentlemen. I'll treat you like regular employees. As I recall, some of you have to do jobs on the side now, to make ends meet?"

"Yeah, once in a while," Danny said, and Derrick gave him a fierce look to quiet him.

"If you work with me, you'd no longer have to do that," Camille said.

"Why are you willing to do that for us?" Derrick asked her, as though there had to have been a catch.

"I'm not as greedy as they are," Camille replied with a smile. "To me, this is more than about making money, it's about a family legacy."

Pat and Danny nodded at her reasoning, but Derrick didn't react.

"I don't believe you," Derrick said. "I don't believe you would give us that kind of money."

He still didn't trust her, and Camille contemplated a way to convince him, and they all stared at her, with Pat and Danny having expectant looks on their faces and Derrick watching her like she was a liar.

"If you can give me a handshake, then I'll trust your word, and I can give you all an advance," she said after a moment.

"Where are you getting this money from?" Derrick asked her.

She almost said, "That's none of your business," but she said, "The Italians are on my side, as I'm sure you already know, as are the Russians. My business is growing splendidly. That's another thing you ought to consider—Catherine's in jail, and they've lost the Italians—they seem to be losing a lot lately, don't you agree?"

"And you're the winner?" Derrick said, and he finally smiled, and he had quite a charming smile at that.

"I am," Camille said with confidence. "And I'll keep winning."

"Why?"

"Because I'm doing it in honor of someone, it's personal."

"When you say more power, what do you mean exactly?" Derrick asked after few moments.

"You'll have more control over what you do," Camille said, a little more control, because she would still be in charge.

"Meaning?"

"I won't force you to do things you don't want to. You won't be punished for saying no."

Derrick leaned back in his chair like he enjoyed the idea of that. "But you'd still be our boss?" he said as though still a little uncertain.

Camille nodded.

"So, you're not going to get married to Garcia and expect us to listen to him?" Derrick asked.

Camille shook her head.

Derrick sat up. "Thanks, but we're going to pass," he said.

Camille froze in shock.

"If Violet goes to jail along with her mother then the gang is done," she said in desperation.

"Max will take over if that happens," Derrick repeated with a smug look.

Camille quickly turned to Danny and Pat. "What about you two, what do you think?"

Both men looked to Derrick for what to say.

"Can't you speak for yourselves?" Camille said to them. "Think about what I'm offering. I can see your faces; I can tell you're interested. Forget what he says."

"Hey, now," Derrick said, rising.

Camille had left her gun at her apartment because she didn't want it on her at the movies, and she assumed at least one of the three was armed. A few people had been staring at them, knowing that they were rivals, to see what unfolded, and now their focus seemed to intensify, and their conversations halted, and the pub got quiet. Camille could feel their eyes upon her.

27

"**D**errick," Pat suddenly spoke up. "I think we should consider her offer. It seems pretty good."

"Where's your loyalty?" Derrick said to him in disgust, standing. Then he looked at Danny. "What about you?"

Danny glanced at Camille then said to Derrick, "I actually think it sounds pretty good."

"I can't believe both of you!" Derrick shouted.

More people in the pub turned to look at them and the entire place fell silent.

"We don't know her like we know the McCarthys, we can't trust her," Derrick told his men.

"Camille used to work at the pub. We know her from there," Pat said, seeming more confident.

Derrick glared at both men and his posture stiffened. "It isn't the same thing. They're like family to us, and you don't turn your back on family."

"But they aren't really our family," Danny told him.

"You're dead to me, both of you," Derrick said to him and Pat.

He walked away in a fury, pushing past the crowd that

blocked him. "What the hell are you looking at?" he sneered at everyone who dared to watch him, leaving Camille alone with Pat and Danny. Once Derrick exited, slamming the door as he went, the people who had been watching them resumed their chattering.

"That leaves you, gentlemen," Camille told Pat and Danny. "Are you with me or not?"

Neither hesitated when each answered yes.

"Terrific," Camille said with a smile. "Let me buy you a drink."

Did she trust them? Not entirely. But, then again, she never trusted anyone entirely, and they'd have to earn their place in her gang before she gave them responsibility, but both she and they would learn over time. At least she had two of them now and would try Max tomorrow morning, but convincing him would be even harder than Derrick, and she had failed at Derrick. But she reasoned that if she could convince Max, somehow, then Derrick would be convinced as well.

She bought Danny and Pat a round of drinks and when they were done, they shook hands and went on their way. Camille returned to her apartment and was glad to be away from the noise of, first, the pub, then the city street. She had a terrible headache and knew she wouldn't sleep well tonight because of the business with Johnny. She entered her apartment just as the phone rang. She closed the front door and raced to answer. Was it Johnny?

"Hello?"

"Camille?" her mother said. "Honey, it's me."

"Oh, hi." She didn't plan to tell her mother that she and Johnny were over, at least not now. They hadn't spoken since Camille visited her after her mother banished Vito. But presently she did have a bit of good news to share with her. "I convinced two of Violet's guys to come work with me."

Sheila said, "What about the other ones?"

Camille sighed. "Can't you just be happy? The others will come around."

"I am happy for you, but with guys like these, honey, it's better to have them all on your side."

"Even Max?"

"Him I'm not so sure about."

"All of this time, why didn't you ask Vito to take care of him?"

"I did, sweetheart, but Vito said no, said he didn't want to start a war. And he said 'unnecessary killings' can do that. He didn't care about your father like we do, and if it was up to me, then Max would have been dead a long time ago."

"I'll take care of him," Camille promised her mother. "I'm not sure when, but I will."

"Was he the one who said no about working together?"

"I haven't asked him yet. One of the others said no."

"You're a clever girl, trying to get Max over to your side before getting rid of him, betraying him like he betrayed your father, that's the perfect revenge. Your father couldn't have done it better himself. He'd be proud of you, Camille."

She thanked her mother but inside it somehow felt wrong that he'd be proud of her for that. "Speaking of Vito, I wonder where he's gone to," she said.

"I don't care, he can rot."

"I told Joe Alfonsi what he did, and he says I won't have to interact with Vito, but he says he can't just throw him out of the mafia."

"Of course not. Men protect themselves; you remember that, sweetheart. Don't let your guard down ever."

"Did Vito come to collect his belongings?" Camille asked after a moment.

"He didn't have to. I tossed them out the window down to the street." Her mother howled with laughter and Camille smiled. "It's what he deserves," Sheila said with more seriousness.

"Why did you call me?" Camille asked after a while.

"Can't a mother call to see how her daughter is?"

"I'm sorry, it's just that, are you going to be asking me if I've been taking my medication? Because sometimes you ring to ask me that."

"I wasn't, but are you?"

"Of course," she said, but even if she hadn't been, she would have lied, as she didn't want to concern her mother. She understood the difficulty her mother must have been going through after banishing Vito. Sheila had enjoyed a high status as the wife of a mafia man, and now that was done.

"When are you going to approach Max?" Sheila asked after a moment.

"Tomorrow morning, actually."

"Are you going to go there alone?"

"Yeah. Why, do you think I should take somebody with me?"

"Max is a smart bastard, and one never knows what he'll do."

Her mother was correct, of course, as she usually was.

"Don't forget how he tricked your father," her mother added.

"You've convinced me," Camille said, and she knew she'd ask Danny to go with her, since he seemed more astute than Pat, whom she knew as strong and capable and violent when he needed to be, but not smart.

"It's late," Sheila said. "I'm sure you want to get to sleep. You have a big day ahead of you."

"Good night," Camille told her mother. "Mom?" she started to say.

"Yes, sweetheart?"

And she almost said, 'Johnny and I are finished', but she didn't say that, instead she said, "Nothing. Goodnight."

"Goodnight, sweetheart."

Camille spent most of the night with the television in her bedroom turned on low and not really paying attention to it, but she couldn't sleep. Instead, she thought. She thought a lot, because she missed Johnny, and she almost turned to drink but resisted the temptation. She had seen too many people she knew growing up turn to drink during difficult times and then they were destroyed because of it.

She rose from bed early the next day, eager to get the meeting with Max completed. Of course, he wasn't expecting her, and she felt that was best, because if he knew she was coming, she wasn't sure he'd see her. She'd called up Danny late the night before, when she couldn't sleep, and for a moment was tempted to ask the handsome Danny to come over and keep her company, but she knew he would never fill the void losing Johnny had left, so she only asked him to meet her outside her apartment in the morning to come along with her to Max's, and he'd agreed.

She showered and dressed and made herself a cup of coffee but no breakfast, and when she looked out her window and saw Danny waiting outside on the sidewalk, she left the apartment to meet him.

"Camille," he said. "I hope you had a good night's sleep."

Camille smiled to herself at the inelegance of his words, as though he, too, recognized the attraction between them, which had started at the pub, but she knew it wouldn't materialize and she suspected he also grasped that.

"I did, thanks," she lied. "I'm glad you decided to come with me. Remember, when you're working with me, you have more say."

"I know that," Danny said, "but I thought that maybe I could help you out with Max since he likes me."

"Good," she said. "That could come in handy." She paused and they started to walk to the shop Max's friend owned where he had an office in the basement. "Were you surprised I wanted you to start work right away?"

"No, not really. You seem like a prompt lady."

Camille chuckled at how he'd call her a 'lady'.

The sun radiated like a sparkling jewel on that morning and she shielded her eyes from the intense light as she walked. The street was crowded with people going to work. A few people in the neighborhood stopped to say hello to her out of respect, and Camille enjoyed her new status as the 'queen' of the neighborhood. She liked winning, and as far as she was concerned, Violet and her mother were old news. She and Danny didn't say much to one another during the rest of the way to Max's, rather they had a mutual silent respect, and when they arrived close to the shop Camille stopped in the street and turned to Danny.

"This is how it's going to work," she told him. "I know he likes you, but I'm going to take the lead when we go inside. But feel free to interject and help me out as needed."

Danny nodded. "Sure thing," he said.

The door to the basement was ajar with a stone keeping it open, letting in the summer air, but Camille knocked before entering.

"Who is it?" Max called from inside, and she heard him approaching the door.

"It's Camille O'Brien. Is now a good time?" she asked, but she could see inside and saw that Max was alone.

"What do you want?" he asked.

"Why, I want to see you, of course," Camille said pointedly.

"I don't like sarcasm," Max said, appearing in the doorway and glaring at her.

"I think it's time you and I had a talk," she said.

Danny waved to him, but he ignored Danny, and Camille

figured he knew that Danny had moved over to her side, and he probably knew about Pat as well.

"I doubt there's anything for us to discuss. Anyway, I'm busy."

"No one's here," Camille observed. "How busy can you be? Unless you're placing bets for ghosts these days?" She smiled.

Max scowled and Camille realized she might have gone too far in insulting him.

"We still have business," Max declared. "Less than usual, but we still have some. We're doing okay."

"That's not what I heard, I heard that ever since you lost the Italians to me and your nice little gambling ring, that you've been hurting badly. Catherine's gone, and from what I'm hearing, the word on the street is that Violet could be next. What are you going to do when that happens?"

People in the neighborhood had contacts in the police department and were gossiping.

"I'll take over if that happens," Max told her.

"I won't let you, and I have the Italians on my side, so they won't let you."

She tensed and Max tensed, and she kept her eyes on him, to make sure he wouldn't pull a gun. She had a gun and she had Danny there for backup, who was also armed, but one could never be sure what kind of tricks Max had up his sleeve.

"Is that what you came here to do, to threaten me?" Max held her gaze, but Camille didn't back down.

"No, I'm making you an offer to work with me."

Max laughed. "Are you kidding me?"

"No."

"Why would you want me to work with you, after everything?" he asked.

"Can we come inside?" she said, gesturing to her and Danny.

Max looked from her to Danny, as if unsure.

"Derrick called me last night and told me you got some of our guys," he said to Camille.

"Yes, Pat and Danny here."

"I'm disappointed in you," Max said to Danny with a ferocious stare. "But I'm even more disappointed in Pat, who has known the McCarthys for quite some time. I always knew you were a little punk," he said to Danny.

Danny bolted forward as if he would hit Max and Camille blocked his way. So much for Max 'liking' Danny.

"Calm down," she told both men. "I'm here to talk, that's all, to see if we can come up with an arrangement. I promise you that it's worth your time to hear me out."

She didn't know Max well despite seeing him around the pub, but he was a gangster, and she knew that like many gangsters, he liked the sound of a good deal.

Max nodded. "Come in," he said, and Danny entered first followed by Camille.

Inside, Max had a simple, unadorned office and it looked like he had just set up shop. He had a table with two phones and a few chairs and a large chalkboard to keep track of bets. He gestured to the chairs, but Camille shook her head. She didn't trust him well enough to sit down and relax.

"We'll stand," she told him.

"Fine, but I'm sitting," Max said, and did just that.

Camille had the urge to ask him what her father's last moments were like—had he suffered or gone quickly?—because she had always wondered, now that she had him one on one. But she knew that asking him that question would make her appear vulnerable in his eyes and she didn't want him to have the upper hand; she wanted to control Max.

"Make it quick because I'm busy," Max told her with a smirk.

"I don't see anyone," she said.

"I got people coming in soon."

Danny stood to her right and stayed quiet as she'd instructed. "You've told me that you would run the McCarthys' racket if Violet gets sent away," Camille said to Max.

"That's right."

"But I won't let you, and the Italians will help me make sure of that."

"Listen," Max said, sitting up and looking at her. "There's no point in your being here. I'm loyal to Violet and her mother. I'm loyal to their whole family, especially Violet's kid, and have always been. That's not going to change. Violet needs me right now, and I'm not going anywhere."

Camille had noticed over the years that Max had a soft spot for Violet's son.

"You'd risk the Italians wrath?" she asked him, thinking that he wouldn't dare.

"No one knows for sure if Violet's going down with her mother."

"Regardless, she's going down, and I'm making sure of that. You might as well be on the winning side, right?"

"Why do you hate Vi so much? I know why you don't like me, but I thought you were friends with her."

They stared at each other with a simmering hatred, as each was very much aware of the unspoken conflict between them.

"She's a part of that family, that's why," Camille said.

"But you're willing to work with me? I'm the one who . . ." Max didn't finish his sentence but Camille knew what he'd been about to say.

"I don't like you," she told him. "This is strictly a business strategy. If I get you, then the rest of Violet's guys will follow you, and then Violet's all alone and I take over the neighborhood."

"And what happens to me?" Max asked, as though he doubted she'd let him live after everything he'd done.

"You continue to work with me."

"Why?"

"I'm willing to forget some things for the sake of my business, that's why."

"You're willing to forget what I did to your father?" Max asked with a skeptical look.

"I won't ever forget it, but I'm willing to overlook it."

"You're like ice," he observed, "like your mother."

"Don't talk about my mother that way," Camille said, stepping closer to him, and Derrick moved with her.

"Your father had a softer heart, but not very," Max said.

Max didn't get to talk about Camille's parents, especially her father, not after what he'd done, but at the same time she knew that to show emotion would make her appear weak and she didn't want Max to think he'd gotten to her where it hurt the most, although he had.

"Pat and Danny are with me," she reiterated.

"But not Derrick," Max said, looking at the clock on the wall, as though he really was expecting someone. "What did you give them to get them to turn on Violet and her mother? A little something extra?"

The innuendo in his voice disgusted her but she couldn't let him get to her. "More money. More power," she said, as if that was her slogan.

"Of course, you did," Max said. "And I'm not surprised they fell for it. Danny here doesn't know the McCarthys very well and so his loyalty is thin, and Pat is an idiot. Derrick is a sharp man, though, as am I, especially since, with Derrick still in, I know I'm not the only one. So, no thank you, Miss O'Brien."

He'd insulted her and she knew it, and she detested him more than ever. For a few moments they glowered at each other.

"Come on, Danny," she said. "We're leaving," and he followed her out.

"Good—bye," Max sang to them and she wanted to turn

around and eliminate him once and for all. But a good gangster used restraint, and so at that very tense moment, she did. But she did tell him, "You're making a big mistake."

"You should stop, Camille," he replied.

But Camille didn't stop, although that wasn't the last she saw of Max. She'd lost Johnny but business still had to be dealt with, and with Catherine in prison and Violet under the police's scrutiny, and with Pat and Danny and the Italian mob already on her side, she had a golden opportunity to move in permanently. She began collecting 'protection' money from some of the businesses in the neighborhood, so that they could do business without anyone bothering them, including her. Then she moved in on the McCarthys's—and Max's—neighborhood loan shark business, and one day Max confronted her in the street as she was on a way for a meeting with her crew at a local pub. She'd hoped that soon they would no longer have to meet in the backrooms of generous pub owners, as she had her eye on a few pubs of her own to purchase, and had the cash needed to do so.

"You can't do this," Max shouted at her, preventing her from crossing the street.

"I have the Alfonsis on my side, so I certainly can," she told him with a shrug. "Please move out of my way."

"I get you want to punish me, but why do this to Violet and her mother?"

"They were a part of what happened to my father." Camille tried to walk past him, but he wouldn't let her. A few people in the area recognized them and stopped to watch the confrontation unfold. "I made you an offer, Max, and you said no."

"I don't trust you," he said, "that's why I said no."

"That's too bad because I was being honest with you, and I meant what I said."

"I can't work with you, not after your father."

"I already told you that I'm willing to forget."

"You should know that your father wasn't a saint. He did bad things, like me. I'm no different from him, really," Max said with uncertainty—and a little fear—in his voice.

"I don't want your opinion of him," she stated calmly but inside she swelled with hatred for the man blocking her way.

"I heard you ended things with the Cuban." He smirked. "Sorry to hear that."

Camille wanted to hit him, but not in the street, so she restrained herself and stared him in the eye.

"It's a shame because something could happen to him, or to your mother," Max said.

Fury, and fear, shot through her entire body. "Are you threatening them?"

Max shrugged. "I ought to kill you for what you did, for taking my business," he said.

Camille figured he meant that she'd moved in on his loan shark business.

She recoiled but scowled. "Careful, Max, I doubt the Alfonsis would like that," she told him.

"Maybe I don't care," he threatened. "A man has got to have pride. You can't hide behind them forever, Camille."

She frowned at his veiled threat. "I don't like what you're saying, and I'd be careful if I were you."

"See, I knew that you hadn't gotten over the history between your father and me," Max said. "You can't fool me."

"Get out of my way," she said, shoving past him.

"I'm watching you, Camille," he shouted out to her as she walked away, and the crowd thinned out. She took his words to mean, 'I'm going to get you.'

Not if I get you first.

28

Violet had noticed Detective Seale watching her over the past few days—she was certain that the man in the car was him—but she didn't think he had enough evidence to charge her with anything since he never approached her. The last Violet had heard, the wife of Joseph O'Connor, the man who had owed Max, was too afraid to call the police.

Catherine was set to go to trial for murder and racketeering charges, and Violet knew that wouldn't be the end of it, that Seale would continue to watch her. One thing was for certain, though, she knew her mother would never rat on her, for if there was one thing that Catherine McCarthy was not, that was a stool pigeon, and so far, Frank O'Rourke had only implicated her mother. Violet wasn't sure why that was, exactly, it wasn't as though she and O'Rourke were close, but he was aware that she had a young son, and so Violet liked to think that maybe that was why he hadn't said anything about her to the police. But she couldn't be sure, so Seale's constant, close presence still put her on edge.

Her plans to move to the suburbs had been derailed, and she didn't even have enough money to rebuild her pub, and the local construction workers who, through Max, had offered their assistance free of charge, had withdrawn their offer. They'd told her they didn't want to get on Camille O'Brien's 'bad side.' So, that's how it was now. Camille was queen. Violet thought that maybe Camille had something to do with it, that she had told them not to work for her, but she didn't have proof. Camille hadn't just taken some of her men, she'd taken most of her business, including, recently, the 'protection' money she made from local businesses and the money she made from loansharking.

Violet wondered how far Camille would go. Would she kill Violet? And how far should she, herself, go? Should she kill Camille? She might not have a choice. But didn't want Tommy to be left alone if that happened and Violet was caught. She had a lot to lose.

Which was why one day Violet rang her grandmother who lived in the country, from a payphone, in case Detective Seale was listening in, and asked her to take Tommy.

"I've been meaning to come to the city to visit my daughter," her grandmother told her. Her grandmother's voice was the opposite of a sweet older lady, as was the rest of her. "How is your mother doing?" her grandmother asked her.

"Better than you might expect. She's optimistic, and so is her lawyer, but I don't know." Violet paused.

"Violet, what is it?" her grandmother asked. "Do you need money?"

Violet did, but she didn't want to ask her grandmother, because she knew her grandmother hadn't been left with much after her grandfather's death, due to his lavish spending.

"I'm all right, gran," she said.

"You're sure? I know you don't have any money coming in from the pub," her grandmother said, though that wasn't where Violet and Catherine had made most of their money. They'd made most of their money from the businesses that Camille had stolen. Violet's grandmother already knew about Camille because she'd told her.

"That girl is still giving you trouble?" her grandmother asked.

"Yes, she's practically taken everything. Just you wait, next thing she'll buy a pub," Violet joked, yet cringed at the thought, because it was possible.

"And you've just let her?" Her grandmother spoke in a tone that implied, 'What are you going to do about her?' because her grandmother and grandfather had a lot in common.

"The Italians are on her side," Violet said. "There's not much I can do."

"You can get rid of her. That's what your grandfather would have done. Get rid of her and then the Italians will be back to working with you."

"I'm not sure if they'll like it if I get rid of her, they'll view me as having stepped out of line."

"They might be angry at first, but after a while they'll forget about it and you'll be back in with them."

"Hold on a second," Violet said, and put more money into the payphone. "Ever since Mom's arrest, I'm being watched by this cop. If I get Camille, he could catch me. So, I don't think I can do anything at the moment. But I need you to take Tommy for a little while."

"In case you end up in jail?"

"Yeah, or she kills me. I don't know how far this woman will go."

"Do you think she could harm him?"

"Maybe. She's dangerous."

"I'll take him," her grandmother said, seeming very concerned. "I'll speak to the school here to get him enrolled. He can stay with me for as long as you need him to."

"Thanks, grandma."

"Anytime, sweetheart. How are things with your fellow? Sam?"

"He's stayed with me," Violet said. "That's the one good thing that's happened to me lately."

"That counts for something. He's a good man. He'll make a good father to Tommy."

"Tommy doesn't like him."

"He'll learn to. It always hard for boys at first when their father is gone."

"I'm worried about Tommy. He's been through so much. But thank you for taking him. Please look out for him for me."

"You know I will, sweetheart."

A few days later she sent Tommy on a bus to the country to stay with his grandmother. Tommy wasn't happy leaving his friends behind but went. Violet only hoped that he would forgive her someday.

Flush with cash, Camille bought an old neighborhood pub that she'd always liked—it had been the first pub she'd gone to—and planned to renovate it and turn it into a playground of sorts for herself and her crew. She planned to run her operation out of the pub and to launder her profits through the legitimate business.

Camille was there with a local carpenter one day when the bell at the top of the door sounded. She looked away from the carpenter's rough hands wiping sawdust off the bar he worked on, to see who'd entered.

"Hello," Johnny said. "I heard you own this place now."

"Yeah, I bought it recently," she replied, stunned to see him, having only dreamt of this moment, and not sure what to do now that he was there.

"Congratulations," he said with a smile.

"Thanks."

Camille told the carpenter he could take a break and the man stepped outside. "What are you doing here?" she said to Johnny when he'd left.

"I've missed you. I wanted to see you. How are you?"

"I'm . . . okay." She paused. "It took me a long time to get over what happened, but I have." Her words were untruthful because every bit of her still longed for him.

"I haven't gotten over you," he said.

Camille stepped behind the bar. She could see the carpenter smoking a cigarette on the sidewalk outside. "I was just about to make coffee," she said to Johnny, but she hadn't been, really, but she wanted to physically distance herself from him to resist the temptation to reciprocate his sentiment. She'd lied to him, but he'd hurt her, and she wanted to protect herself.

"Camille," Johnny said, stepping closer and reaching out, as if to touch her, though he couldn't at that distance. "Don't walk away."

"I'm not going anywhere, I'm making coffee," she replied quietly.

"I'd never hurt you or your family," he told her from where he stood in front of the bar.

"I know that," she replied and felt the truth in her heart.

"I said some things that were untrue, and I want to apologize."

"You don't have to. You were angry. I understand."

"Please, let me."

Camille nodded at him to go on.

"I'm in love with you, Camille, and I'm sorry I said those

things. I was angry, and I didn't mean any of them. And I can't stand not being with you."

"You had every right to be angry," she told him. "I shouldn't have kept that secret from you. It was terrible for me to do that, so I'm sorry as well. But why would you ever want to be with me after what my father did?"

"Because I love you, Camille. You aren't your father, just as I'm not mine. We're our own people."

"And my mother, you don't want anything to happen to her?" she asked him.

"Of course not," Johnny said, and moved to embrace her over the bar. "I love you, Camille, and so I love your family."

Camille stood still then hugged him, and he buried his face in her hair and held her tightly.

"But we can't be together," she said, pulling away.

"Why?" Johnny asked, hurt evident in his voice.

"Not after what my father did. I don't believe that you could ever move past it."

"But I have," Johnny insisted, reaching out to her.

"No, it will always come between us, I just know it. I love you, Johnny, I do, but I don't believe we should be together." It pained her to utter the words, but she knew they had to be spoken. She'd dreamt of this very moment, of him returning to her, but, in the end, she felt that the idea of them wasn't in her cards.

"Camille, please don't say that. How can you say that? You must not mean it. You're upset, and I understand, but can't we —" he said desperately.

"Please, go, Johnny," she told him, looking away and waiting for him to walk out the door.

Then he got down on his knees and belted out Jimmy Ruffin's "What Becomes of the Brokenhearted" to her from the other side of the bar. And Camille covered her hands with her mouth to hide her grin because his voice was terrible, just awful, and he seemed to know that, but he continued to sing anyway, and so he must have really loved her. His display of vulnerability endeared him to her.

As he struggled to finish the song, she motioned for him to stop. She didn't want to laugh at him, but then he got up and started laughing and so she did also. The carpenter was staring at them through the window. Camille walked out from behind the bar and embraced Johnny.

"All right," she said, looking at him. If he was willing to forgive her big secret, then he must have loved her.

Sheila eventually came around and accepted that Johnny would be in Camille's life and he wasn't going anywhere. Camille had told her mother that Johnny knew about their fathers but still wanted her in his life. "Yes, I already know," she'd said when her mother gave her a look.

"How?" Sheila had asked.

"It's not important," Camille had replied.

Then Johnny did something that Camille was certain he'd never thought was possible: he joined forces with her. Out of his love for her. This was despite initial resistance from Rafael and from Pat and Danny. But in the end, each managed to convince their respective crews that the partnership would mean larger earnings for all, and each were willing to forget for the sake of money, because, in the end, money always won.

There still was one problem: how to deal with Max. Camille had never forgotten what he'd done to her father, or how he'd threatened her mother and Johnny, and she knew she wouldn't stop thinking about Max until she did something. She saw Violet's continued bad luck as an opportunity to take over, and Max stood in her way. It was Johnny who suggested they get rid of him. At first, he'd said it jokingly, but when she told him that she had considered it, he warmed to the idea. It would be Camille's first time killing someone, but clearly, not Johnny's.

They took Johnny's car and watched Max over a couple of days and became familiar with his routine. Max had a similar routine every night. He'd leave the basement after the shop had closed for the evening and the streets were still, and he'd walk home alone.

One night they waited until Max left the shop then they quietly exited the car, taking care to shut the doors carefully, and approached him from the opposite direction, where he couldn't see them coming. They walked the hot, quiet street with their guns at the ready and Camille's forehead damp with sweat. She'd convinced Danny and Pat that it had to be done, that there was no other way.

"Max," she called out, and he stopped walking and turned around, slowly. There was nobody else out on the street, as far as she could tell, and even if someone had seen them, most people who lived in the neighborhood wouldn't ring the police, especially if they knew who she was.

The streetlamp illuminated Max's fear when he faced them. He stared at them with their guns pointing at him and his hand placed over what Camille assumed was his gun.

"Don't even think about it," Johnny told him.

Max removed his hand from his side but never took his eyes off them.

"Put your hands up," Camille told him.

For a moment it seemed he wouldn't then she shouted at him and he put his hands in the air. Then Johnny approached him while Camille kept her gun pointed on him and Johnny took Max's gun from him. Johnny tucked the gun into his back pocket then retreated to Camille.

"Walk," Camille ordered Max, directing him to Johnny's parked car.

"I'm not going to beg for my life," Max told them as he walked. "I'm not scared of you," he said when they ignored him, but his voice wavered. "I knew this time would come, but you'll never get away with it. Violet will know it was you, and she'll kill you for it." He raised his voice when they continued to ignore him. "Do you hear me?"

"Be quiet," Johnny said calmly. He glanced at Camille, and, despite her trembling, she imagined that if they could have held hands then they would have, so bonded were they by this moment.

If Max made a run for it then both knew they would have to shoot him right there—they had discussed that possibility beforehand—and when they reached the car without incident, Camille felt relieved. Johnny opened the car trunk and ordered Max to crawl in.

"Are you fucking kidding me?" Max said, backing away from the car.

"No," Camille said. "Get in." She motioned at him with her gun.

Max grumbled then approached the car again and raised one leg over the other and got inside, kneeling, and she ordered him to lie down.

"What are you going to do with me?" Max asked. "You're going to kill me, aren't you, because of what I did to your father?"

"No," Camille said, because she didn't want him to panic. "But you could cause trouble for us and we need you to go away."

"So, you're going to, what, drive me somewhere and drop me off?"

"Yeah," Johnny said. "And you can't return, we want you to stay away."

"But I don't have anything with me, clothes, money," Max pleaded, surprising her.

"We'll give you some money when we drop you off," Camille told him.

"I don't believe you," he said. "You're going to kill me; I can see it in your eyes."

"Lie down," she instructed, but her voice shook.

"Not until you're honest with me."

"This is taking too long," Johnny whispered to her in a panicked tone and Camille looked around nervously.

"Lie down!" she yelled at Max in fear, shaking her gun at him.

"I don't believe you," Max told them both then he complied.

Johnny went around to the backseat to get the rope and tape they had brought and bound Max's hands and feet, and put a piece of tape on his mouth.

"Where are you taking me?" Max asked before Johnny placed the tape over his mouth.

"You'll find out soon enough," Johnny told him. "Be quiet while you're in there, okay?"

Max nodded. Johnny shut the car trunk and they got inside the car, with Johnny driving. The streets were quiet given the late hour, with the occasional car or taxi speeding past them. Johnny drove at a normal speed, so as not to attract attention from the police. A few minutes later, they arrived at the abandoned pier where Johnny had taught her to shoot and Johnny turned off the headlights so they wouldn't be seen. He parked close by the river, dark and shining in the moonlight, and they exited.

They'd discussed their plans beforehand and had decided to get the grisly task over with quickly, and Johnny opened the car trunk and Max's eyes bulged with fear and his body shaking as he protested behind the tape, his screams muffled, as Johnny shot a single bullet into his forehead. Camille flinched and turned away. Max's end was not pleasant, of course, as death never was, but it was fast, and more humane than her father's had been, as she'd heard that he'd died slowly.

Beforehand, Camille had offered to complete the unpleasant task, but Johnny had insisted it be him, as he hadn't wanted her to 'have to live with that burden.' Which meant that Johnny loved her enough to kill for her, which meant that he loved her more than anyone had before, except for her mother and father, of course.

Johnny turned to her with the task completed. "See those big rocks over there?" he asked, gesturing. He seemed calm.

Camille looked at the rocks by the waterfront. Then she felt like she would vomit and clutched her stomach. The reality of hurting someone was very different than planning to do it. Johnny rubbed her back until she calmed herself.

"We'll gather those rocks and put them inside here," he said, rummaging around the car trunk and pulling out an empty duffel bag. "Then we'll tie the bag to his feet with some of the same rope I bound him with and put him in the river and the rocks will weigh him down. It'll be months before he's found, if ever."

Camille wondered if they should think more far ahead, such as, what would happen after those months past and the body was found? Would they come under suspicion? But she knew, as any gangster did, that you could only think so far ahead. Sometimes you had to take a risk, even if it was very big.

She helped Johnny pull Max's body out of the car and he landed on the ground with a *thud*. Some of Max's blood had trickled onto her arm and Camille used her spit to clean it. They rolled Max's body over to the old wooden pier and the slats creaked from his weight. Then Johnny ran back to the car and got the bag and the ropes, and they filled the bag with rocks and used the rope to tie it around Max's legs, so that he would float upright down in the water. She and Johnny heaved him off the pier face-forward, into the river, with a loud *splash*, which sprinkled water into her eyes and Camille blinked to dry them. Bubbles rose to the surface as Max's body submerged.

"Do you think anybody saw us?" she asked Johnny on the walk back to the car.

"No one really comes down here, that's why me and my crew like it."

But what if, Camille wondered in dread, someone had seen them?

But she saw new opportunity in Max's demise, and she started her own bookmaking operation in the neighborhood, to replace Max's, and used some of the money she made to buy a car, a brand-new black Cadillac.

29

Max never reappeared, and Violet knew that Camille had something to do with it, but she couldn't prove that. In her business, sometimes people just disappeared and you never found them. She had an extra set of keys and had found Max's car parked near his office, so she inherited it, since he didn't have any family that she knew of. She contemplated filing a missing person's report but refrained from doing so since she felt that the police would look at her even more closely if she did. With Tommy away, and with her mother in prison and Max vanished, she started to drink more.

"She bought her own pub," Violet complained to Sam when he came by her apartment after work to check on her. "That bitch is copying me."

"I'm worried about you," Sam said, "that's why I'm here. I haven't seen you in days, and you aren't answering your phone. I know Max doesn't seem to be around these days, and I know that's devastating for you, but you need to leave the apartment once in a while to get some fresh air."

She'd been cooped up for days afterwards, grieving over

Max, and missing Tommy, blaming and resenting Camille for causing all of it, and drinking to help her cope with her grief and anger.

"I'm worried something could happen to you," Sam told her. He'd made her tea and he sat on the couch, close by her, as she pretended to drink it.

"You think she could hurt me?" Violet asked. "I'll never let her."

"I'm worried that something could happen to you like what happened to your mother."

"You're worried I'll kill Camille and end up in jail?"

Sam furrowed his brow and nodded in silence. "Why does she dislike you so much?" he asked her after a moment.

"It doesn't matter," Camille said, looking away.

"I want to be with you," Sam told her, "but it's hard for me to be with you when you're like this, and when you won't tell me what's going on."

Sam handed her a tissue from a box on the table and she took it from him. "The truth is," she said, wiping her eyes. "It has to do with our families, there's a history. I don't want to discuss it."

"You can tell me," Sam said, and she wanted to confide in him. "I'm here to listen, I want to help you."

"Thanks, Sam, but there's no way you could help me with my situation with Camille."

"Why not?" Sam asked thoughtfully.

"Because I'm a gangster, that's why. You wouldn't understand how to help me, and I don't want you to get involved with this, I don't want to put you at risk."

"What *is* the story between you two?" he asked, moving closer to her, as if to embrace her.

"My family was involved in her father's death, in his

murder," she told him when it became clear he wouldn't stop talking about it.

Sam's eyes widened and he pulled slightly away from her. "You know this? How?"

"She told me, and then I confirmed it. She wants revenge, and she thinks that everything I have should be hers. She hated Max especially, because he was directly involved," Violet said, unwilling to divulge the entire truth about Max. "She's not going away."

"If she's threatening you, then you should go to the police," Sam suggested, touching her arm.

"That's not how it works for people like me, we don't go to the police. There's a street code, there are certain rules, and one of them is you don't rat to the cops."

"Right," Sam said, seeming at a loss for words. "Have you tried talking to her? Maybe I can talk to her?"

"Absolutely not," Violet told him, sitting up straight and looking at him. "You're not going near her. So far, you've managed to stay off her radar, and I don't want you putting yourself at risk."

"She's not going to do anything to me," Sam said confidently.

"I wouldn't be sure of that. I think she killed Max."

"Why would you think that?"

"Max wouldn't just leave without telling me, he's always been there."

"Maybe he had a family emergency."

"Max doesn't have any family, he only has us. Anyway, I've already tried talking to her and she's not interested."

"When was that?"

"Before Max disappeared."

"Maybe she'll act differently now that he's gone."

"No," Violet said firmly. "If she killed Max, I want nothing to do with her. I don't trust her, that's one of the reasons I'm staying home." Sam knew she had a gun, but even with a gun she feared Camille's wrath.

"Then what are you going to do?" Sam asked her. "You can't just stay inside here all the time, hiding from her. Nobody could live like that."

"I'm not sure what I'll do, but I'll think of something."

Violet did leave her apartment eventually, when she decided to use Max's car to watch Camille as Camille made her 'rounds' in the neighborhood, picking up protection money from the local businesses with Danny and Pat, and sometimes Johnny Garcia, in tow. Violet knew the police could be observing her, but she'd gotten to a point in her life where she no longer cared.

One day Camille was alone, and Violet decided to take things a step further by following Camille in Max's car when she drove away. Rock music quietly played on the radio and Violet had the windows open as she drove. She was a car behind Camille then when the other car made a turn, she was directly behind her. She didn't care if Camille saw her, and she knew that Camille would recognize Max's car. Camille stopped at a light and Violet braked behind her. She could see Camille watching her in the rearview mirror. She *had* noticed her. Violet revved the engine and planned to smash into the back of Camille's car when the light turned green again. Then she looked in her own rearview mirror at the car behind her, she hadn't been paying attention to it before, and she noticed a man who looked a lot like Detective Seale driving the car. The light turned green, and before Violet could get a chance to react, Camille had driven off.

Afterwards, with Seale continuing to follow her, she parked Max's car near her apartment and went upstairs. She went inside and called Sam at work before doing anything else.

"They're following me," she told him when his secretary connected her to him.

"Who is?" Sam sounded concerned.

"The police, because of my mother, they're trying to get me too."

"Violet, what are you saying? Are you okay?" Sam didn't understand, and why should he have? He was a normal guy, and she was a gangster.

"I followed her, I followed Camille. I almost hit her car."

"Violet, what did you do? Is everything okay? I can't come there right now. I have a very important meeting. Maybe I can stop by later, but I'm not sure."

But from the tone of his voice she knew she'd never see him again. Sam cared about her, but even he had his limits. She tried to comfort herself with the logic that Tommy hadn't liked him, and so maybe she'd be better off. Part of her had known all along that their different worlds would tear them apart.

That same day, she decided she would eliminate Camille. She needed to ensure Tommy's future. It would be her first killing, and she considered that once Camille ended up dead, Sam could go to the police and tell them what he knew and she'd be a suspect, and she thought that maybe she would have to eliminate Sam as well, if it came to that. But she loved Sam, and couldn't harm him herself, and she wasn't like her grandfather in that respect. But if she got sent to jail, she would need someone to look after Tommy, and with Max gone, she couldn't ask Sam to do that, so she rang her grandmother from a payphone.

"How's Tommy?" she asked her.

"Tommy misses his friends, and you, but he's fine. School's been hard for him, but I expect he'll adjust soon."

"Grandma, I need you to promise me something."

"Sure, what is it, honey?"

"I need you to promise me you'll look after Tommy no matter what happens," Violet said, because she was going after Camille, and she didn't care if she got caught.

There was silence.

"Gran?" Violet said.

"Why are you talking like that, sweetheart? I'm worried."

"Because I don't know what will happen, and I need to know that you will do this for me."

"So, it's come to that, then?"

"Possibly," she replied, without elaborating.

Her grandmother breathed out, then she said, "You can count on me, honey."

Next, Violet rang Derrick and her other only remaining man, and asked them to seek out Camille and tell her that Violet wanted to surrender, and to summon her to a meeting at an old warehouse on the waterfront that she and her mother still owned, and which had very little property value given it's undesirable location, but they kept it to use in certain circumstances. She told Derrick to tell Camille that they would negotiate the transition of power at the meeting, and she asked that Camille meet her alone, no associates. She knew Camille would have a gun on her, but Violet was a better shot, and she was counting on that.

Max's murder put Camille on edge and made her look behind her shoulder outside to see if she was being watched by the police, and it made her think that maybe she wasn't cut out for the harsher side of the gangster business, but her mother assured her that her father had to get used to the nastier side of things as well, and he had.

She had recognized Max's car, and for a moment it had alarmed her, then she saw Violet driving. She could have confronted her about the incident afterwards, but she hadn't, because she almost felt sorry for Violet, whose life was such a wreck. And now Violet had sent what was left of her men to ask Camille to meet her alone at a warehouse. What exactly was Violet up to? Camille was suspicious and hesitant to agree, but she had said yes.

Violet had asked to meet alone, but Johnny didn't trust Violet, so he and Pat came with Camille, and Valeria had sent Anton and the Alfonsis sent Billy. They gathered in front of Camille's apartment early that night and squeezed into Johnny's car for the drive to the warehouse. Camille planned to go in unaccompanied to meet Violet and the men would wait outside as backup in case something went wrong.

When they arrived at the address Derrick had given them, in a remote, industrial part of the city that appeared very dark, almost as if untouched by moonlight, Camille noticed Derrick and another man waiting across the street and figured Violet had the same idea as her.

"Are you sure you don't want me to come inside with you?" Johnny asked her as he parked outside, eyeing Derrick and the other man.

"No, I'll be fine. I don't think she's got anyone inside with her," Camille replied. She had to go in immediately, for she knew she might not have the courage to go in at all if she waited, so she opened the car door in the front, where she sat with Johnny.

Billy touched her shoulder from the backseat. "I want to let you know I'm not going anywhere, Camille, because I love you," he told her, as though these could be her last moments on earth.

Johnny yelled at him and pushed his hand off Camille.

"What do you think you're doing?" he asked Billy.

Billy told Johnny to keep his hands off him.

Camille stopped and looked at both men. "Enough," she said to calm them. "I can't deal with this right now. We'll talk about it when I return."

"Are you saying—" Johnny said.

"When I get back," she cut him short, then she stepped outside and closed the door, glancing at Derrick as she crossed the quiet street.

Johnny and the other men waited in the car, with the engine running and the windows down so they could hear.

Camille heard the crunching of her shoes treading over broken glass. The summer heat felt thick and sticky on her bare arms as she walked to the warehouse. Did she trust that Violet would be alone inside? Camille had her gun with her, of course, and she assumed Violet would have hers. The warehouse looked large and ominous in the night, and without the guidance of the moonlight, Camille struggled to find the door in the dark. Then a door opened, and she saw light and heard Violet's voice.

"Camille."

She approached Violet carefully, with her hand over her gun tucked in her waistband.

"Are you armed?" Violet asked her.

"Sure."

Violet didn't say whether she was also, and from her silence, Camille confirmed she was.

"Thanks for coming," Violet said. "I'm surprised you came."

"I wanted to see what you had to say," Camille said, but Violet looked at her warily.

"You didn't have to kill Max, you know."

"Oh, yes, I did."

Violet watched her in silence with a look of hate on her face. Then she invited Camille inside.

In the warehouse, Violet didn't look well, she looked like

she'd been up all night drinking and perhaps she had been. Violet shut the door.

~

Violet finally had Camille standing in front of her, alone. Their voices echoed in the open space. Camille stared at her in silence, as though she was debating how to proceed, then she said, "I can give you some money."

"That'd be great," Violet said, and forced herself to smile. She carried her purse with her, with her gun inside. She reached in for it.

"What are you doing?" Camille shouted, and her hand disappeared as she reached around for what Violet assumed was her own gun.

Violet's purse fell to the floor from her hands and the noise of it dropping filled her ears. "You really thought I'd ever negotiate with you?" Violet laughed as she pointed her gun at Camille, who now aimed her own gun at Violet.

~

Camille perspired heavily as she stood facing Violet, their guns drawn, and she knew that whoever was the better shot would win. Violet probably assumed she was the best, but Camille had practiced regularly with Johnny.

"This is for everything, and for Max," Violet said, her voice sounding especially harsh in the bare room.

Camille's hand that gripped the gun tensed then she pulled the trigger. An astringent smell filled the air. Then she felt a sharp pain in her chest and something wet, and she saw bright blood seeping through her shirt.

Violet touched her neck and fell to the ground. "You shot

me," Violet screamed as Camille's legs gave out and she collapsed to the floor. She heard the door opening, footsteps, and Anton calling Violet's name and Johnny's voice.

THE END

A NOTE FROM THE PUBLISHER

Thank you for reading this book. If you enjoyed it please do consider leaving a review on Amazon to help others find it too.

We hate typos. All of our books have been rigorously edited and proofread, but sometimes mistakes do slip through. If you have spotted a typo, please do let us know and we can get it amended within hours.

info@bloodhoundbooks.com

ABOUT THE AUTHORS

Best-selling authors E.R. Fallon and KJ Fallon know well the gritty city streets of which they write and have understanding of the localized crime world.